A complete list of books by James Patterson
is at the back of this book.
For previews of upcoming books by James Patterson
and more information about the author, visit
www.JamesPatterson.com

Now You See Her

Now You See Her

A NOVEL BY

James Patterson
AND
Michael Ledwidge

DOUBLEDAY LARGE PRINT HOME LIBRARY EDITION

LITTLE, BROWN AND COMPANY
NEW YORK   BOSTON   LONDON

This Large Print Edition, prepared especially for Doubleday Large Print Home Library, contains the complete, unabridged text of the original Publisher's Edition.

For the Gilroys, Ledwiths, Murphys, and Tighes—M.L.

——————————————

Little, Brown and Company
Hachette Book Group
237 Park Avenue, New York, NY 10017

Little, Brown and Company is a division of Hachette
Book Group, Inc. The Little, Brown name and logo
are trademarks of Hachette Book Group, Inc.

The publisher is not responsible for websites (or their
content) that are not owned by the publisher.

ISBN 978-1-61129-503-0

Printed in the United States of America

This Large Print Book carries the
Seal of Approval of N.A.V.H.

Prologue

LIES AND VIDEOTAPE

One

I'd already tossed the driver a twenty and was bouncing up and down like a preschooler last in line for the potty when my taxi finally stopped across from the Hudson hotel on West 58th. I didn't wait for change, but I did nearly get clipped by an express bus as I got out on the street side and hightailed it across Eighth Avenue.

I didn't even look at my iPhone as it tried to buzz out of my jacket pocket. By this point, with my full workday and tonight's party of all parties to plan, I was more surprised when it wasn't going off.

A sound, deafening even by midtown Manhattan standards, hammered into my ears as I made the corner.

Was it a jackhammer? A construction pile driver?

Of course not, I thought, as I spotted a black kid squatting on the sidewalk, playing drums on an empty Spackle bucket.

Luckily I also spotted my lunch appointment, Aidan Beck, at the edge of the crowded street performance.

Without preamble, I hooked elbows with the fair, scruffily handsome young man and pulled him into the chic Hudson. At the top of the neon-lit escalator, a concierge who looked like one of the happy, shiny cast members of *High School Musical* smiled from behind the Carrara marble check-in desk.

"Hi. I called twenty minutes ago," I said. "I'm Mrs. Smith. This is Mr. Smith. We'd like a room with a large double bed. The floor or view doesn't matter. I'm paying cash. I'm really in a rush."

The clerk took in my sweating face and the contrast between my sexy office attire and my much younger companion's faded jeans and suede jacket with seeming approval.

"Let's get you to your room, then," the über-happy concierge said without missing a beat.

A cold wind hit me as I came out of the hotel with Aidan an hour later. I looked up at the New York spring light glistening off the blue-tinged towers of the Time Warner Center down the block. I smiled as I remembered how my daughter, Emma, called it the world's largest glass goalpost.

I looked at Aidan and wondered if what we just did was right. It didn't matter, did it? I thought as I dabbed my eyes with the sleeve of my knockoff Burberry jacket. It was done.

"You were amazing. You really were," I said, handing him the envelope as I kissed his cheek.

He gave a theatrical little bow as he tucked the thousand into the inside pocket of his suede car coat.

"Hey, it's what I do, Nina Bloom," he said, walking off with a wave.

"It's Mrs. Smith to you," I called as I hailed a taxi back to my job.

Two

"OK, Mom. You can open your eyes now."

I did.

My daughter, Emma, stood before me in our cozy Turtle Bay apartment in her sweet sixteen party dress. I took in her luminous skin and ebony hair above the sleeveless black silk and began to cry for the second time that day as my heart melted.

How had this magical, ethereal creature come out of me? She looked absolutely knockdown amazing.

"Really not bad," I said, catching tears in my palms.

It wasn't just how beautiful Emma was, of course. It was also that I was so proud of her. When she was eight, I encouraged her, as a lark, to take the test for Brearley, Manhattan's most prestigious girls' school. Not only did she get in, but she was offered an almost complete scholarship.

It had been so hard for her to fit in at the beginning, but with her charm and intelligence and strong will, she stuck it out and now was one of the most popular, beloved kids in the school.

I wasn't the only person who thought so, either. At a classmate's birthday party, she'd wowed the mom of one of her friends so much with her love of art history that the gazillionaire socialite MOMA board member insisted on pulling some strings in order to get Em into Brown. Not that Em would need the help.

I was practically going to have to get a home equity loan on our two-bedroom apartment in order to pay for tonight's 120-person party at the Blue

Note down in the Village, but I didn't care. As a young, single mom, I had practically grown up with Em. She was my heart, and tonight was her night.

"Mom," Emma said, coming over and shaking me back and forth by my shoulders. "Lift up your right hand and solemnly swear that this will be the last time you will puddle this evening. I agreed to this only because you promised me you'd be Nina Bloom, *très chic,* ultrahip, cool mom. Hold it together."

I raised my right hand. "I do so solemnly swear to be a *très chic,* ultrahip, cool mom," I said.

"OK, then," she said, blowing a raspberry on my cheek. She whispered in my ear before she let go, "I love you, Mom, by the way."

"Actually, Emma, that isn't the only thing," I said, walking over to the entertainment unit. I turned on the TV and the ten-ton VCR that I'd dragged out of the storage bin when I came home from work. "You have another present."

I handed Emma the dusty black tape box that was on top of the VCR.

"TO EMMA," it said on the index card taped to its cover. "FROM DAD."

"What?" she said, her eyes suddenly about the size of manhole covers. "But I thought you said everything was lost in the fire when I was three. All the tapes. All the pictures."

"Your dad put this in the safety deposit box right before he went into the hospital for the last time," I said. "I know how badly you've been dying to know who your dad was. I wanted to give this to you so many times. But Kevin had said he wanted you to get it today. I thought it would be best to honor his wishes."

I started out of the room.

"No, Mom. Where are you going? You have to stay and watch it with me."

I shook my head as I handed her the remote. I patted her cheek. "This is between you and your dad," I said.

"Hey, Em. It's me, Daddy," a deep, warm, Irish-accented voice said as I left. "If you're watching this, it must mean you're a big girl now. Happy Sweet Sixteen, Emma."

I turned back as I was closing the

door. Aidan Beck, the actor I'd hired and filmed with a vintage camcorder at the Hudson that afternoon, was smiling from the screen.

"There are a few things I want you to know about me and about my life, Em," he said in his brogue. "First and foremost is that I love you."

Three

Down the hallway, I went into a large closet, otherwise known as a Manhattan home office, and shredded the script I'd written to fool my daughter. I sifted the confetti through my fingers and let out a breath as I heard Emma start to sob.

No wonder she was crying. Aidan Beck had performed the script impeccably. Especially the accent. I'd met and hired the young off-Broadway actor outside the SAG offices the week before.

As I sat there listening to my daughter crying in the next room, some part of me knew how cruel it was. It sucked having to be a Gen-X "Mommie Dearest."

It didn't matter. Emma was going to have a good life, a normal life. No matter what.

The ruse was elaborate, I knew, but when I spotted Emma's Google searches for Kevin Bloom on our home computer the week before, I knew I had to come up with something airtight.

Kevin Bloom was supposed to be Emma's idyllic, loving father who had died of cancer when she was two. I'd told Emma that Kevin had been a romantic Irish cabdriver / budding playwright whom I'd met when I first came to the city. A man with no family, of whom all trace had been lost in a fire a year later.

The fact, of course, was that there was no Kevin Bloom. I wish there were more times than not, believe me. I could have really used a romantic Irish playwright in my hectic life.

The truth was, there wasn't even a Nina Bloom.

I made me up, too.

I had my reasons. They were good ones.

What I couldn't tell Emma was that nearly two decades ago and a thousand miles to the south, I got into some trouble. The worst kind. The kind where forever after, you always make sure your phone number is unlisted and never ever, ever stop looking over your shoulder.

It started on spring break, of all things. In the spring of 1992 in Key West, Florida, I guess you could say a foolish girl went wild.

And stayed wild.

That foolish girl was me.

My name was Jeanine.

Book One

THE LAST SUNSET

Chapter 1

March 12, 1992

Party till you drop, man!

Every time I think back to everything that happened, it's that expression, that silly early-eighties cliché, that first comes to mind.

It was actually the first thing we heard when we arrived in Key West to start the last spring break of our college careers. As we were checking into our hotel, a very hairy and even drunker middle-aged man wearing goggles and an orange Speedo screamed, "Party till you drop, man!" as he ran, soaking wet, through the lobby.

From that hilariously random moment on, for the rest of our vacation it was our mantra, our boast, our dare to one another. My boyfriend at one point seriously suggested we should all get "Party till you drop, man!" tattoos.

Because we thought it was a joke.

It turned out to be a prophecy.

It actually happened.

First we partied.

Then someone dropped.

It happened on the last day. Our last afternoon found us just as the previous afternoons had, giddily hungover, lazily finishing up burgers under one of our hotel beach bar's umbrellas.

Under the table, my boyfriend Alex's bare foot was hooked around mine as his finger played with the string of my yellow bikini top. The Cars' classic song "Touch and Go" was playing softly from the outdoor speakers as we watched an aging biker with a black leather vest and braided gray hair play catch with his dog off the bar's sun-bleached dock. We laughed every time the collie in the red bandanna head-butted the wet tennis ball before belly flopping into the shallow blue waves.

As the huffing, drenched collie paddled back to shore, a stiff breeze off the water began jingling the bar's hanging glasses like wind chimes. Listening to the unexpected musical sound, I sighed as a long, steady hit of vacation nirvana swept through me. For a tingling moment, everything—the coolness under the Jägermeister umbrella, the almost pulsating white sand of the beach, the blue-green water of the Gulf—became sharper, brighter, more vivid.

When Alex slipped his hand into mine, all the wonderful memories of how we fell in love freshman year played through my mind. The first nervous eye contact across the cavernous Geology classroom. The first time he haltingly asked me out. The first time we kissed.

As I squeezed his hand back, I thought how lucky we were to have found each other, how good we were together, how bright our future looked.

Then it happened.

The beginning of the end of my life.

Our wiry Australian waitress, Maggie, who was clearing the table, smiled as she raised an eyebrow. Then she casually asked what would turn out to be the most important yes-or-no question of my life.

"You motley mob need anything else?" she said in her terrific Aussie accent.

Alex, who was leaning so far back in his plastic deck chair that he was practically lying down, suddenly sat up with a wide, strangely infectious smile on his face. He was average-sized, slim, dark, almost delicate, so you wouldn't guess that he was the place kicker for the nationally ranked University of Florida Gators football team.

I sat up myself when I realized that he was sporting the same slightly touched, let's-get-fired-up smile that he wore before he took the field in front of seventy thousand people to drill a fifty-yarder.

Or to get us into a bar fight.

Our vacation had been everything the travel brochure headline—"Five Days, Four Nights in Key West!"—had promised. No school. No rules. Nothing but me and my friends, the beach, cold beer, Coppertone, loud music, and louder laughs. We'd all even managed to stay in one piece over the previous, hard-partying four days.

Uh-oh. What now? I thought.

Alex looked around the table at the four of us slowly, one by one, before he threw down the gauntlet.

"Since it's our last whole day here, who's in the mood for some dessert?" he said. "I was thinking Jell-O. The kind Bill Cosby never talks about. The kind served in a shot glass."

The Cars song broke into a frolicking guitar riff as an expression of piqued interest crossed my best friend Maureen's face. My pretty roommate and fellow co-captain of the Gators women's varsity softball team was apparently game. So was her boyfriend, Big Mike, judging by his enthusiastic nod. Even our studious, usually pessimistic, sunburned pal Cathy looked up from her paperback at the interesting suggestion.

"Jeanine?" Alex said as my friends turned to me in silent deference.

The questionable decision was all mine.

I pursed my lips in worry as I looked down at the sand-covered bar floor between my sun-browned toes.

Then my face broke into my own mischievous grin as I rolled my eyes. "Uh…definitely!" I said.

All around the bar, people turned as my friends whooped and high-fived and pounded playfully on the sandy table.

"Shot, shots, shots," Mike and Alex started to chant as our waitress quickly turned to get them.

As a responsible 3.9 GPA English major and student athlete, I was well aware that vodka and gelatin was a highly hazardous afternoon snack. But then again, I had an excuse. Actually four of them.

I was a college kid. I was in Key West. And not only was spring break '92 quickly coming to a close, but it was three days after my twenty-first birthday.

Yet as I sat smiling, looking through the happy, crowded bar out over the endless Tiffany blue Gulf, I still had the slightest moment's doubt, the slightest moment's wonder if maybe I was pushing my luck.

The feeling was gone by the time Maggie returned with our drinks.

Then we proceeded to do what we always did. We raised our paper cups, tapped them together, and screamed, "Party till you drop, man!" as loud as we could.

Chapter 2

I saw a video once of the 2004 Indian Ocean tsunami. It was recorded at some beachfront resort in Sri Lanka, and in it, as the ocean bizarrely recedes, a group of curious tourists wander down to the beach to see what's going on.

Staring at the screen, knowing that the receding water is actually already on its way back to kill them, what disturbs you the most is their complete innocence. The fact that they still think they're safe instead of living out the very last moments of their lives right in front of you.

I feel that same sick way whenever I go over what happened to me next.

I still think I'm safe.

I couldn't be more wrong.

Several hours later, the Jell-O shots had done their job and then some. By seven thirty that evening, my friends and I were sardined into the packed Mallory Square for Key West's world-famous outdoor drunken sunset celebration. The gold of our last sunset warmed our shoulders as cold beer splattered and stuck our toes to our flip-flops. Cathy and Maureen were on my right. Alex and his Gator outside linebacker buddy, Mike, were on my left, and with our arms around one another, we were singing, "Could You Be Loved" with as much gusto as Bob Marley himself.

In front of the outdoor reggae band, I danced in my floppy bush hat, bikini top, and cargo shorts. I was as drunk as a skunk, laughing hysterically, forehead to forehead with my friends, and the feeling I'd had at the beach bar returned, on steroids. I had everything.

I was young and pretty and carefree with my arms around people I loved who loved me back. For a fleeting moment, I felt truly ecstatically happy to be alive.

For a split second.

Then it was gone.

When I woke, the cheap hotel room clock read 2:23 a.m. Turning over in the cramped, dark room, the first thing I noticed was that Alex wasn't beside me. I quickly fumbled through my last memories. I remembered a club we went to after the sunset, loud techno, Alex in a straw cowboy hat he'd found somewhere, Alex twirling beside me to Madonna's "Vogue."

That was about it. The intervening hours, how I had gotten back to the hotel, were an impenetrable alcohol-induced fog, a complete mystery.

A ball of panic began to burn at the lining of my stomach like guzzled vodka as I stared at Alex's empty pillow.

Was he OK? I thought groggily. Passed out somewhere? Worse?

I was lying there, breathing rapidly in

the dark, woodenly wondering what I should do next, when I heard the sound.

It was a giggle, and it had come from the bathroom behind me on my right. I rolled myself up onto my elbows and tilted my head off the bed to look through the crack of its slightly open door.

In the light of a strange, low glow, I spotted Alex leaning against the sink. Then I heard another giggle, and Maureen, my best friend, appeared in front of him holding a lit candle.

At first, as Maureen put the candle down onto the counter and they began to kiss, I truly wondered if I was still asleep and having a nightmare. Then I heard Maureen moan. Realizing that I was very much awake, the enormity of what I was watching walloped into me like an asteroid into a continent. It was my worst fear, everyone's worst fear.

My boyfriend and my best friend together.

Crippling waves of anger and fear and revulsion slammed through me. Why wouldn't they? Primordial betrayal was being enacted right in front of my locked-open eyes.

I heard Maureen moan again as Alex began to peel off her T-shirt.

Then they were cut from sight as the bathroom door closed with a soft, careful click.

A T. S. Eliot quote from my last Modern Poetry class popped into my mind as I blinked at the closed door.

This is the way the world ends
Not with a bang but a whimper.

Or a moan, I thought, turning and looking at the clock again: 2:26.

If my premed boyfriend wasn't currently busy, he could have marked it down.

Time of girlfriend's death.

I didn't scream as I sat up. I didn't look for something heavy and then kick the door in and start swinging.

In retrospect, that's exactly what I should have done.

Instead, I decided not to bother them. I just simply stood.

Barefoot, I grabbed my jacket and

stumbled out of the bedroom and through the hotel room's front door, closing it behind me with my own soft, careful click.

Chapter 3

I waited until I was outside the hotel's empty lobby before I started jogging. After a minute, I broke into a sprint. Down the middle of the pitch-dark street, I huffed and puffed, sweating like a marathon runner, like an action movie star escaping an impending nuclear explosion.

I was fast, too. Maureen was the tall, blond, long-limbed pitcher. Cathy was the short, tough catcher, and I was the lean, mean, in-between fast one. The now-you-see-her, now-you-don't, lay-one-down-the-third-base-line-and-beat-you-to-first-base fast one.

And at that moment, I needed every ounce of my speed to take me away from what I'd seen.

Because what I'd witnessed wasn't just the two-for-one end of my relationships with my boyfriend and my best friend.

I guess you could call it the proverbial last straw.

My dad, a Maryland state trooper, had died in the line of duty when I was eleven. All dads are special, of course, but my dad actually was an extremely special human being. Exceedingly kind, deeply moral, and a gifted, natural listener, he was the person everyone he came into contact with—coworkers, neighbors, the mailman, complete strangers—turned to for comfort and advice.

Which was what made his unexpected death even more devastating. It tore something deep and fundamental inside of my mom. Once an intensely religious teetotaler, she started drinking. She put on eighty pounds and

stopped taking care of herself. Everything came to a head in the spring of
my junior year in college when she
committed suicide in my dad's old Ford
F-150 with the help of a garden hose.

Maureen and Alex had bookended
me throughout my mom's funeral arrangements. Since I had no brothers or
sisters or close relatives, they had been
more than best friends to me. They had
been the only family I had left.

The trip down here had actually been
Maureen's idea. She knew the anniversary of my mom's passing was approaching, and she wanted to cheer
me up.

It was all too much. The pain of the
betrayal I'd just witnessed hit me again
like a wrecking ball. I began crying as I
ran. Tears mixed with the sweat that
began to drip off my face and onto the
sandy blacktop and the tops of my bare
feet.

I dropped to my knees onto the sand
when I arrived at the beach. It was
empty, just me and the dark ocean and
the star-filled sky. Staring out at the
black water, I remembered when I'd al-

most drowned at an Ocean City beach when I was nine. I'd been caught by a riptide, but my dad had saved me.

I breathed the night air in and out and listened to the lap of the waves, feeling more alone and desperate than I ever had in my entire life.

There was no one at all to save me now.

About twenty feet to the right beside me, I noticed a fat, concrete buoy-shaped marker.

SOUTHERNMOST POINT, CONTINENTAL U.S.A., was painted on it. 90 MILES TO CUBA.

I was standing, soul wrecked, about to take a shot at swimming those ninety miles, when I stuck my hand into the pocket of my shorts and realized something fascinating.

I had Alex's car keys.

The keys to his Z28 Chevy Camaro, which had brought us down here from the University of Florida in Gainesville. He'd gotten his "baby," as he called it, from sweating four summers at his dad's landscaping business. I'd sweated four years, trying to get his numb jock skull through premed, so the sudden idea of taking the sleek red car out for a little spin instead of going for a swim seemed eminently logical. To my shattered heart, it seemed downright brilliant.

I ran even faster back to the hotel parking lot. After I sailed one of Whorereen's bags out the window, I gunned the Z28's engine like I had pole position at the Indy 500.

Then I did what any self-respecting, suicidal, recently orphaned, currently being-cheated-on twenty-one-year-old girl would do.

I neutral-dropped my boyfriend's Camaro out of the lot in a cloud of rubber smoke.

Chapter 4

After a few fishtailing turns, I found an open road next to a beach and drove the Camaro properly—namely, like I'd stolen it. I didn't drop the hammer. I very nearly busted it through the meticulously vacuumed floor.

Its 5.7-liter V8 engine roared hungrily, demonically, as it rose in pitch, the intro to a heavy metal song.

"Crazy Train," I thought as I slammed back into my seat. Or was it "Highway to Hell"?

Parked cars that I blurred past started

making that zip zip zip zip NASCAR sound.

I tried to decide what I wanted to wreck more at that moment: Alex's pride and joy or myself. The notion of ending the utter silliness of my bad-luck life seemed very tempting. From where I was sitting without a seat belt, life was pain, and I was seriously think-ing about ending mine as visibly and messily as possible.

The Z28's speedometer was hitting three figures, its rear end starting to rise like an airplane on takeoff, when I caught some movement on the dark beach to my right.

I squinted at the motion through the windshield. It was a blur, something small running. Was it a rabbit?

No, I realized as I got closer very quickly. It was a dog, a collie with a red bandanna around its neck. I recognized the belly-flopping dog from the bar at the exact moment it changed course, like a guided missile, and shot out into the beach road.

Directly in front of the car.

Immediately, instinctually, I slammed

on the brakes and spun the steering wheel to the right, trying to avoid it. A high howl of evaporating tire rubber filled the car as the Z28's rear end fishtailed to the left like it was on ice. I tried to straighten it, but I must have overcompensated because the car suddenly reversed momentum and went into a rubber-barking, skidding, counterclockwise spin.

Shit!

I'd lost complete control of the car. My head flew back onto the headrest heavily, helplessly, like I was on a carnival teacup ride. I held my breath as I felt the right side of the car swell, threatening to flip. Instead, it did a 180 and kept right on rotating. It was when the car completed a full 360 that I saw what was looming ahead.

And I screamed.

Lit in my pinwheeling headlights, as if he'd been conjured there by a magician, was the dog's owner, the biker from the bar with the gray braided hair.

The last thing I remember was pumping the brake again and again, savagely, as the ridges of the spinning steering wheel flickered painfully over the insides of my fingers.

I closed my eyes as the Camaro's swinging front end clipped the man in the waist with a sickening, heart-skewering thump.

There was a brief crumpling sound of rolling weight onto the metal hood followed by a squeegee-like squeak as the man slid up the ramp of the windshield.

And then there was silence. Nothing but horrible, deafening silence.

Chapter 5

I forced myself to open my eyes.

The Camaro had come to a shuddering stop another fifty feet to the north.

I stared at the empty road in front of me, my foot pinned down on the brake, my hands as tight on the steering wheel as a pair of vise grips. The only sound was my panicked breathing as sweat seemed to pour from everywhere at once, the inside of my elbows, the backs of my knees, even my ears.

The Camaro idled in the empty road, its engine chugging loudly like an animal catching its breath. I thought the windshield would be cracked, but it was unmarked. So was the hood. Besides losing a couple of inches of tire rubber and brake pad, the car seemed to be doing fine.

It was as if nothing had happened at all.

As if.

I didn't want to look in the rearview mirror. I stared at Albert, Alex's stupid grinning orange University of Florida Gator logo air freshener instead. Albert wasn't offering any suggestions. I sucked in a hard breath, like a diver before going under, and finally looked.

The biker lay in the middle of the right lane behind me. He was facedown on the asphalt beside my skid marks, his thick gray braid half undone, his arms flung out in a Christlike spread. Traffic cones and stanchions from a work area along the side of the road were scattered around him like nailed bowling pins. He wasn't moving.

When I noticed the dark, inky splotch in his gray hair and on the street beside his head, various parts of my body started to shake simultaneously, my knees, my hands, my lips. I let out my sour, rum-scented breath and covered my face with my quivering hands. My trembling, clenching fingers clawed at my skull like a rock climber searching for purchase.

"What have I done?" I asked myself between hysterical gulps of air.

Killed a man, came a stone-sober answering thought in response.

You just killed a man trying to save his dog.

I glanced up at the open road through the windshield. It curved away out of sight in the moonlit distance, beautiful, dreamlike, beckoning like the Yellow Brick Road in *The Wizard of Oz.*

That's when the cool, rational, very sober-sounding voice in my head delivered two words, a sound bite, an ad slogan.

Just go.

It wasn't your fault, my interior voice-over continued. *You were trying not to hit the dog. There was nothing you could do. Besides, no one saw. Take your foot off the brake and move it onto the gas. Don't look back. Don't be stupid. Just go.*

It was true that no one had seen it, I realized with a swallow. I was on an empty stretch of road near the airport with nothing but the deserted beach on the right. The only structure was an abandoned-looking concrete industrial building a couple of hundred feet up on the left.

The only witnesses to the incident were a silent armada of yellow school buses parked behind a chain-link fence across the street. Their dead eyelike headlights seemed to stare at me as if wondering what I was going to do.

I looked around for the biker's dog. It was gone.

It was as if I came back online then. Having thought the unthinkable, the spell was broken, and I could once again focus.

I slid the car into park and turned it off.

I had to help this poor man. I needed to do what my father would have done. Start CPR, stop his bleeding, find a phone.

Go? I thought, disgusted, as I fumbled with the door latch. How could I
have even considered such a thing? I
was a good person. I'd been a lifeguard,
a candy striper. *That's my good girl,* my
daddy used to say as I'd help him off
with his high-gloss police oxfords.

I was getting out of the car when I
noticed a pair of headlights approaching in the distance behind the injured
man. Before I could breathe, an unexpected and dazzling flash of brilliant
color crowned the headlights.

I stared, paralyzed, mesmerized, as
the night suddenly blazed with a fire-
works burst of police lights, blinding
bubbles of blood red and vivid sapphire
blue.

Chapter 6

The flashing police cruiser was strangely silent as it rolled to a slanting stop half-way between me and the fallen biker. As the metallic squawk and chitter of its police radio reached my ears, my chin dropped to my chest like a condemned prisoner's, waiting for the ax.

I looked up as I heard the heavy crunch of a footstep by the cop car's open door. I couldn't see the officer's face, which was backlit by the blinding roof lights. The only thing I could make out was his large, squarish, dark outline against the crazily strobing lights.

"Stay there and keep your hands where I can see them," the cop said like the voice of God.

I immediately complied.

Over the trunk of the cop car, I watched the officer quickly approach the injured man and squat by his side. The next thing I knew, the cop was looming over me.

He was unexpectedly handsome, with short black hair and pale blue eyes in a lean face. He was six two or three, early thirties, powerfully built. His all-American physical attractiveness made the whole situation worse somehow. Made my guilt sharper, my despair more vile.

"He's dead," the officer said.

Something at my core faltered.

"Oh, no," I whispered like a crazy person into my lap. "Please, God, no. I'm sorry, I'm sorry, I'm so sorry."

I buried my shaking head deeper into my hands as the recruitment-poster police officer leaned down beside my face and sniffed.

"And you're dead drunk. Stand up and put your hands behind your head."

Chapter 7

When my father died and I saw his coffin for the first time, I remember thinking, *This is it. Nothing will ever be this bad.*

I was wrong.

The officer cuffed me and put me into the back seat of the cruiser. I was surprised at how clean it was. It smelled new. The rubber floor mats were as immaculate as the ones in Alex's car, the seat was deep, plush almost. Except for the kind of black plastic mesh separating the front from the back, you wouldn't think it was a cop car. Despite the fact that my father was a cop, I'd never been in one before.

My right leg started shaking like a newly caught fish. Was I having a stroke? I wondered, staring at my jitterbugging thigh. I hoped so. Because anything was better than facing this.

I snorted back a wet, spasming sob.

Anything.

I glanced at the back of the cop's head as he lowered himself into the police cruiser's front seat. Like everything else about him, his head was neat, ordered, squared off. You could probably have balanced a level on his broad boxer's shoulders. He had good posture, bearing, my mother would have said.

Had he been in the military? my haywire brain wanted to know. I read his backward name tag in the rearview mirror. Fournier.

Officer Fournier put his head down as he typed my driver's license information into his boxy front-seat computer terminal. Then his cropped head suddenly leveled again.

"This right?" he said without turning

around. "Your twenty-first birthday was just a few days ago? You down here for spring break?"

I noticed for the first time that there was a slight Northeast-city inflection to his voice. Boston, New York, Philly maybe. Then I had another, less distracted thought. What color prison jumpsuit would they give me?

"Yes," I said, choking back another sob. "I'm a senior at UF."

I suddenly wanted to be back there so much I almost moaned. If only I could click my heels and be back to Frisbee and meal cards and the note-scribbled onionskin pages of my *Norton Anthology of English Literature.*

There'd be no more school, no more softball, no more nothing at all. I'd loved books my entire life, and ever since high school I'd dreamed of becoming an editor at a New York City publishing house. I'd vaporized my future, too, I thought. Annihilated it like a mosquito into a bug zapper.

I was now one of those people that you read about in your pajamas, a name you shook your head over in the local newspaper's police-beat section as you turned back to your coffee and thought about what to wear to work.

My life as I knew it had become a thing of the past.

Chapter 8

"Who do you want me to talk to first? Your mom or your dad?" Officer Fournier said, making eye contact for the first time in the rearview.

He really was easy to look at. Not pretty and dark like Alex. His was a paler, more angular, badass white man sort of handsome. His eyes were a strikingly light, almost silver blue.

"They're both dead," I said.

Officer Fournier let out a sigh. "You don't want to lie to me, Jeanine," he said sternly. "I think you understand your situation here. You really don't

want to make this even worse for yourself."

"It's true," I said, sounding calm and
sober suddenly. "My dad was a Maryland state trooper. He was killed in a
line-of-duty roadblock car crash in
1982. I have his prayer card in my wallet. My mom died last year."

Officer Fournier went into my wallet.
He turned all the way around a moment
later, suddenly much less imposing,
with my dad's prayer card in his hand.

"How'd your mom die?" he said.

"She committed suicide," I said. I realized it was the first time I'd ever said
it out loud.

"Wow. That's rough," Officer Fournier said, sounding almost sympathetic
as he absorbed that. "Any brothers or
sisters?"

I shook my head.

"Whose Camaro?"

"My boyfriend's. He's back at our
hotel," I said.

I sat there for a second.

"Having sex with my best friend," I
added quietly.

Officer Fournier shook his head as he looked back at the biker.

"Wow," the blue-eyed cop said. "You're all partying, and he cheats on you, so you took his car. I see."

"The man had a dog. It ran out in front of the car," I said quietly. "I was trying to swerve out of the way of the dog, and I went into a skid. I guess I was going too fast so I started to spin, and then the man was just...there."

I lost it again. I folded like a lawn chair as I started crying.

After about a minute, I wiped my wet face on my thigh. When I sat up, Officer Fournier was staring at me in the rearview mirror with a look I couldn't quite read in his pale eyes.

We held eye contact for a long, startling electric beat. I guess it was a strange time to feel attraction toward someone, but there it was. I couldn't look away. He cut away first, tapping my dad's prayer card to his chin.

"What if?" he said after a moment.

I had my own what-ifs going through my head right at that moment. Like, what if I hadn't had Jell-O shots for lunch? What if I hadn't taken Alex's car? What if I'd never been born?

That's when the officer suddenly opened his door and got out. Then there was a snap and a click and the door beside me opened, too.

"I'm making a judgment call here," he said as he undid my cuffs. "Get back in your car and get out of here. Go back to school, Jeanine. This never happened."

Chapter 9

I stood up in the street beside the police car, rubbing my wrists, trying to
absorb exactly what was happening.
My head was spinning faster than the
Camaro had, faster than the blinding
carnival lights on top of the cop car.

I looked forward past Alex's Camaro
at the open road. Beside the empty
beach, the dark water was as still as
glass.

"I don't understand, Officer Fournier,"
I said.

"That's funny. I'm having a little trouble understanding what I'm doing my-

self," he said, putting the cuffs back on his belt and passing a hand through his cropped black hair. "And you can drop the 'Officer' there. My name's Peter. Saint Peter, in your case, since I just saved your life. Now get back in your car and get out of here before somebody comes or I change my mind."

"But how can I just go?"

"There aren't any witnesses, and I haven't called it in yet, is how," he said.

"But I'm responsible."

"Listen to me," Peter said. "The state of Florida is waging a war on drunk driving, with extremely strict sentencing guidelines for vehicular manslaughter. Once I make you blow into the Breathalyzer, you're looking at jail time. It's a ridiculously stupid, politically motivated law. But the jury won't see that, and neither will the judge. You can't survive jail, Jeanine. You won't make it."

"But that poor man is dead. I can't just walk away."

"Let me tell you a little about that poor man," Peter said. "His name is Ramón Peña. He was a hard-core meth and heroin addict who just got out of jail. We collared the repeat offender a couple of years ago, climbing out of an old lady's window. He raped and robbed an eighty-three-year-old woman. Broke her jaw."

Peter nodded at my surprise.

"When Ramón couldn't find a drunk to roll, he'd bum money from tourists on Duval Street with his dog. That's basically his obituary. Besides, it wasn't even your fault. He was probably so high that he dove out in front of your car thinking it was a swimming pool. Ramón's hurt enough people in his life. Don't let his death take you out, too. You're a decent person who was in the wrong place at the wrong time. Now take your boyfriend's keys and get out of here."

"But...," I said.

"I'm not asking you," Peter said, putting the keys in my hand. "I'm telling you. Now go."

Chapter 10

I was staring at the keys, now miraculously back in my palm, when Peter's police radio let out a long beep. A voice on the radio began chattering something I couldn't decipher. Peter cocked his head, listening intently.

"What is it?" I said.

"Wait, wait," he said, leaning back into the car, listening.

"Unbelievable," he said when the radio voice stopped. He shook his head as he turned, his face crestfallen.

"What?" I said.

"Your boyfriend's Camaro just came

up over the radio as stolen. He told dispatch that not only did you take his car without permission, but that you're drunk. First thing the DTs will do when they pull up is ask for all the overnight calls that came in. Next, they'll want to see your boyfriend's car, which for sure has blood on it. Which leaves no way out of this after all. I can't believe this. I actually can't let you go. I have to call this in now."

Alex had called his car in as stolen? After what he did to me with Maureen, he actually called the cops on me? I felt incredibly weak suddenly. I felt like lying down on the asphalt next to the cop car and closing my eyes. Instead I just started to cry.

"Wait, wait, wait," Peter said, putting his hand on my shoulder. He stared at me, his blue eyes as big as saucers. "Please don't cry. I think we can fix this. I have an idea," he said.

Peter made a dismal face as he slowly glanced over his shoulder at the fallen man, then back at me.

"We could get rid of Ramón's body," he said.

Chapter 11

"What?" I said, wincing.

"I live a few blocks from here. I have a boat at my house," Peter said. "I'll take care of everything."

My leg started hopping again like a Mexican jumping bean.

"But that's nuts," I said. "You know that, right? How nuts that is?"

Peter nodded with an almost comic enthusiasm. "You don't have to explain it to me," he said.

"But I mean...," I said, hesitating.

"Look, Jeanine. It's our only option. I'll put him in the Camaro's trunk. You follow me in the Camaro back to my house. I'll take it from there. I'm working the graveyard shift. No one will even know I'm gone."

"This is crazy," I said, looking around.

"We're out of time," Peter said. "If a car comes by, I won't have a choice. I'm trying to do you a favor, but if you're not up to it, I completely understand. I'm not real jazzed about the possibility of going to jail myself. It's entirely up to you."

I stood there looking at him as he checked his watch. He blinked as he stared back, waiting calmly for my answer. Even with his big hands resting on his bulky gear-laden hips, he suddenly seemed friendly, a nice teddy bear of a guy, a drinking buddy, a big brother sticking his neck out for me, trying to do me a solid.

Had my father ever done something like this for someone? I wondered. Maybe he had, I thought.

I closed my eyes. There it was before me. The rest of my life. Jail or freedom. Right or wrong.

I thought about looking over again at

the man I'd struck, but in the end I decided not to.

I opened my eyes.

In the silence, Peter clicked the cuffs together. Like the final tick of a scale coming to rest. Like the click of the bathroom door with Alex and Maureen behind it, I thought.

Then finally, I nodded.

"OK, then. Hurry up now," Peter said. "Back up the car, pop the trunk, and follow me."

Book Two

ENDLESS SUMMER

Chapter 12

It must have been around noon when I woke up, but I didn't open my eyes right away.

As I pretty much always did over the last two years, I lay still, my breath held and eyelids sealed, momentarily unsure and afraid of where I might find myself.

Then I opened my eyes and let out a sigh of relief.

Because I was OK.

I was still free.

I wasn't in a prison cell.

Not even close.

Yawning, stretching, blinking in the

bright, hazy morning light, I sat up in bed, slowly taking in the white-on-white bedroom. From left to right, I scanned the driftwood sculpture on the side table, the seashell shadow box, the book-filled beadboard bookcases.

And, as usual, my waking inventory ended at my left hand. Or more precisely, at the diamond engagement ring and wedding band that had somehow become attached to my ring finger.

Standing, I stopped and shook my startled head at the mirror above the bedside table. From all my sea kayaking and windsurfing over the past two years, my light skin had turned a deep shade of brown. My brown hair, on the other hand, had become lighter, now striped with blond streaks.

I'd somehow become a version of myself I'd never even considered. Jeanine, surfer chick. Malibu Jeanine.

Failing to wrap my head around that one, I crossed the room and opened the vertical blinds on the sliders. I squinted as I took in the lazily leaning king palms, the expanse of Crayola teal water, the forest of boat masts.

My backyard, replete with two white seaward-facing chaise longues, could have been the set of a Corona commercial. I smiled at the muscular arm resting on the edge of the right chair.

Since we were out of Corona, I had to settle for putting an ice-cold bottle of Red Stripe into the big hand as I stepped up.

Two years of healing. Two years of love. No one was luckier than I.

"How's the fishing there, Mr. Fournier?" I said.

"Slow, *Mrs.* Fournier," Peter said, grinning at me impishly behind his Wayfarers.

Chapter **13**

Yep. You guessed it. Peter and I had gotten married.

Or maybe you didn't. I don't blame you. I sure as hell hadn't seen it coming.

I came down for spring break, and I never went home.

"Fish don't seem to be biting today," Peter said, putting the beer bottle down next to his sea rod and grabbing my ankle. "But hey, wait. I think I got something."

For a scary second, I worried that I'd fall onto our concrete seawall or off it.

But then I was on my back, across Peter's lap, screeching ecstatically as he mercilessly tickled my armpits. Over the last two years in Key West, I was basically *majoring* in ecstatic screeching.

"You honestly think I'd let you fall in?" Peter whispered as he caught my earlobe in his teeth. "After all we've been through? It took me my whole life to catch a real-life mermaid. I'd never throw you back. No way."

"In that case," I said, sighing, as I lay back in the neighboring chaise. I smiled up at the merciless blue tropical Floridian sky. "I'll just have to put up with you mortals for one more day."

What *hadn't* we been through? I thought as I closed my eyes, remembering the night of the accident.

It seemed like a million years ago.

After we had pulled into Peter's carport, he brought me inside and sat me down on his living room couch and told me to sit tight. About ten minutes later, I heard his boat start up. I fell asleep waiting for him to return and woke to the sun coming up and Peter, back from his night shift, in the kitchen making us breakfast.

He'd taken care of everything, including delivering the Camaro back to Alex and persuading him to drop the car theft charge. It was as if the night before had never happened at all.

When I went back to the hotel that afternoon, the only thing waiting in the lobby were my bags. My friends were gone. Not just Alex and Maureen, but Mike and even Cathy had left. They hadn't left a message.

I remembered singing "Could You Be Loved?" with them. The answer in my case was apparently a big fat no. Life wasn't an episode of *Friends,* it seemed. Not one of them had "been there" for me, that was for sure. Not one of them had given a shit whether I lived or died.

Driving me to the bus station, Peter had taken one look at my face and told me that he had a tiny room above his garage that he sometimes rented.

"If you're not ready to go back to school just yet, you could stay for a couple of days," he said.

A couple of days.

Key West's most famous last words.

When two days turned into a week, Peter said he had a friend, Elena, a female cop, who was part owner of the island's largest catering company and was always looking for people.

I took the catering job the next day and withdrew from school the day after that.

I knew it was a rash, probably borderline crazy thing to do. I also knew things were different now. That I was different. It wasn't just the accident. With the break from my friends, the last vestiges of my old life had been cast away. One door had closed, and something in the Key West air told me to sit tight until the next one opened.

And that's exactly what happened.

From the beginning, Peter was a perfect gentleman. Really more like a father or an extremely protective brother. He was always making sure that I used sunscreen and ate enough and got enough exercise and enough sleep. He was constantly leaving things on the rickety landing outside my door, videotapes, bags of fruit, books.

By far, my favorite offering was a battered, secondhand copy of seventeenth-century English poets, Herrick and Marvell. At night I'd lie in my tiny bed and read, rediscovering why I'd become an English major in the first place. Rose petals and winged chariots, eternal youth and beauty. It was uncanny how well Peter seemed to know me.

Peter actually stuttered the first time he asked me to come to dinner. He served in the backyard with a tablecloth and china. He even wore a jacket with his Bermuda shorts. The lamb chops were burnt, the mashed potatoes were runny, but by the end of the sunset, even before he reached across the table and held my hand, I knew.

We both knew. Despite our ten-year age difference, we'd both known it from pretty much the moment we looked at each other through his cruiser's backseat mesh.

He proposed two weeks later. Teaching me how to fish, he asked me to reel in the line so he could change the bait.

Only instead of a hook, my ring was tied to the end of the line, and I turned to find Peter down on one knee.

We were married in a city hall wedding six months after that.

I knew the whole thing was crazy. I knew that I was too young, that things were happening too fast, that I was being impulsive. But the craziest thing of all was that it kept working.

"Jeanine?" Peter said.

I opened one of my eyes.

"Yes, Peter," I said.

"I thought you mermaids never wore shirts."

"That's only under the sea, silly," I said. "On land among you mortals, we have to keep the devastating, beguiling power of our boobies in check or nothing would ever get done."

"Except you?" Peter said.

I closed my eye. "Now you're getting it."

"Jeanine?" Peter said, laying down the sea pole.

"Yes, Peter?"

"You know what I'm in the mood for?"

"Devastating beguilement?"

"How'd you know?" he said.

"Mermaids know," I said, standing and taking my husband by the hand.

Chapter 14

Back to the present, and I'd just put in a load of whites when I heard the beeping. I padded into the kitchen and turned off the microwave timer before I headed to the rear of our cozy beach bungalow and into the master bath.

Then I took a monster breath and held it as I turned and lifted the pregnancy test off the toilet lid.

Time and my heart stopped at the exact same moment as I stared at the display window with its two identical blue lines. My breath whooshed out of me as though I were a seven-year-old blowing out birthday candles.

Because I'd already read the math on the box.

One blue line plus one blue line equaled one pregnant Jeanine.

Over the past two weeks, I'd been in panic mode. More and more as another day passed and I didn't get my period. I kept thinking about those three pills that I'd somehow missed. I must have experienced brain freeze in the middle of last month's cycle.

Peter had elected me the head of the contraception department, and I'd definitely dropped the ball. Talk about a whoops.

I also thought about what a baby would do to my twenty-three-year-old body, my twenty-three-year-old future.

But as I stood there, staring down the two blue lines, something odd and unexpected happened. A warmth started in the center of my chest and for a quicksilver second, I could actually feel my baby, skin on skin, soft in my arms.

Why not? I thought, suddenly daz-

zled with the life-affirming awesome-
ness of it. Why couldn't Malibu Jeanine
bring a Malibu baby to the luau? Hell,
why not two? I'd always wanted kids.
Peter and I had planned for some in
the vague future anyway, so why not
start early?

Life was crazy. You had to roll with it.
If the last two years and Key West had
taught me anything, it was that. *Mi vida*
really was *loca*. Besides, plans were for
making God laugh.

I dropped the test, sending the trusty
stick flying, when there was a pounding on the door followed by a deafening electronic squawk.

What the?

"THIS IS THE POLICE!" Peter called
through a police megaphone. "WE
KNOW YOU'RE IN THERE! COME OUT
WITH YOUR HANDS UP AND YOUR
PANTIES OFF!"

I couldn't stop laughing. He was always so crazy and funny, a holy terror
of a rascal. All he did was make me
laugh. When he wasn't making me do
even better stuff. I knew right then that

Peter would make the best dad on earth.

Should I tell him about the test? I thought. No, I quickly decided, hiding it under the sink. In two weeks we were going up to the Breakers in Palm Beach, where we'd spent our honeymoon. I'd drop it on him at dinner. Blow his doors off. Knock his socks off. Then his pants.

He might be a little thrown off, but not for long. I'd show him. I loved him and he loved me. We could definitely make this work.

"I'm coming out," I said a moment later.

"GOOD MOVE!" Peter squawked. "AND NO FUNNY BUSINESS!"

I unlocked the door. Then I sailed my Victoria's Secret bra and thong onto the megaphone, right into Peter's dumbfounded blue eyes.

"Don't shoot," I said, wearing nothing but my smile.

Chapter 15

It was the following Friday when I decided to clean Peter's boat.

Peter liked to go fishing by himself on Fridays after work. It was his way to blow off steam, clear his head, transition from the stressful workweek to the weekend. He'd usually come back in at around nine, and we'd end up having a late dinner of freshly caught wahoo or sailfish or blackfin tuna.

So as a surprise, I wanted his boat to be shining when he came home after his shift.

My hair up in a bandanna, wearing

stylish yellow kitchen gloves and holding a soapy mop bucket, I boarded his twenty-five-foot Stingray at around eleven that morning. It was a white cabin cruiser, squat and powerful, almost like a speed- boat but with two berths for sleeping and a small galley under the bow.

An enormous seagull cried from atop the mast of a small sailboat across our canal as I stood on the softly swaying deck. As a breeze came off the electric blue water, I suddenly felt a strange lifting sensation in my stomach, guilt mixed with pleasure, like a child playing hooky. My life consisted of pretty much nothing but playing hooky, didn't it? I was loving every millisecond of it.

I smiled as I glanced at the CD in the boat's topside boom box. It was by the seventies one-hit wonder Looking Glass. As silly as it was, the old jukebox staple about a sailor torn between the sea and his beloved bar wench, "Brandy," was our wedding song.

I didn't even know why. I guess because it was fun and goofy and yet deep down seriously romantic, just like Peter and me.

Looking at the powerboat's sleek lines, I thought for the millionth time how much Peter impressed me. As funny and fun-loving as he was, he was an even harder worker. And because he came from meager circumstances in, of all places, the Bronx, New York, his accomplishments were nothing short of amazing.

Without the benefit of a college education, he'd managed to buy this boat, not to mention this beautiful house in paradise that he'd redone himself. All the while becoming hands down the most well respected, competent cop on the island since the moment he'd transferred down from the NYPD seven years before.

Peter was the real deal, the big-city go-to cop that all the other cops called when the shit hit the fan. Unlike my ex-boyfriend, Alex—who had proven himself to be nothing but a completely self-centered jock, faithless and irre-

sponsible, unwilling to deal with anything his talent didn't easily overcome—
Peter was a traditional guy who actually
sought out the hard stuff, took on every challenge the world had to offer,
the more difficult the better, knowing it
to be the thing that, in fact, made him
a man.

There was no doubt that I loved my
Saint Peter. I loved him as much as you
can love someone who is not only your
lover and friend but your hero. If he
hadn't existed, I would have had to in-
vent him.

"Brandy," the groovy seventies sing-
er's voice crooned as I hit the boom
box's Play button, "what a good wife
you would be. But my life, my lover, my
lady, is the sea."

By noon, I had finished polishing and
waxing everything topside and I headed
belowdecks. It was hot even by Key
West standards, and down in the
cruiser's dim, claustrophobic cabin, the
warm, icky, hazy air stuck like Saran
wrap on my sweat-drenched skin.

I was putting away some paper tow-

els under one of the galley's lower cab-
inets when I noticed something curious
lashed with bungee cords to the underside of the sink.

It was a gray plastic box, hard and
flat like one that a tool set might come
in. I was surprised by how heavy it was
as I grabbed its handle and slipped it
out. I sat on the cabin steps, set it on
my lap, and popped its clasps.

My entire body went slack with a
sharp intake of breath as I stared down
at what was inside it. I pulled off my
bandanna and wiped the sweat out of
my eyes.

I'd been expecting some sort of first
aid kit, but sitting in the gray foam pad-
ding was a gun. It was matte black,
greasy with oil, a little larger than a pistol. A nasty-looking hole-filled tube sur-
rounded the barrel, and there were a
few wraps of gray duct tape around its
grip.

The words "Intratec Miami 9mm"
were stamped in the metal in front of
the trigger. In the foam beside it were
two thin rectangular magazines, the

reddish copper jackets of bullets winking at their brims.

Being the daughter of a cop, guns
didn't faze me. I actually used to duck-
hunt with my dad, so I knew how to
use the shotgun and two nine-millime-
ters Peter kept in the locked gun cabi-
net in our bedroom closet.

But wasn't it a little strange to have a
machine pistol on the boat? Wouldn't a
shotgun make more sense? Why hadn't
Peter told me about it?

I tightly closed the lid of the box and
put it back where I found it before heading back into the house.

Inside, I was startled to find Peter by
the kitchen sink in his police uniform
home early.

"Peter?" I said.

Then he turned around, and I saw
the scowl on his face. I covered my
smile with my hand as I saw that his
entire front, from chest to crotch, was
covered in the residue of white, rank-
smelling puke.

"Go ahead. Laugh it up," he said with
a wide grin. "Look what a nice drunken
lady tourist gave me over by the La

Concha hotel. Nice of her, wasn't it? Smells like she had the clam chowder for lunch, don't you think? Did I ever tell you how much I love being a Key West cop?"

I quickly decided that now probably wasn't the most opportune time to have a sit-down about Peter's choice of firearms. It was probably just a rah-rah-cop gung ho throwback to his bachelor days anyway. He probably used it to shoot beer cans with his buddies when they went fishing.

"Let me get a garbage bag," I said as the puke stench hit me. "On second thought, I'll get some lighter fluid and a match." I laughed.

"What are you talking about, Jeanine? I thought you said I look hot in my uniform," Peter said, mischief gleaming in his blue eyes.

I knew that look.

"Don't you dare," I screamed, running as he came quickly around the kitchen island with open arms, puke emanating from his shirt front.

"Come here, Brandy. Where are you going, Mermaid?" he said, laughing as he ran after me into the backyard. "Time to give your husband some sugar, baby doll. Stay right where you are. We need to hug this thing out."

Chapter 16

On the edge of the manicured lawn, I sighed as a cello, flute, and violin trio played Pachelbel's Canon in D with perfect, aching precision.

Work, work, work, I thought, filling another long-stemmed glass with two-hundred-dollar-a-bottle Krug brut champagne. The aristocratic wedding guests at the reception we were catering seemed every bit as elegant as the crystal as they laughed and hugged around billowing, white-draped tables arranged on the emerald grounds.

Even to a jaded veteran caterer like

me, the wedding on the sprawling front lawn of the Hemingway Home was breathtaking. The famed Spanish colonial in the background had its hurricane shutters flung wide, as if Papa himself might come out at any moment onto the second-story veranda with a highball and offer the lucky couple a toast.

The bubbly that I dispensed in perfectly folded linen was '92 Krug to be exact, the year the sleekly beautiful, dark-haired couple, a convertible bond arbitrager and an art dealer, both from New York, had met. Between refills, I watched them as they smiled, hand in hand, on the western fringe of the lush lawn, taking pictures to capture the Key West Lighthouse in the background.

One day I'd probably finish my English degree, I thought, as I sighed again. But until then, I had no problem chilling out here in wedding world, where it was forever Saturday afternoon, complete with classical music, popping corks, raised champagne flutes, eggshell and ivory, eternally blue skies.

Of course, I would have preferred to spend all day fishing with Peter, but he'd been working overtime on Saturdays for the last two solid months with a DEA task force. It was undercover work, which I knew was dangerous and I hated, but I also knew my husband. Peter was a hard-driving superstar cop, more than capable of taking care of himself and his buddies. It was the bad guys who needed to worry.

"Your wedding was better," my boss and Peter's coworker Elena Cardenas said, hip-butting me as she passed with a tray of sesame chicken.

"Yeah, right," I said, rolling my eyes. "Which part did you like more? When Peter faked throwing me off the bar's dock or his drunken rendition of 'Paradise by the Dashboard Light'?"

"Hard to decide," the full-figured blond Cuban said with a laugh. "At least he didn't appear to have a pole up his keister like this groom. Anyway, Teo is up to his neck and running low on champagne at the bar. Could you run and grab another box of Krug out of the van?"

"Aye, aye, captain," I said.

"And remember, watch out for the

Jump Killer," Elena called as I went toward the iron street gate.

The Jump Killer *was* on my mind and probably that of every young woman in South Florida that summer. An ongoing Channel 7 news story told about spooky abductions up-in North Miami, missing prostitutes, an unsuccessful attack in which a man tied up a woman with parachute cord. The words *serial killer* were being used, though no bodies had been found.

Gee, thanks for reminding me, Elena, I thought as I walked down the deserted street toward the van.

I was coming back up the faded sidewalk with the champagne when I spotted a man in the beat-up black Jeep across the street.

He reminded me of the tennis player Björn Borg, with long, dirty blond hair and wraparound sunglasses. He also sported a blond Jesus beard. I glanced at the windshield, and though his face was pointed away, I got the impression that as I approached he was watching me from behind the glasses. He took something out of the pocket of his cutoff denim shirt and started playing with it. It was a gold lighter, and he started clicking it in rhythm to the clink of champagne bottles as I walked past.

I swallowed, suddenly afraid. The guy was definitely creepy. As I picked up my pace and made it back to the gate, the Jeep roared to life and peeled out, its big tires screeching as it took the first corner.

What the hell had that been about? I thought, hurrying back toward the white tent.

Teo didn't so much as grunt a thank-you when I dropped off the heavy case by his busy bar, which was par for his course. I couldn't decide what I disliked more about the young, handsome Hispanic with frosted hair: the several occasions I spotted him coming out of a bathroom rubbing his runny nose or the way he constantly tried to look down my shirt. If he wasn't Elena's cousin, I would have complained. I was definitely losing my patience.

I found Elena with her business partner, Gary, the chef, in our staging tent.

She smiled as she pulled a tray of puff pastries off the portable oven's rack.

"Hey, you made it back," she said, winking at Gary. "See any dangerous-looking parachutists?"

I actually was about to tell her about my evil Björn Borg sighting, but the way she said it, like I was a complete idiot, checked me. It would only lead to more teasing. I liked Elena, but sometimes her tough-chick sarcasm was a little hard to take. I decided to keep the creepy encounter to myself.

"Ha-ha. At least you have a gun," I said. "Speaking of dangerous, I've been meaning to ask you, Elena. How dangerous is that DEA task force thing at work?"

"Are you kidding me?" Elena said, handing me an hors d'oeuvre—packed silver tray. "You have to be a stone-cold supercop like your husband to even think about doing undercover work. Besides, you mean how dangerous *was* that DEA task force thing. They rerouted the DEA agents back to Miami, like, two months ago. Fed funding dried up. Sucks, too. I did surveillance for them for almost two weeks. The overtime was kick-ass. Take those out now. The yuppie natives look like they're getting restless."

Over? For the last two months? I thought as I stumbled out onto the grass, the tray almost slipping from my hand.

Then where the hell had Peter been going on Saturdays only to come home at three in the morning? I wondered.

For the last two months.

Chapter 17

Peter blinked when he turned on the kitchen light and saw me sitting ramrod straight with my arms folded at the table at five thirty the next morning.

"Jeanine, you're up," he said.

Two months, I thought, noticing that he was showered. I didn't know whether to scream or cry or hit him. I was ready for all three at once.

Why had Peter been lying through his teeth to me for over two months!?

"I'm up all right," I said. "All night, in fact. I wanted to ask you a question. Um, I wonder how I can put this delicately. Where the *FUCK* have you been going every Saturday for the past two *FUCKING* months?"

Peter held up his hands, a completely floored expression on his face. "What in the name of God are you talking about? Where do you think I've been? Mexico? I've been at *work*."

"Then why did Elena tell me that the DEA task force returned to Miami two months ago?"

"She what?" he said. He actually laughed. "It's OK, Jeanine. Don't shoot. I can explain. It's simple. For a cop, your boss, Elena, is one hell of a caterer. She doesn't know what she's talking about. You didn't tell her, did you? That I was still involved with the DEA?"

"No," I said, confused. "Don't change the subject."

"Listen to me for a second, all right? The DEA only said they were going back to Miami. They have a confidential informant who said there's a leak in the department. Some bad cop is leaking stuff to a suspected drug smuggling operation. That's why the chief hand-selected me. It was stupid not to explain it to you. I should have told you. The important thing is not to tell Elena about it. Don't tell anyone."

"You think Elena might be a bad cop?" I said.

"Who the hell knows?" Peter said, shrugging as he took the orange juice out of the fridge. "Somebody in the department is. We can't rule her out."

"Are you sure about all of this, Peter?" I said, staring into his eyes. "I mean, are you really sure you're sure?"

"Am I sure?" he said, laughing again as he stared right back. "Christ, Jeanine. Look at you. I thought cops were suspicious. You want to look at my pay stubs? Check our phone records. If you want, I'll bring home a CSI kit so you can take prints."

"It's just..." I began and then started crying.

Peter stepped over and opened his palms.

"Hands," he demanded.

I gave mine over.

"Look in my eyes," he said. "There.

Much better. Now, I have a question. Why do you think I married you?"

"You love me?" I said.

"Ya think?" he said. "Look, Jeanine. I never told you this before, but you weren't the only one that night on the beach who was seriously thinking about calling it quits. I was sick of it. Being a cop, Key West, people, partying. I don't know, being alive, everything. It all seemed so meaningless and stupid." He smiled down at me.

"Then I rolled up and looked into your eyes, and I haven't been inside a church since my Communion, Jeanine, but it felt holy, you know? Like God sent me an angel down from heaven. After I got to know you and realized how incredible we were together, I knew it was true."

"Not an angel, a mermaid," I said, sniffling.

"Exactly," Peter said, wiping a tear off my nose. "You're the first thing in a long time, maybe the only thing ever, that actually makes me want to get out of bed and floss my teeth and balance my checkbook. You understand? I'm not Alex. I'm not some asshole. I'd do anything. I'd die before hurting you. I'd burn this shit-heel, sunburned tourist trap to the ground, if you wanted me to. I'd—"

"Oh, Peter," I said, crying as I kissed him. "I know. I'm sorry. My Saint Peter, my love," I said, burying my face in his shoulder.

Chapter 18

On Friday night, exactly one week before our trip to Palm Beach, I was sitting on the couch, thinking about going to bed early. But at the last second, I decided to throw caution to the wind and put my flip-flops on and head out to the island's only Blockbuster, half a mile away on North Roosevelt Boulevard.

Peter was pulling a double, directing traffic at some road construction on the Overseas Highway up in Big Pine Key, so I was flying solo. Being much more of a classic movie buff than he was, I decided I couldn't waste the home-alone opportunity to indulge in a late-night Alfred Hitchcock double feature. I snagged *The Birds* and *North by Northwest* off the shelf.

I was a foot out the door when I hit the Unlock button on my car key fob and heard the faint bloop-bloop.

No, wait, I thought as I suddenly spotted my battered blue Vespa at the curb. What was I thinking? I'd taken the moped. Our new Toyota Supra was still with Peter at work.

I stopped and stared down at my car key fob, confused. Why had I heard the car beep, then?

I scanned the parking lot as I thumbed Unlock a second time. I turned to my left as the double bloop sounded out faintly again.

What the heck? It seemed to be coming from across the street.

I stepped past my Vespa to the edge of the sidewalk that rimmed the strip mall's lot and hit the fob one last time.

In a parking lot directly across North Roosevelt Boulevard, a parked car's lights went on and off with the familiar electronic bloop.

I stared across at it. It was sleek, black, brand-new. What the hell? I squinted at the Florida license plate. Yep, it was ours. It was our Supra.

But why was it there? I thought. Shouldn't it be parked at police headquarters? Shouldn't it be at Peter's job?

Then I made the mistake of reading the lit sign on the building behind the car.

A sickening numbness sprouted in the pit of my stomach and began expanding upward, outward, filling my chest like a swallowed balloon.

BEST WESTERN, the sign said.

Chapter 19

Cars went back and forth on North Roosevelt as I stood there, staring at the shiny black hood of Peter's car sitting in the Best Western parking lot.

OK, I finally thought as my shock eased up slightly a long five minutes later.

Slowly now, I urged myself.

Think this through.

I tried. Nothing would come. It was fruitless. There wasn't anything to think about. Even an idiot like me knew what finding your husband's car in a motel parking lot meant.

One word surfaced in my swirling mind. It made sense that it had four letters. As I stood there, it was as if each one was being struck into the surface of my brain with the heavy-handed pound of an old-fashioned typewriter.

L-I-A-R.

Peter was a liar.

There was no construction job at Big Pine. No overtime. I also figured there was no DEA assignment and never had been. Peter *had* lied about the other night and about all the other double shifts over the last two months.

As I stood on the sidewalk in the dark across from the Best Western, the thing that struck me most—more than hurt, more than even anger—was the sudden knowledge of exactly how vulnerable I was.

Because my whole life revolved around Peter, I realized. The house was his, and so were the car and the boat. In the last two years, my six-dollar-an-hour, off-the-books catering job had paid for what? Some clothes from the Gap? The occasional meal?

I had nothing, I realized. Not even the

University of Florida academic scholarship I had blown off when brilliant old me decided to throw caution to the wind and pull a Jimmy Buffett and take that last plane out.

I'd put all my chips on Peter, and it didn't take a genius to figure out that his car across the street meant that I'd lost big time.

No, wait a second. Correction, I thought, cupping my stomach.

It wasn't just me who had lost big time.

So had my brand-new baby on board.

Well, what did you expect, Jeanine? screeched my next thought.

This new internal voice was my mother's, I realized. The unforgettable tone was her black, drunken raging that occurred more and more after my dad's death.

Are you really that stupid, Jeanie Beanie? What kind of cop would cover up a man's death? What kind of cop would get rid of a body? An Eagle Scout? Did you really think you could make a bloody mess and not have to pay for it? And while we're on the sub-

ject of bloody messes, what's up with the machine pistol *you found on your handsome husband's boat?*

A hair-raising pulse of terror gripped the back of my neck like a claw. I reared back until my shoulder blades found the video store's wall. I started sliding down it until my butt touched the cold, hard concrete.

The traffic went by obliviously on the dark street as I covered my face with my hands like a toddler trying to make herself disappear. At that moment I realized something for the first time.

It had somehow completely escaped me.

I had taken everything Peter had told me about himself at face value.

I really had no idea at all who Peter was.

Chapter 20

It was about ten soul-annihilating minutes later when one of the motel's ground-floor rooms opened and a man exited.

Even though I'd been expecting it, it still felt like an uppercut to the chin when I saw that it was Peter.

That wasn't the only blow, either. Peter was wearing a suit. It was a tailored dark blue one I'd never seen before, an Armani maybe.

I started sobbing. How could this be happening? How could the man who'd introduced me to "Brandy" and *The*

Princess Bride and the joys of Japanese beer be the world's biggest lying scumbag?

I watched Peter as he scanned the parking lot carefully. Seemingly satisfied, he pulled the motel room door closed behind him and headed for the Supra.

I turned and broke into a run for my moped as he opened the car door.

Was whoever he was with still in the room? I wondered, still flabbergasted. Or maybe they hadn't met yet. Maybe he was going to pick her up?

"Hey, can I be the fifth wheel on your date, you son of a bitch?" I said to myself, truly losing it as I gunned my Vespa to life. "Thanks, Peter. Don't mind if I do. Sexy suit, by the way."

Duval Street, Key West's main strip, was staggering room only as I buzzed onto it two cars behind Peter's Supra a few minutes later.

With its packed bars and outdoor street stalls that sold beer and rum the way Coney Island sold hot dogs, Duval Street was to Key West what Bourbon Street was to New Orleans. Except in

Key West, it seemed that Mardi Gras was every night.

I pulled to the curb in front of a crowded bar as Peter turned the car into a side alley beside a T-shirt shop and parked. What now, Peter? I thought. Some drinking and dancing? A late dinner perhaps?

My clenching hands shook on the moped's sweat-slicked rubber handlebars. I *still* couldn't believe this was happening.

I sat waiting about a block back, scanning the Friday night sidewalk parade of navy aviators, drag queens, college kids, beach bums, and trendy millionaire couples on vacation. Peter appeared a few moments later from the alley. He was holding a small green duffel bag now, I noticed.

How do you like that? I thought as he headed south through the crowd. Maybe Peter's alter ego was now going to hit the gym?

A double shift? I thought, absolutely stunned, as I gunned my moped to life and started to follow him again.

It was more like Peter was working a double *life*.

I came to a hard stop, scraping my moped and ankle off the curb, when I saw Peter turn the corner onto Fleming Street around the south side of the more shabby than chic La Concha hotel. I hopped off, keeping in the shadows beneath the storied art deco hotel's awning, as I jogged to the corner and peeked around the side street.

Peter was standing on the brightly lit sidewalk in front of a Hibiscus Savings Bank ATM. As I watched, he took a thick envelope out of the bag and slipped it into the bank's deposit slot.

A late-night deposit would have been normal enough, I suppose.

Except Hibiscus Savings wasn't *our* bank.

Our savings account was with First State. At least the account that I knew about, I thought, shaking my head.

I was trying to process that revelation when a small silver Mazda Z with tinted windows pulled past me. It slowed and made the turn onto Fleming. Peter turned as its horn honked and ran around to the passenger side and got in.

I ran back to the moped.

Peter's night was apparently just getting started.

Chapter 21

A new possibility slowly occurred to me as I tailed the Mazda Z off crowded Duval and onto the darker side streets of the adjoining Bahama Village neighborhood.

It was actually a comforting one. Definitely soothing, considering the current circumstances.

Maybe this was the DEA thing after all, I thought.

Maybe Peter really had to work undercover and had just invented the story about traffic duty in Big Pine so I wouldn't be worried. Sure, he'd still lied to me, but maybe it wasn't as bad as I had first thought.

Please let that be the reason, I prayed as I buzzed along behind him like a complete maniac through Key West's pitch-black streets.

Ten minutes later, the car pulled into the empty parking lot of Fort Zachary Taylor State Park. I waited on the street by the park's walled entrance, watching as the Mazda stopped in the center of the lot and sat idling. After a moment, its lights dimmed and went off.

Were they staking someplace out? I wondered. Doing a deal? Waiting for someone?

Wind began blowing through the darkened, creaking palm trees as I crouched along the stone wall, watching the car. As I stared down the deserted street at my back, I remembered Elena warning me about the Jump Killer. About how some people thought he was from Key West.

Great, I thought. Thanks again, Elena. Really appreciate it. I really need something else to freak out about around now.

I sank down behind the wall as the car suddenly started and screeched out of the lot.

I lost the car as I was getting back on the moped, so I decided to drive back to Peter's car parked in the alley on Duval. The silver Mazda was letting Peter out beside the alley when I made the corner half a block north ten minutes later. I pulled to the curb in front of the crowded corner bar to see what would happen next.

The first thing I noticed was that instead of the green duffel I'd seen him with, Peter was now carrying a much larger black leather knapsack.

A feeling of desperate, last-ditch hope floated in my chest. Did that mean there really had been some kind of DEA work? I wanted so badly to believe that what I had just seen was Peter working undercover.

The Mazda Z pulled onto Duval and rolled to the red light where I sat idling. Spanish music began to blare out of it as its tinted passenger window zipped down. I listened to horns and bongo drums racing each other as I laid my wide eyes on the two people inside.

I squinted in surprise and shook my head. That couldn't be right, I thought.

I knew them both.

Teo, the skeevy bartender with the frosted hair, was behind the wheel doing what he seemed to do best, rubbing at his nose.

Even more surprising, beside him, my boss, Elena, sang along to the salsa with her eyes closed as she drummed on the dashboard to the beat.

Then the light turned and the tricked-out Mazda peeled off and disappeared into the traffic of upper Duval.

Still sitting on my buzzing moped, staring at its red running lights, I tried to piece together what I had just seen. For a moment, the fact that I knew everyone involved in the odd encounter gave me a feeling of relief. I actually wondered for a silly second if they were doing all this sneaking around for my benefit, as if they might be planning some kind of surprise party for me.

Then reality took hold. There was no party. Quite the opposite.

My husband is a bad cop? I thought.

No, I realized. It was Elena! Elena was the bad cop. Peter was working a case against her and Teo. I knew for a fact that Teo did coke and he probably dealt it, too. That had to be it!

That's when the car behind me laid on its horn.

I turned the handlebars and throttled to get out of its way, but I must have given it too much gas. The back wheel spun out, the bike tipped, and I went down hard. I lay there for a moment, my elbow and knee in agony, my head in the gutter. Then I scrambled out from underneath the moped and sat on the curb.

I stared fascinated at my torn-open knee. A thin line of blood rode down the ridge of my shin and took a left as it reached my ankle.

As I watched myself bleed, the Rick James song "Super Freak" floated out into the street from the crowded bar behind me.

"When I make my move to her room, it's the right time," the drunken crowd sang along. "It's such a freaky scene."

"Hey, you OK? Can I help you?" called a beery male voice from somewhere on the sidewalk behind me.

I shook my head as I lifted the bike, got back on, and headed home.

Chapter 22

It took me twenty minutes to get home. I took a shower and bandaged my knee. When I got into bed, I lifted the remote off the night table and turned on the TV. I was determined to stay up until Peter came home, but after only a minute or two I found myself nodding off.

The sky outside my bedroom sliders was the dark gray of predawn when I woke up. The TV was showing an aerobics program: thin young women with too much makeup, smiling like Miss America as they counted off toe touches.

Then the doorbell rang.

I stumbled out of bed. Was it Peter? Did he forget his key?

I was even more confused when I saw a squad car in the driveway outside the living room window.

I opened the door. It wasn't Peter. It was a short female officer in a Key West PD uniform. I thought I knew all of Peter's fellow cops, but I'd never seen her before.

"Jeanine Fournier?" she said.

Even in a dazed fugue, I could tell by her demeanor, by the intense look in her eyes, that something was seriously wrong.

I suddenly felt tired and powerless, thoroughly unprepared for whatever I was about to be told. Staring at the woman's hard face, I felt like going back into my bedroom and lying down. The sun broke as I stood there, light rapidly filling the sky.

"Yes?" I finally said.

"You need to come with me, Jeanine," she said.

What the? What was this?

"I'm so sorry to have to tell you this," the lady cop said. "It's your husband. Peter. He's been involved in a shooting."

Chapter 23

A shooting?!

That one stupid thought kept repeating in my numb mind as I sat in the passenger seat of the speeding cruiser. Every few seconds, I would try to form another thought, but my indignant, stubborn brain wouldn't have it.

A shooting? I thought. A shooting?

That meant that Peter had been shot, right? I stared down at the cop car's incident report–covered carpet. It had to. Otherwise, the red-haired lady cop behind the wheel wouldn't be involving me.

I needed to talk to Peter. To find out what was going on. Now he'd been shot? I didn't know what to think as the cop car's tires cried around a curve. What did it mean?

If I thought I'd been disoriented riding in the cop car, it was nothing compared to the skull slap I felt as we screeched to a stop beside a Shell gas station on North Roosevelt.

It looked and sounded as if the world was coming to a violent end. Besides a half-dozen siren-screaming patrol cars, there were three ambulances and a fire truck. Yellow evidence tape strung across the pumps wafted in the breeze from the nearby north shore. The whole block around the station looked like a huge present wrapped in the stuff. A crowd of tourists and beach bums stood silently, shoulder to shoulder, behind the yellow ribbon like spectators at a strange outdoor sporting event that was just about to get under way.

It seemed like every cop in the department was there. I glanced from face to face, marking the people I knew. At our pickup softball games and bar-

becues, these men had been so happy
and laid-back. Now, as they secured
the crime scene in their stark black uniforms, they suddenly seemed cold,
heartless, angry, almost malevolent.

What the hell had happened here?

"She's here," a cop and good friend
of Peter's named Billy Mulford said as
he saw me.

The last time I saw Billy, a blond,
middle-aged fireplug of a man, he was
doing a cannonball off a booze cruise
boat at a retirement party. Now he
looked about as fun-loving as a con-
centration camp guard.

"It's Peter's wife, Jeanine. Let her
through," he ordered.

I was too stupefied to question what
was happening as the evidence tape
was lifted up, and I was beckoned under. Why were they treating me like a
first responder? The deafening siren of
yet another arriving ambulance went
off as Mulford quickly led me over the
sun-bleached asphalt and past the
pumps.

Just inside the door of the food mart,
half a dozen EMTs were kneeling down

beside someone I couldn't see. My hands started shaking as I tried to figure out what was happening in all the commotion. I grasped them together in a praying gesture.

"Come on, come on! Give me some fucking space here," a big black medic barked as he retrieved a syringe from a bright yellow hard-pack first-aid case.

"Coming out!" someone else yelled in a high, panicked voice a moment later. There was a tremendous clatter as a trauma stretcher was clicked into rolling position. The crowd of cops and medics began to part in front of it, letting the stretcher through.

My knees almost gave out when Mulford moved out of my line of sight and I finally saw who was on the stretcher.

I staggered back, shaking my head.

Something caved in my chest as Peter was rolled past me, his eyes flat and unfocused, his face and chest covered in blood.

Chapter 24

Cops made a tight circle around Peter, shielding him from the public as he was rolled toward a reversing ambulance.

I noticed several things at once. He was sheet white. A thin spiderweb of blood was splattered across his cheek and neck. His uniform shirt had been cut open, and I could see more blackish blood caked on his arm, dripping off his elbow.

Peter didn't just look shot, I thought, staring at him as he was lifted into the back of the ambulance. Peter looked dead.

"Let her through," Mulford said, dragging me forward. "It's his wife."

"Not now, goddammit," the burly black medic said, stiff-arming him away.

"Oh, God. Oh, God," Mulford said, shaking his head as Peter was borne away. He squeezed my shoulder. "I'm so sorry, Jeanine. This shouldn't be happening."

"What happened?" I said.

"We're not sure," he said, ashen-faced, as he shrugged his shoulders. "I just got here myself. We think Peter came in here to get some coffee during his shift. Walked into the middle of a robbery. Two Jamaican males. They had some kind of machine gun. Our guys were ambushed. We're looking for them now."

Mulford wheeled around as a wiry, startlingly muscular female EMT with bloody sneakers emerged from the food mart door.

"How is she?" he asked her.

She? I thought.

I stepped to my right and looked farther into the store. That's when I saw the rest of them. Three more EMTs were surrounding *another* body.

When I stepped forward and saw the spill of blond hair beside a fallen police cap, I felt like I'd walked face-first into an invisible electric fence. For absolutely no reason, I began slowly nodding to myself.

My boss, Elena, her throat shot to ribbons, was lying in a pool of blood, dead on the floor.

Chapter 25

One of Elena's unmoving eyes, the one that wasn't shot out, was wide open, staring up at the ceiling. Blood was everywhere as if a mop bucket filled with it had been overturned. On her uniform. On a bunch of knocked-over plastic jugs of blue windshield-wiper fluid. On the surgical gloves that one of the EMTs snapped off with a loud curse. Ink blots and dashes and horrid smears of copper-smelling crimson red blood.

"I'm so sorry," the female EMT said to Mulford. "Poor thing took at least half a dozen in the face and neck and another four in the lower abdomen. She'd lost too much blood by the time we got here. She's gone."

"And the other one?" Mulford said to the EMT, pointing to his left. I followed his finger to the pair of bare brown feet that poked out from the end of the aisle like the wicked witch's from under Dorothy's house.

"The station clerk?" the medic said with a shake of her head. "He took a long burst in his throat, looks like. Died instantly."

I slowly nodded again at the new knowledge. There was a third victim?

I gaped at the blood-and-brain-splattered food racks, the brass shell casings, the broken glass. In the air was the strong hospital stench of voided bowels. I'd never been that close to so much violence and death. It was literally a bloodbath.

I stumbled behind Mulford back outside to get away from the smell and noticed that the crowd beyond the tape seemed to have doubled in size. A tall, shirtless middle-aged man in cutoff shorts and a panama hat suddenly reached under the crime scene tape and lifted a shell casing to his red-rimmed eyes.

"Hey! Put that down!" Mulford yelled, running toward him.

That's when I noticed the gun.

On the fuel-stained asphalt, halfway between the first pump and the gas mart's front door, beside a bright yellow police evidence cone sat a flat black pistol.

When I took a step forward to look at it more closely, I saw that I was mistaken. It wasn't a normal pistol. It was a larger black submachine pistol with little holes around its barrel. It had gray duct tape around its grip and scuff marks beside the words "Intratec Miami 9mm."

I stood there bent over, staring at the weapon. I couldn't take my eyes off it, in fact.

Because it wasn't just *like* the gun I'd seen on Peter's boat.

It *was* the gun from Peter's boat.

"That's a roger," Mulford said into his radio as he arrived back beside me. "Get those detectives down here ASAP.

It looks like the goddamn Valentine's Day massacre. Tell them that Officer Cardenas has been killed in a robbery-homicide. See if that gets them moving."

As I stood there, the white masts of the sailboats at the Palm Avenue marina across the street from the gas station suddenly became supervivid against the blue sky.

Peter's gun? Why was Peter's gun here? Was it really his?

"Come on, Jeanine. They took Peter to Lower Keys Medical. I'll take you right there," Mulford said.

We walked to his cruiser and got in. I jumped as the feisty little cop suddenly punched the steering wheel.

"Those fuckers," he said. After a moment, I realized he was crying. He quickly wiped his face and got the car started.

"Sorry, Jeanine," he said. "Elena was just awesome, you know? How can she be dead? At least they got Peter's bleeding under control. We can thank God for that."

"They what?" I said, sitting up as if

Mulford had punched me instead of the steering wheel.

"What? No one told you?" Mulford said. "The EMTs got the bleeding under control. It looks like Peter's going to make it."

Chapter 26

They'd brought Peter to the Lower Keys Medical Center five minutes from Key West on Stock Island. I was told by a male ER nurse that Peter had been taken directly to surgery.

For the next couple of hours, I sat in a cop-filled waiting room on the hospital's second floor.

After a while, the surrounding cops started drifting out into the hallway and stood in clusters speaking softly to one another.

From the cheap TV above the door, I watched a *7 News* special report about the Jump Killer. A Filipina massage therapist from Marathon, Florida, had gone missing, and speculation was that the Jump Killer had struck again.

The special report had just been replaced by *Family Feud* when a tall, gray-haired uniformed cop entered the waiting room.

"Jeanine?" he said as he crossed the room in two quick strides. "I'm Chief John Morley. Peter's boss. I can't tell you how sorry I am about all of this."

I shook his hand. I'd seen Morley's picture in the local papers before, but this was the first time I'd actually met him.

"Thank you, Chief," I said.

"Please call me John. How's Peter?"

"Still in surgery," I said.

He pulled over a chair.

"You must be going through hell," the chief said with a sympathetic shake of his head. "It looks like Peter and Elena interrupted a holdup in progress, but when a police officer is shot, it could be anything. You mind if I ask you a few questions?"

"No, of course," I said.

"Has Peter had any disagreements with anyone that you know of? A neighbor? Anyone who might be holding a grudge against him? Strange phone calls? Can you think of an unusual reason why this happened?"

I thought about everything I'd seen last night, Peter's bizarre behavior. I decided not to mention it until I spoke to Peter.

"I'm not really sure. I don't think so," I said with a shrug.

Morley kept eye contact as he patted me on the knee.

"It could be anything, Jeanine. Has Peter been acting strangely at all lately?"

I squinted at him. He seemed to be pressing me a little. Frantically wondering how to respond, I was relieved when an attractive Asian woman in green doctor's scrubs came through the doorway a moment later.

"I'm Dr. Pyeng," she said. "Your husband is out of surgery and in stable condition. Please come with me, Mrs. Fournier.

"We were able to retrieve the bullet intact," Dr. Pyeng said as I quickly fol-

lowed her out into the hall. "The gun-
shot tore up a lot of deep muscle tissue in his shoulder, but thankfully it
missed bone. Also no major blood ves-
sels or nerves were cut, so I'm confident there won't be any permanent
damage."

Instead of heading into the elevator
as I expected, we made a right through
some automatic swinging doors. Dr.
Pyeng stopped at the first room beyond an empty nurses' station and
opened a door.

The room inside was narrow and
dim. Beside the bulky hospital bed, a
glowing white heart monitor beeped
softly next to a half-full IV drip. Peter
was lying on the wheeled bed with his
eyes closed. There was a thin, pink-
tinged tube under his nose. There was
also a huge bandage on his left shoulder and an IV inserted into his uninjured
right forearm.

"His blood pressure is looking good,
so I think we're out of the woods in
terms of shock," Dr. Pyeng whispered
as she led me inside and closed the
door.

Peter's eyes were glazed. I glanced at the IV bag. DIAZEPAM SOLUTION, it said in bold red letters, and in smaller type, I spotted the word VALIUM.

He squeezed my hand. Then he stared at me, sighing as he broke into a wide, serene grin. "Mermaid," he whispered.

There he was again, my big teddy bear, my drinking buddy. Even lying there in a hospital bed, he was handsome. He gave me his boyish Brett Favre winning-in-overtime smile.

I held my breath as I stared down into his groggy blue eyes. They were his best feature, as pale and soft as faded denim.

His eyes closed after a few seconds, and he started snoring.

"It's the painkiller," Dr. Pyeng whispered in my ear. "He should probably get some rest now. He'll be more lucid tomorrow when you come back."

Chapter 27

"You knew Elena as well, didn't you?" Chief Morley said as we pulled out of the medical center's parking lot in his department Bronco.

Morley had been standing in the hallway directly outside of Peter's room when I came out. He'd insisted on driving me home. Not being able to come up with a valid excuse, I'd finally reluctantly agreed.

"We worked together catering," I said. "I can't believe she's gone."

"None of us can," Morley said as we turned south on the Overseas Bridge back to Key West. Then he nodded with a frown. "Don't worry. We have an APB stretching from the Lower Keys all the way up to Miami. Catching these pieces of garbage is only a question of time."

Morley cocked an ear as something garbled squawked over the dash-mounted police radio. He lifted the handset to say something but then seemed to reconsider and placed it down again. He gave me a weary smile. "How did you and Peter meet, if you don't mind me asking? You seem, well, a little young."

"I was down here on spring break two years ago," I said. "I met Peter, and I never left."

"Ah, love at first sight. That's awesome. Was he off duty?" Morley said with a grin. "Or did you fall for the uniform?"

"It was all about the uniform," I said with a weak smile. "I ran a stop sign with my rental scooter, he pulled me over, and the rest is history."

It was the lie Peter and I had agreed on.

"Romance at the scene of the crime, huh?" Morley said with a nod. "That's how it happens with cops. Occupational hazard. You slap the cuffs on somebody one night at the beach, and the next thing you know you're letting them go and giving them a diamond ring."

I shot a look over at the police chief. For the second time, I got the impression that he was prying, trying to rattle me in some strange way. But his eyes were on the road. There was no trace of irony or accusation.

Still, I held my breath as the words *slap the cuffs on somebody one night at the beach* kept looping through my mind. Was the phrasing just coincidental, or did he actually know my secret?

The inside of the police SUV suddenly seemed hot, airless. Drops of sweat started to bead on my neck and underarms, along my lower back. I tried to zip down the electric window. Nothing happened. Morley must have had the child lock on.

Who was Morley really, anyway? I wondered dizzily. Who was he to Peter? Just a boss? Or was he a friend? An enemy like Elena? An accomplice?

We suddenly slowed and stopped. I looked out the window. We were in front of my house now.

"Thanks for the ride," I said, getting out.

"Any time, Jeanine," Morley said. "Sorry we had to meet under such bad circumstances. Remember, anything at all you can think of that might help us understand why Peter and Elena were shot, don't hesitate to call. Day or night."

"Will do," I said.

The cool trade breezes that make Key West bearable felt ice-cold as I resisted running to my front door. Once inside, I locked the door behind me and went to the living room window.

Morley was still sitting there, idling in the street in front of my driveway. After a gut-churning three or four minutes, he slowly pulled out. I'd never been so relieved in my life.

I continued to stand there for the next few minutes, scanning out the window up and down the street. I looked out across our sandy little lane at the palm fronds waving in the wind for another five minutes before I turned to go.

I stopped as something inched into my peripheral vision. Outside the window down on the corner of the block, Morley's PD Bronco slowed and stopped.

My face began to tingle, pins and needles in my cheeks, my lips.

What the hell was this?! Morley was watching the house now? Watching me?

I backed away from the window in disbelief, fighting for breath. My back hit a chair, and I collapsed onto the Mexican tile.

Chapter 28

It was sunset when the sound of seagulls woke me from the living room couch. Two of them were fighting over something along the backyard seawall. I watched them with horrific fascination as they cawed and hacked at each other with their beaks.

I gulped down a glass of water at the sink. I couldn't remember the last time I'd eaten. I was opening the fridge when I heard a car and the crunch of wheels in our crushed-shell driveway.

I ran to the living room window in a full-blown panic. Morley's black-and-white Bronco was gone, but instead, there was a police cruiser pulling into the driveway.

The cruiser's passenger door opened, and I almost passed out.

The cruiser backed out of the driveway as Peter, his left arm stiff, walked to the door.

Peter?

Why was he here? Wasn't he supposed to be in a frigging hospital bed!? Why the hell would they let him come home so soon? He'd been shot!

I backed away from the window, swallowing hard as his keys jingled at the door.

The lock clicked open as the knob turned.

Peter stopped like a kid playing freeze tag when he spotted me from the doorway.

I was frozen as well. Everything was strange, slightly off kilter. Even the light was wrong. It didn't feel like sunset. It felt like the morning.

Peter closed the door behind him. Then his keys dropped from his hand as his blue eyes beaded with tears. He squatted and then collapsed onto the front hall tile.

"Those assholes at the hospital told me to stay, but no way," he said, squinting up at the ceiling. "Soon as I woke up, I pulled that shit out of my arm and left. Fuck them and fuck those assholes who tried to kill me. I made it. I win. They lose. I'm home, Jeanine."

I thought about everything then. All the strange things I'd seen. Everything Peter had been keeping from me. I knew that what Peter was up to probably wasn't by the book, but I also knew that whatever it was, there had to be a good reason behind it.

Maybe he was in over his head, I thought suddenly. He did the finances. Maybe he'd made a bad investment and was trying to make up for it by doing something not exactly legal. Couldn't his nocturnal activity be his way of trying to protect us?

After all, I, of all people, knew he wasn't exactly a by-the-book sort of guy. Peter was a risk taker. He'd certainly taken a risk on me. If I didn't like it, I shouldn't have married him, right?

A pang of love and sympathy for him went through me then. I didn't want him to go to work ever again. I wanted him to stay here in our house, where it was safe. To stay here in our sanctuary, where bad things were kept away and all mistakes were forgotten.

I walked over and sat down beside him. I held his hand as he buried his face in my hair and cried.

"I was so afraid, Peter," I said. "I thought I lost you."

Chapter 29

Elena's wake was the following evening at the Dean-Lopez Funeral Home on Simonton Street. Peter and I were instantly swamped by the block-long line of dress-uniformed law enforcement on the sidewalk.

Peter, too, was wearing his crisply ironed uniform, his hat pulled low over his eyes, his dress blue coat draped over his wounded shoulder like a cape. I walked beside him in my somber black dress, holding on to his good arm.

Hundreds of hands patted Peter

softly on the back as we walked through the parted crowd.

"We'll catch those bastards, man," a bald state trooper with a twirly circus-strongman mustache said.

"Hang in there, buddy," said a short black female cop in a Marathon PD uniform.

Down the other side of the block, a crowd of saddened black people were also filing into the funeral home. I spotted young black boys in starched white shirts and bow ties, young girls in what looked like Communion dresses. There was even a Creole band playing for the mourners from the flatbed of a parked pickup.

They were there for the store clerk who had been killed, a fifty-three-year-old Haitian immigrant by the name of Paul Phillip Baptiste, who was being waked tonight as well. It seemed like the entire island had turned out.

Peter nodded with solemn concern as the gathered mourners embraced him and gave him their condolences.

"I couldn't get through this without you at my side, Mermaid," Peter whispered to me as we finally entered the funeral home.

I gave his hand a squeeze. "Where else would I be, Peter?" I said as we waited in line to sign the viewing room book.

Yesterday had actually been wonderful. I couldn't remember the last time we'd spent so much unbroken time together. We ate in, and when we weren't in bed, we were watching the sunset. A couple of times it seemed as if he wanted to tell me what was going on, but then he changed his mind and the subject. I didn't press him. I don't think I wanted to know. I just wanted us to be together. The world be damned.

Besides, I knew he would tell me everything eventually. We were best friends.

There *was* one odd moment this morning. As I returned to the kitchen after drinking my morning coffee in the yard, Peter was standing with his back to me, speaking softly on the phone. I stopped, frozen in the doorway, when he suddenly raised his voice.

"Fuck your plans, Morley," Peter

barked in a tone that managed to be fierce and cold at the same time. I'd heard Peter speak that way only once before. The night he'd arrested me.

"You just be there," I heard him say very distinctly as I went back outside. "I won't tell you twice."

It seemed odd that Peter would speak that way to his boss. I remembered Morley watching the house. It was hard to understand.

When it was our turn to pray, Peter and I walked together over to Elena's closed, flower-covered casket and knelt down. There was a hush in the room behind us as people realized what was going on. Out of the corner of my eye, I watched Peter remove his hat. After a moment, his face crumpled as if buckling under an unbearable interior torment, and I took his hat from him.

Peter and I became separated as he stayed and spoke with Michael Cardenas, Elena's husband.

I shook hands with the priest beside him and some more people I didn't know.

"Jeanine, there you are," Gary, the chef

from work, said as he scooped me up in a painful hug. "Can you believe any of this?"

"No, Gary. It's just horrible," I said looking around. "I don't see Teo. Is he taking this very hard?"

"He's gone," Gary said, shaking his head. "It's the craziest thing. Teo called me the night after the shooting. He said that he got a hotel job in the Dominican Republic and that he was leaving immediately. Elena's death must have been too much for him to take. You had to hear him on the phone. I felt so bad for the guy. I went by his apartment with his check the next day, but the landlord said he was already gone. Left his clothes and everything."

Peter's hat dropped from my hand as I remembered the last time I'd seen Teo. It was the night I had tailed Peter. Teo had been behind the wheel of the Mazda with Elena.

Elena was dead, and now Teo was just gone?

As Gary greeted someone else, I turned toward the front of the room by the casket. Morley had arrived, and Peter was standing with him. They were speaking quietly but intensely.

"Mrs. Fournier?" someone said.

I turned around. For a moment, I panicked. Standing very close beside me was a handsome man with long, dirty blond hair and a Jesus beard. It was the Björn Borg look-alike who'd scared me outside the Hemingway Home when I was catering. That now seemed like a thousand years ago.

"Do I know you?" I said, taking a quick step back.

"No," the man said in a voice deeper than I expected. "But I know you. Sort of."

What the hell was this? I thought. "Are you a cop?" I said doubtfully.

"I'm actually an FBI agent," he said, discreetly tucking a business card into my hand.

After a shocked moment, I looked at it. It had a raised FBI logo. "Special Agent Theodore Murphy," it said, with a phone number.

"Why are you giving this to me?" I asked.

Continuing to scan the room, he

shrugged his shoulders. "Nice to have help when you're in a tight spot," he said. He nodded at the card with his blond chin. "Hide it now before someone sees."

"What?" I said. "Before who sees?"

Murphy looked up at the front of the room where Peter and Morley were talking. Then he shrugged again. "You need to be very careful, Jeanine," he said, and then he turned and walked away.

Chapter 30

It was seven in the morning, a week after Elena's funeral, when I heard the engine on Peter's Stingray growl to life. Coming out of the shower, I dropped my towel and ran to the window.

Through the blinds, I saw a man rolling a large cooler across our backyard toward Peter's fishing boat. A tall man with cropped gray hair. It was Chief Morley.

As he boarded the boat, I remembered Peter's strange phone call: *Fuck your plans, Morley. You just be there. I won't tell you twice.*

There was a soft knock on the bedroom door.

"Jeanine! Whoa!" Peter said, poking his head in and seeing that I was naked. "You made me forget what I was going to say. Oh, right. I totally forgot to tell you that Chief Morley and I are going on a fishing trip."

A what?

"I know, I know. I should have said something. Bad Peter," he said, slapping the back of his hand. "It was the chief's suggestion. He thought this would give us a chance to clear our heads after the shooting and maybe get to know each other a little better. Sounds good, right? Hanging with the boss man. Who knows? Maybe it'll lead to a promotion. Don't worry about my shoulder. I'll let the old buzzard do most of the heavy lifting." Peter kissed me on the forehead softly and let me go.

"Thank you for being so supportive this week, Jeanine. You're the best. I can't wait to go to the Breakers with you. Steak au poivre, a nice red. Love you," Peter said, closing the door behind him.

"Wait," I said.

Peter smiled as he came back in.

"What is it? A quickie?" he said, hugging me. "Sure, but we need to hit it double time. Can't keep the boss waiting."

"No, idiot," I said, giving him a faux pound on his chest. "This is so sudden. What time will you be back?"

"I don't know. The usual. Sundown?" Peter said. "We'll grill. We badass about-to-be-promoted cops like to eat what we kill, you know."

I nodded. "See you at sundown," I said.

"Not if I see you first," Peter said, pinching my butt before he left.

Chapter 31

Two hours later, sweating not just from the rising heat, I waited on the coral pink steps of Key West's public library on Fleming Street. At nine thirty on the dot, I finally heard the lock turning behind me, and I jumped up, lifting the couple of large Dunkin' Donuts coffees I'd brought.

The tiny librarian, Alice Dowd, smiled in surprise as I approached the reference desk and handed her one of the coffees.

"Jeanine, bearing gifts," my elderly friend said with a smile. "What can I do

for you, my dear, on this lovely morning?"

"Actually, Alice, I needed to do some
research on my late father," I lied.

"Research, I see," Alice said, placing
the coffee I gave her onto a tissue she
produced from her desk. "Well, you've
come to the right place. Where do you
want to start?"

"Do you have access to the Boston
papers?" I said.

"You're in luck," Alice said, standing.
She gestured for me to follow her
through a book-lined corridor behind
her desk and into a little room. "We just
got these new computers with new
software called Netscape. It helps you
surf the World Wide Web, thousands of
newspapers and magazines and data-
bases and archives. Here, let me show
you how to use it."

After setting me up at one of the
computers, I waited until Alice was
back at her desk before I took a sip of
my bitter black coffee and contem-
plated my next move.

Then I made it.

I took out the card that Björn, or

Agent Theodore Murphy, or whoever he was had given me at Elena's wake.

Then I turned it over and read what was handwritten on the back.

> **Boston Globe, September 22, 1988**
> **Boston Globe, October 29, 1988**
> **You're not safe. I can help. Call me.**

I'd felt disoriented and tense ever since he'd given me the card. What did the *Boston Globe* have to do with me? And why had I been approached by an FBI agent? Was he watching Peter? Had he been doing surveillance when I spotted him the first time at the Hemingway Home wedding? Of who? Elena? Me? Was he trying to recruit me or something?

I didn't have answers, but I had kept the card hidden.

I took a breath and typed "Peter Fournier" along with "Boston Globe" into the search engine and hit Enter.

The screen blinked. I began to cough as two links popped up.

Both were from the *Boston Globe*. The dates matched those on the card.

I quickly clicked on the first one before I could think of a reason not to.
The screen blacked out for a second,
and a little hourglass icon appeared. I
was about to get up to ask Alice what
was wrong when an image appeared.

Boston Globe
September 22, 1988

ROOKIE COP'S WIFE KILLED
IN ROBBERY

Chapter 32

September 22, 1988

ROOKIE COP'S WIFE KILLED IN ROBBERY

Amanda Fournier, wife of Boston Police Department rookie Peter Fournier, was killed in a holdup of a Boston delicatessen on Thursday. Around noon, witnesses say, a masked man entered the establishment, brandishing a shotgun and demanding money. The assailant grabbed for Mrs. Fournier's purse, and

during the struggle the gun discharged, killing the twenty-year-old instantly. The suspect fled in a blue Chevy pickup truck. The Fourniers, police sources said, were planning to start a family.

I swallowed involuntarily, my hand shaking. I felt like throwing up, like I'd been kicked in the stomach.

Coffee shot out of the lid of my cup, scalding my jittery hand, but I couldn't feel it.

The date seemed to make sense. It was Peter. I could feel it in the marrow of my pregnant bones.

He'd had a wife? A wife who'd been killed?!

Why didn't he tell me that he was a widower? I wondered. He *did* tell me I was the first girl that he'd ever dated for more than a month. He'd also told me he was from New York, not Boston. Which I'd accepted at face value despite the suspicious fact that he was a die-hard Red Sox fan.

"No!" I actually said out loud to the screen.

I wiped sweat from my face with my wrist. When I turned, Alice was looking at me funny from her desk.

"Everything OK in there?" she said.

"Fine," I lied again as I looked back at the screen.

So what? I thought angrily. What did this prove? It was just a coincidence. Someone named Peter Fournier was a cop in Boston. There were lots of Peter Fourniers in the world. It was just a co-incidence.

What was I doing here anyway? I wondered. Wasting my time was what. Driving myself crazy was what.

I stood and grabbed my barely touched coffee. I needed to get out of this cramped concrete box and go for a jog on the beach or a long swim. Maybe in the afternoon, I'd head down to one of the wharves in Old Town and buy some freshly caught wahoo in case Peter and Morley came back empty.

Maybe he was doing something he shouldn't be doing, but we could deal with that. Checking up on him like I was

Nancy Drew was too out there. Screw Björn and his cryptic bullshit. My trip to Crazyland was over. I needed to go where I belonged. Home. Now.

As I stood, I couldn't help but remember the second link on the screen.

I clicked on the back arrow and stared at the Enter button as if it meant "Self-destruct." Then I put my coffee back down and clicked.

"Come on already," I said, nervously flicking the coffee's plastic lid with my thumb as I waited for the screen to change.

There was a hum, and then my stomach dropped as the black screen turned to white. The first thing that appeared as I began to scroll down to the article was a smudgy photograph.

I stopped scrolling, my whole hand trembling on the mouse.

It was Peter.

He was a few years younger, and he was wearing a Boston PD uniform.

As I looked into Peter's eyes, it felt like my throat was slowly closing, garden hose to coin wrapper to bar straw.

I finally closed my eyes to make the

picture and the rest of my rapidly disintegrating world disappear.

Unbelievable, I thought, keeping my eyes closed.

I assumed I'd calm down after a while, but it wasn't happening. The office chair beneath me suddenly felt wobbly, as if all the screws had been removed.

I'd thought that I'd grown up on the day my father died, but I'd been wrong. Sitting there in front of the picture of my husband that proved he was a liar, I felt my heart concede and my head take over.

I shook my head at my wedding and engagement rings. I had to get it out of the sand. I needed to wake the hell up.

There was no more denying it. Pictures didn't lie.

Fact: Peter was from Boston, not New York.

Fact: Peter had been married before to a woman who was killed.

Fact: Peter had been lying to me from day one.

Fact: I was in some deep shit.

It felt like time stopped as I glanced

down and spotted the new headline beside Peter's picture. My eyes ran over the five words, and it felt like the rapidly spinning world had stopped dead right there under the public library fluorescents.

I didn't think that it could get worse.

God, was I so very wrong.

"Cop Questioned in Wife's Death," the headline said.

Chapter 33

Boston, MA

COP QUESTIONED IN
WIFE'S DEATH

Authorities in the Boston Police Department have questioned the husband of the woman killed in a delicatessen holdup last month. Peter Fournier, who is a rookie patrolman on the Boston Police force, refused to answer reporters' questions as he left headquarters with his lawyer late last night.

Twenty-year-old Amanda Fournier was killed by multiple shotgun blasts during the midday holdup on September 21. A receptionist in a pediatrician's office on Crescent Street, she entered Jake's Deli next door a little before noon. Witnesses say a masked assailant entered behind her and that she was shot several times when she hesitated to give up her bag. No one else was injured.

The autopsy report released from the Suffolk County coroner's office confirmed that Mrs. Fournier was pregnant.

Detectives would not reveal if the questioning was routine or not. But a source close to the investigation described the events surrounding the murder as "suspicious."

Neighbors of the couple described the Fourniers as close and were shocked to learn of the questioning of Mr. Fournier.

As were Mr. Fournier's fellow Boston PD officers, one of whom described the twenty-six-year-old rookie and former U.S. Army Ranger as extremely competent and "a cop's cop."

I stopped reading. The world turned gray, as if a dimmer switch had been hit. I blinked, unable to breathe, waiting for my heart to start beating again.

I noticed that there was another photograph at the bottom of the article. I shuddered as I looked at the picture of the young woman above the "Amanda Fournier" caption.

The young woman had a lot of high hair and some dark eye shadow. I realized two things about this photograph simultaneously. It looked like the girl's high school picture, and she looked *a hell of a lot like me!*

I thought about what Peter had said when I confronted him about his double shift.

Then I...looked into your eyes, and I haven't been inside a church since my

Communion, Jeanine, but it felt holy...
Like God sent an angel down from
heaven.

I'll bet! I thought as I sat there, unable
to pry my eyes away from the photo of
the deceased young woman on the
screen.

I didn't actually remember printing
the article or leaving the library. Or
starting my Vespa, for that matter. The
first place I found myself after my shock
subsided enough for me to form a
thought was the main post office on
Whitehead Street.

A Coppertone-colored bum making
a straw hat on the curb glanced up as
I swerved to a dust-raising stop. There
was a pay phone inside the post office,
I remembered. It was inside a dark,
old-fashioned phone booth with a door
that closed, like a confessional. I had
actually called my college from this se-
cluded booth to tell them I wasn't coming back.

That was exactly what I needed now,
I realized. Privacy, darkness, confession.

I thought of another headline as I entered the post office, like a movie zombie.

"Cop's Wife Goes Nuts."

Chapter 34

As if in a trance, I pushed into the post office and fished out a bunch of quarters. I collapsed in the circa 1930s phone booth in the corner and closed its folding door behind me. Quarters rang off the dusty marble between my feet as I dropped several while dialing 411.

I needed to know what happened after Peter had spoken to the detectives. I needed to go to the primary source, get to the bottom of this.

If it had a bottom.

I got the Boston PD number from information, dialed, and began feeding the phone quarters.

One fact actually made me dry-heave as it kept repeating in my mind like a news crawl across the bottom of a TV screen.

Amanda Fournier was pregnant.

Just like me.

My sweat almost made me drop the receiver as the last quarter bonged home and the phone rang.

"Boston."

"Hello. May I speak to Detective... Yorgenson?" I said, reading from the printed article in my hand.

"Hold on," said the gruff Boston cop.

"Yorgenson," said an even gruffer voice a moment later.

"My name's Jeanine Baker," I said with a convincing Southern twang. My current state of insanity apparently was a wonder for my acting chops. "I work for Tony's Bail Bonds down here in Miami. We're doing an employment check on a Peter Fournier. Rumor has it he was involved in some kind of homicide. I got your name from a *Boston Globe* article. Can you give me some clarity on Mr. Fournier?"

Even at that point, I was hoping for some good news. Even after the lies and strange behavior, I was hoping that there was some reasonable explanation. That it was all one big mistake.

"Miami?" Yorgenson said. "So that's where that virus Fournier turned up. I'd be delighted to give you some clarity on Petey. The son of a bitch killed his wife and got away with it. He should be in a jail cell."

Chapter 35

I opened the booth door at the dusty post office, unable to breathe. The air had a strange new pressure, a new weight, as if the room had been suddenly filled with water when I wasn't paying attention, and now I was drowning.

"A shock, isn't it?" the cop said. "I know. Pete doesn't look like a psychopath, does he? He's a real charmer, especially with the ladies."

"How can you be so sure he did it?" I said.

"After his wife turned up dead, we

went by the book, looked at Pete straight off the bat more to clear him than anything else," Yorgenson said. "But we found out some very interesting things about Mr. Rookie of the Year.

"Like how he had dozens of brutality complaints. Like how he was rumored to love to party with nose candy. Like how he and Amanda had been separated. One of Amanda's friends told us it was because of the baby. He wanted her to abort it. She filed for divorce instead. He'd been harassing her for months before the shooting. Stalking her at work. Following some of her male coworkers home. 'If I can't have you, nobody will,' he told her on several occasions."

Yorgenson paused, letting it all sink in.

"I don't remember if it was in the papers, but Amanda was shot several times. The first time in the abdomen. The first officer to arrive on scene retired soon after on a psychiatric disability pension. I hear he lives in the subway station down at the Government Center now."

Yorgenson chuckled bitterly.

"Think Petey Boy was nervous when we came to question him? Think again. He sat there with those big cold baby blues of his and a shit-eating grin, like we were best buddies watching a Sox game at the corner watering hole. Had his alibi information ready and waiting for me. He didn't even bother asking if we had any other leads. The whole thing seemed to amuse him."

"But why didn't he—?" I started.

"Go to jail?" Yorgenson finished. "I ask myself that every day. Classic stalker-husband-kills-wife open-and-shut case, right? Wrong. The DA wouldn't prosecute, wouldn't even help us get a search warrant to look for the murder weapon.

"If I had to bet, Peter's uncle, Jack, who was the head of Boston PD's Internal Affairs, used every dirty secret and favor and string he had to squash our case. At least the stink I made got the punk to resign from the force."

I closed my eyes, my forehead banging against my knees as all the breath escaped my lungs.

"If you ask me—" Yorgenson started.

Then my time had elapsed and the phone went dead.

The phone clicking back into its cradle sounded like a pistol shot in the silence. A bullet right through my brain. I stared down at my hands as they shook in time with the painful thump of my heart.

I wandered outside dazed. Blinking in the sunlight, I felt weary, drained, like I'd just completed a stint of hard labor. The sun-blasted steps and sidewalk were empty. The George Hamilton lookalike bum who'd been weaving palm frond hats was long gone.

What a coincidence, I thought, glancing up into the painfully blue sky. So was my mind.

I left my moped where it was and decided to walk. I headed south past a construction site where a bunch of black and Mexican laborers sat in the shade of a king palm on a metal tool cart, staring blatantly, silently, and rapaciously. Usually I was nervous about such scenes, but that morning, I stared back defiantly, daring them to whistle, to say something to me, to set me off.

Where was I going? I wondered as I made a turn and wandered down a picket fence–lined street. I didn't have a home anymore. I'd never had one, in fact.

How stupid could a person be? I thought. Red flag after red flag had been raised, and I'd pushed them aside time and time again. It was over. I'd been duped, scammed, fleeced. The strangest and by far the worst part of all was that I was the one who'd conned myself.

Peter wasn't my best friend, wasn't the love of my life. I thought about the happy life of ease and suntan lotion on the deck of Peter's Stingray I'd been envisioning less than twenty-four hours ago, and I started laughing. Instead of tanning myself topside, I was in a hole as black and deep as they come, and I had no idea how to get out of it.

It was a rabbit hole, I realized as I walked down the sunlit street, skating along the edge of my sanity. And I was Alice. Peter was the White Rabbit. Who had Elena been? The Queen of Hearts, I thought. And off went her head.

Key West was actually Wonderland, I thought. The theory made a lot of sense, especially if you've ever been to Duval Street after midnight.

Chapter 36

I retrieved my moped and got back to the house twenty minutes later. I went straight to the bedroom closet and took down a suitcase. I opened it on the floor of the closet and threw in some underwear, my shirts, my jeans.

I glanced up at the top shelf at the big white box that contained my wedding dress and shook my head. That was staying. All yours, Peter!

By Greyhound bus, it would take about four or five hours to get back to Homestead, my small Florida hometown. My mom was gone, but I knew a couple of people there. I had a grand-aunt I could crash with for a few days. I lifted the phone to call a taxi. Maybe I could get a job at the Gap, where I'd worked summers, until I figured things out.

I dropped the phone back into the cradle.

Wait a second. What was I doing? That would be the first place Peter would look for me.

I was assuming Peter would just accept the fact that I had left him. But hadn't the Boston cop said that Peter had stalked his wife when she tried to leave? I held my head in my hands as I sat down on the bed.

Was that what I had to look forward to? Would Peter stalk me now? Murder me in a staged robbery?

My hand covered my mouth.

Wait a second. No.

Just like Elena.

Jamaicans hadn't killed Elena and the store clerk.

Peter had.

It all clicked into place. Peter had shot Elena with the machine pistol I'd seen on his boat and made up the story about the robbery.

It was over drugs, I realized, nodding my head. Which had to be why the FBI was involved. Peter was under investigation!

As I sat there, I knew it was true. All of it. I couldn't believe how much denial I'd been in.

Peter wasn't my hero. He wasn't the love of my life. He was a corrupt, drug-dealing cop and an ice-cold-blooded killer.

What now, Mermaid? I thought, dropping onto the bed. I lay there for a while, staring up at the ceiling.

Then I sat back up and took out the FBI agent's card.

I turned it in my hand as I stared at the phone.

Maybe I should call him? He knew the jam I was in. He could help me. He said so.

No! I thought, tapping the card to my forehead. Then everything would come out. What I'd done. How Peter had gotten rid of Ramón Peña.

I held my stomach in my hands. Staring down at the bulge that had already started to take over my belly, I envisioned myself giving birth in jail.

Unbelievable! I crumpled the card as I curled up on the bed. I couldn't call the FBI either. I might as well get a taxi to the nearest prison.

It took a little over an hour for the third option to finally dawn on me: What I needed to do. How I could try to go about doing it. It was an absolutely insane idea.

Right up my alley, I thought, getting to my feet.

Chapter 37

The first thing I did was carefully put all my clothes away. After I replaced the suitcase, I went into the bottom of my sock drawer and shook out every nickel of catering-tip money I'd put aside to buy Peter a watch for our anniversary. Two hundred and eleven dollars wasn't much, but it would have to do.

I quickly put the money into the pocket of my jogging fanny pack and changed into a gym shirt and sneakers and shorts. Finally, I went into the bathroom and put on some lip gloss before doing my hair up in a cute ponytail.

I needed to look my best.

I was, after all, going to be abducted by the Jump Killer this afternoon.

It was the news story at the hospital that had inspired me. The missing Marathon woman. The fact that the serial killer was now supposed to be in the Lower Keys.

Nineteen young women had gone missing, as if they'd disappeared into thin air.

I was going to be number twenty.

Peter wasn't stupid, I knew. If my plan was going to work, it would have to be flawless, perfect in every way. The second he found out, he was going to be suspicious. So was my new FBI friend.

But I didn't have a choice. If I wanted to get away from Peter, to get out of the immense hole I'd dug for myself, I had to try. It was my only shot.

I checked myself in the bathroom mirror one more time and then looked at my watch. It was just coming on noon. I went into the bedroom and stared out the sliders at the sunlit water. There was no sign of Peter's boat.

At least not yet. I'd have a six- or seven-hour head start.

I didn't want to be late to my own funeral.

After I locked the front door, I pulled up my gray jogging T and patted my belly.

"Wish us luck," I said to my baby. "Mommy's sure as hell going to need it."

Chapter 38

Ten minutes later, I was cruising at full throttle along Smathers Beach on my moped. Surprisingly, there were only a few people on its sugar white sand. A woman braiding her daughter's wet hair and a couple of pudgy old men the color of leather, casting sea poles into the almost glass-still water. I looked up as a biplane sputtered by: COME TO THE GREEN PARROT! RIGHT BESIDE US 1'S MILE ZERO! THE MOST SOUTHERN BAR IN THE US! read its ad banner.

Mile Zero, I thought. That's exactly

where I was. Make that Mile Less Than Zero.

I suddenly put on the brakes as I spotted what I was looking for. A tall, skinny white kid with dusty blond dreadlocks was sitting on the concrete boardwalk in what looked like a yoga position. Yet another one of Key West's many street kids and skate rats and punk rockers. A young beach bum come down to the country's lower right-hand corner God knew why, escaping God knew what.

I was escaping, too, in the opposite direction, and I needed his help.

"Excuse me," I said, stepping in front of him.

The kid held up a still finger, his eyes closed. After a moment, he stood, a guileless smile on his tan face.

"Mornin', ma'am," he said in a Texas accent. "Just doing a little Zen breath counting there. Sorry to make you wait. What can I do for you?"

Oddly enough, this was the way most Key West conversations went.

"I know this sounds weird," I said,

"but I was wondering if you could buy something for me."

"Drugs?" he said, looking at me suspiciously.

"No, no," I said. "Nothing like that. I need you to buy me some cord."

"Cord?" he said, eyeing me. "Like rope? You gonna hang yourself? I don't go for that kinky stuff."

"Of course not," I said. "It's nothing like that. I need paracord. It's a special kind of rope for parachuting. I use it in my parasailing business, and I'm out. My ex-husband owns the only marina supply store on the island that sells it, and I don't want to give the son of a bitch the satisfaction of going in to buy it myself."

I needed the cord for my escape plan, of course. The ligature was linked to several of the Jump Killer cases.

I knew the request and my explanation sounded fishy, but I also knew it didn't matter. Despite its small size, Key West had a healthy big-city, screw-the-cops, left-wing street vibe. Even if this stoner put two and two together after my disappearance, there's no way he'd go anywhere near the cops. Who better than some burnt-out street kid to be a go-between?

"What do you say?" I nudged him.

"Paracord, huh? That does sound pretty weird," the kid said, adjusting his dreads as he stood. "But I've been down here for a month now and have heard a lot weirder. I happen to be in the cord-buying business this morning. Ten bucks do it for you?"

"Ten bucks, it is," I said, waving him toward my scooter.

Chapter 39

After my young zen-cowboy friend scored the paracord for me, I hit a vintage clothing store in Bahama Village and then a CVS. A thin, homeless, twenty-something girl with sun-and-drug-wasted eyes holding a baby asked me for money as I exited the pharmacy, carrying two brimming bags.

Though I could hardly spare it, I stopped and gave her a dollar, praying that I wouldn't *be* her pretty soon.

I took the Vespa back over to Flagler Street and stopped at my favorite bodega for lunch. I ate my *cubano* slowly as the sun crested almost directly over-head.

I figured it would take until probably midnight for Peter to come looking for me. If I was lucky, he might even wait until morning.

After I finished lunch, I drove back to Smathers Beach, which ran along the southeast side of the island. Near its most deserted end, by the airport, I pulled over and got off the bike and stepped across the sandy path to the dunes.

I walked along the beach to where the beach grass grew about chest high and hunkered down.

There was no one on the beach, no one in the water.

It was time.

The first thing I did was upend my fanny pack, which contained my keys and wallet. Then with a pair of scissors that I'd bought, I cut a length of the paracord and dropped it on top of my CD Walkman.

The next part of the plan was the one I'd been dreading. It was also the most crucial. I took a small package out of the CVS bag and opened it.

It contained razor blades. They flashed like mirror shards in the bright light as I retrieved one and looked down at myself, debating. I swallowed as I finally decided on the back of my left calf.

I bit my lip as I lowered the blade down and sliced myself open. I hissed as I started the incision a little down from the back of my knee. Then teared up as I dug in harder with the blade, parting my skin.

At first, only a little blood dribbled out of the wound, but after I began to flex my calf over and over again, more came until I had a nice red stream going. It began to drip down my leg and off my heel, darkening the sand. I hopped around on one foot, flicking the blood on my fanny pack, the sand, the sea grass, the piece of paracord.

After about ten minutes, the area looked perfect, a total bloody mess.

Why not? Peter had shot himself to make his crime scene look good. The least I could come up with was a bit of self-mutilation.

I hopped back a few feet and sat down in the sand. I cleaned and bandaged myself carefully with peroxide and gauze and bandages that I'd bought at the pharmacy. I was even more careful to retrieve every scrap of trash.

After I was bandaged, I went over and kicked some more sand over everything. Then I stared at the scene for a minute, resting my chin on my thumb like a painter before a canvas.

Finally I stood.

It would have to do.

I crossed my fingers as I turned and walked away.

Chapter 40

It was as dim as a cave. The concrete floor was littered with cigarette butts and some wriggly-looking thing I didn't even want to think about. The smell of urine made my eyes water.

Perfect, I thought, locking the door of the public beach bathroom a ways from my fabricated crime scene.

It was skeevy and scary, but the most important things were that the women's side had a lock on the door and the sink worked. I turned on the sink's rusty tap as I opened the CVS bag.

Twenty minutes later, I looked at myself in the mirror.

My reflection provided some much-needed comic relief.

My still wet, self-cut, bleached hair was already turning platinum, and I had more black around my eyes than a raccoon. In the Catholic-school plaid skirt, black Social Distortion concert T, and Doc Martens boots that I scored from the secondhand store, I now looked like a cross between Courtney Love and a homeless fortune-teller.

My disguise was complete. I could have been any of the punk-rock girl runaways who hung around Duval asking for handouts. Time to go.

There was a city bus to Marathon, but that would be the first place Peter would check if he wasn't convinced by the crime scene. My plan was to hitchhike out, find some tourist passing by who would never link sweet young cop wife, Jeanine Fournier's, disappearance to my new punk-rock persona.

The wind was picking up as I came back out onto the beach, the first gold shadows stretching over the sand.

There was a roar, and I looked up at a small "puddle jumper" passenger prop plane coming in. Happy tourists about to touch down in paradise.

"One piece of advice. Take a pass on the Jell-O shots," I called up to it.

I shook my head as I gazed at the ocean, at the curvature of the world that I was about to enter practically penniless, definitely friendless, with a baby inside of me.

My Doc Martens clopped loudly on the concrete jogging path as I pointed myself toward the first bridge and whatever the hell would come next.

Chapter 41

The speeding stingray rose and dipped like a skipping stone as Peter opened up its three-hundred-horsepower engine full throttle on their way back in. This was Key West at its finest, he thought, looking through the spray at the red-gold sunset. Wind in your hair, cold beer in your hand, cooler bursting with amberjack.

The pink clouds starboard reminded him of the blood in the water when they'd fed Teo's body to the sharks that afternoon.

The product that Peter had bought

from him and Elena was supposed to
have been pure. He'd paid for pure. But
it had been cut. Not a lot. Just enough
to get them both killed.

Peter took another icy hit of his Corona and placed it back into the drink
holder, his blue eyes glued to the hori-
zon. He thought what he always thought
when push came to shove and someone had to go.

Goddamn fucking shame.

It was twilight as they turned into the
bay. Killing the engine, Peter expertly
drew up along the seawall and saw that
all the lights were off in the house. He
hopped out of the boat and went inside as Morley tied up and unloaded.

"Jeanine?" he called.

He noticed that her sneakers were
missing from the closet when he walked
through the bedroom. A glance out the
front door showed her Vespa wasn't in
the carport either.

He went back into the bedroom and
made a phone call. The phone kept
ringing. He hung up and sat on the
edge of the bed, thinking. He looked in

the closet again. All their bags were still there. All of her clothes.

Finally, he looked at their wedding portrait on the shelf beside the bed.

"Fuck," he said.

Morley was at the picnic table, dividing up the catch into freezer bags, when Peter arrived beside him.

"What is it?" Morley said.

"Jeanine," Peter said. "Something's wrong."

Chapter 42

In the rising engine whine of an approaching truck, I scrambled up onto the tiny concrete ledge on the highway bridge's shoulder just in time. Blinded by headlights, road grit biting at the side of my face, I easily could have reached out and touched the side of the rattling, creaking, speeding eighteen-wheeler flashing by.

Or ended up underneath it.

My knees buckled as its swooshing waft of air came close to knocking me over the bridge's shin-high railing and into the water. At least he was kind enough not to hit his eardrum-puncturing air horn as he clattered past like the truck before.

I hopped down off the ledge and soldiered on after the truck's red taillights, swinging my CVS bag up on my shoulder. There wasn't much left in it, half a package of Combos and a dwindling bottle of water. Supplies were definitely running low. My legs were OK, but my feet were killing me, starting to blister now in the Doc Martens after nearly four hours of walking.

Far out at sea, I spotted the red running lights of an anchored tanker. Above them, the clear startling night contained about a hundred billion silver-blue stars. I remembered how Peter and I had lain out in our backyard after our city hall wedding, drinking Coors Light and kissing in the dark like teenagers as we watched for shooting stars.

Now he was probably searching for me.

I figured that I'd covered about 20 of the 105 miles that make up the Overseas Highway, but I still wanted to put a little more distance between me and Key West before I tried to hitchhike. I wanted to be far enough away that any-one picking me up wouldn't think to put me and my planned disappearance to-gether.

After another ten minutes, I stopped and sat in the sand and finished the Combos. I stood immediately after I dozed off for a second. I couldn't put it off any longer, I decided. I had to hitch-hike now. If I didn't, I'd fall asleep on the spot.

Peter was certainly back by now, and there was only one road out of Key West. If I was on it come morning, he would find me. I couldn't let that hap-pen.

I stood as a pair of northbound lights appeared in the distance behind me. I walked to the road, tentatively lifting my thumb.

The vehicle's high beams dimmed as it slowed. I heard loud music coming from the radio.

Who would stop for someone out on this isolated piece of road? I thought, holding my breath. A good Samaritan? A weirdo? Peter?

I bit my lip to stop it from quivering as the lights hit me, and the car rolled to a stop.

It wasn't actually a car, I realized, but a vintage hot rod pickup with windsurfing boards and sails jutting out over the cherry red tailgate. The radio was blasting AC/DC.

I took a breath as I made eye contact with the two people inside of it. The driver looked friendly enough, a young guy with short, reddish blond hair. He wasn't wearing a shirt. Neither was his wiry, older, and meaner-looking friend, who had a bottle between his knees and a well-endowed-mermaid tattoo on his forearm. I winced as I spotted their glazed red eyes and caught the reek of pot.

Damn, I thought. What have I gotten myself into?

"Hey, punk-rock girl. Need a ride?" said the wasted driver, turning down "Hells Bells."

His Red Hot Chili Pepper reject of a friend took a swig of Southern Comfort and burped. "Cab's a little crowded, but let me clear off a seat for you," the tattooed guy said, wiping at his face.

I knew it, I thought, as icy pinpricks of fear made a path down my spine. I should have waited to hitch until I was at a place with more houses, more lights.

"Actually, guys, I changed my mind," I said, walking away. "I think I'm going to keep walking. Thanks. My boyfriend will be here any minute anyway."

I could feel my heart beating madly in my throat as the truck rumbled. I felt like crying as it kept pace alongside me.

The driver called to me, "Honestly. We're more than happy to give you a ride."

The truck suddenly shot off the road and did a half doughnut in front of me.

"Yeah, come on and stop being a bitch already," said the skinny guy with a smile as he opened his door. "We won't rape you. Promise."

Chapter 43

I dropped my bag as I turned and sprinted in the other direction. The skinny bastard laughed and gave a rebel yell as the truck rumbled again. I looked over my shoulder to see the truck reversing.

Were they just trying to scare me? They were doing a damn good job.

I was thinking about heading into the brush to hide when I saw another set of headlights. A car was coming off the bridge to the south. I ran out into the road, waving frantically. It slowed and then stopped ten feet in front of me. It was a dark Mercedes.

"Say, are you OK?" asked the man behind the wheel. He had a British accent. A feisty Jack Russell began barking from the passenger seat behind him.

Before I could answer, the reversing pickup came to a sand-raising stop in front of the luxury sedan. The two shirtless men hopped out.

"Beat it, fool. Before we put you in the hospital," said the mean, wiry guy, brandishing his booze bottle like a club.

Instead of screeching away as I feared he would, the Mercedes driver just leaned out of his window and smiled.

"Oh, I don't want to go to the hospital," he said to them in a campy, whimsical Shakespearean voice. "How about if we just stay here and play doctor in the back of that butch truck of yours instead? I call doctor. Who wants to get examined first?"

He was a member of Key West's vast gay community, I realized.

The wiry guy with the tattoo gave the bottle a deft flip as he stepped over to the driver's side of the Mercedes.

"The only thing that's going to get examined is your wallet, queen. After I knock all your teeth down your throat."

That's when the Mercedes driver opened his door and my jaw dropped.

The handsome black-haired man was massive, well over six feet, his bodybuilder chest and arms stretching his black polo shirt to the breaking point.

"Forgive me for being so forward, young man," he said, stepping toward the windsurfing punk with his veined arms crossed over his fifty-inch chest. "But has anyone ever told you how utterly striking those eyes of yours are? Let me guess: you're a Sagittarius?"

The two windsurfing fools looked at the WWF-sized gay Brit and then at each other in utter horror before racing back to the truck. A boogie board flipped over the tailgate and onto the road as they peeled out.

"I get the hint. Two's company and three's a crowd," the big Brit said to me with a wink and a sigh. "If that isn't the sad story of my life."

Chapter 44

"Sir Frank, at your service, m'lady," the Brit said, walking over to me and offering his hand. "And that little brat in the car there"—he gestured toward his Jack Russell—"is my loyal squire, Rupert. Those weren't friends of yours, I hope?"

"Not at all," I said, shaking Frank's large hand. "Just two jerks who offered me a ride. Thank you so much for stopping. Do you and Rupert always go about rescuing damsels in distress?"

"To tell you the truth, we'd much prefer to rescue a prince, but in your case, just this once, we'll make an exception. Hop in. I'm only heading up as far as Little Torch, but you're welcome to join me."

"First you rescue me, then you offer me a ride?" I said. "If I weren't so road-grimy, I'd hug you."

"If you weren't so road-grimy, I'd let you," Frank said with another smile. "Actually, I have one minor request. Rupert and I have been celebrating a little too exuberantly tonight, I'm afraid. Sometimes there're police along this stretch of the road, and we'd prefer not to get a DUI. You, on the other hand, look sober. Would you drive?"

Drive?! I thought. A Mercedes? Duh. "Not a problem," I said. "Assuming that it's OK with Rupert."

Sir Frank leaned over and conferred with the dog.

"Rupert says hop in and step on it."

I smiled at my tan, muscular friend as I walked around the car to the driver's side.

Gay British Prince Charming to the rescue. Only in Key West, I thought.

The car had wood trim everywhere

and sumptuous leather seats that smelled like expensive cologne. I would have accepted a ride in the back of a chicken truck, I thought, closing the door with a heavy vaultlike clunk. My luck was definitely turning.

I slid the gearshift into drive and tapped the gas. Sand flew as the car roared and lurched onto the road like an uncaged lion.

"Ease up a tad, would you?" Frank said as he produced a silver flask from the glove compartment and took a sip. "I'm afraid I didn't catch your name."

"Nina." I made it up on the spot.

"To you, fair Nina," he said, taking a tipple.

I was really enjoying the car. I'd never been *in* a Mercedes, let alone *driven* one. I liked the way it handled and especially the way it was making the highway railing blur by on both sides, putting distance between me and Peter. My escape plan was working out even better than I had expected.

"Hitchhiking on the Overseas doesn't seem very safe, Nina," Frank said. "Tell me. Are you running away *from* some-thing or *to* something?"

"Neither," I lied again. "I'm just down here on vacation from New Jersey. My girlfriends and I are staying up in Big Pine. Got separated from them at a party in Old Town."

"New Jersey?" Frank said, taking in my Goodwill attire and scrunching his face in doubt. "Yes, well, quite."

"I love your car," I said to change the subject.

Frank smiled as he pushed his rak-ishly cut black hair out of his face. There was an almost Asian cast to his dark eyes. His teeth seemed a little too per-fect. Were they capped? I wondered.

"Funny you mention that," he said. "That's exactly what I said to its owner when he picked me up an hour ago. You wouldn't believe how hard it was to squeeze the big son of a bitch into the trunk."

What did he just say? I thought, laughing tentatively.

I turned to him. He took another sip from the flask and sat staring ahead si-lently. The only sound was the rushing air in the dark. After a long, awkward and tense moment, he laughed loudly.

"Do-do-do-do. Do-do-do-do," he said, imitating the *Twilight Zone* theme before laughing again. "I'm sorry. I couldn't resist. You should see your face. You need to learn to take a joke, fair Nina. Though it is dangerous to hitch. You're lucky I'm a good person. Who knows what some completely crazy wanker might do to you out here in the middle of nowhere."

"Thanks again," I said after I swallowed.

Was it me? I wondered. Or was this getting weird very quickly?

I was doing my best to keep my eyes on the road ahead when there was a flash and a loud click beside me.

Frank, now holding a Polaroid camera, pulled out the advancing instant film and started shaking it.

What the? Now he was taking snapshots?

"Photography's a little hobby of mine," he said, blowing on the film. "You know what my favorite American expression is? 'Take only snapshots, leave only footprints.' You look shocked. Don't tell me a pretty girl like you doesn't like getting her picture taken?"

That's when a snatch of the Jump Killer news segment I'd watched in the hospital came to me. My lungs stopped working as I almost ran off the road.

The car theft and the body in the trunk may have been jokes, but the wrapper for Polaroid film was found at the site of one of the prostitute abductions!

"Say cheese," Frank said, raising the camera again.

Chapter 45

"You have nice bone structure," Frank said, shaking the second instant film sheet as we drove along. "I have a friend who does some model scouting. Would you like a makeover? I could do wonders for you. Take some head shots. After I do something with that vile hair. Did a blind person color it? You could shower at my motor home."

At the mention of the words *motor home,* my throat closed, as if it had been stuffed with a rag. The Jump Killer was speculated to have one of them as well. For the first time, I noticed the key chain dangling from the ignition.

No.

I closed my eyes as my hands started shaking on the leather steering wheel.

It was an eagle on a black shield. I'd been around enough military down in Key West to know that it was the Airborne symbol. Airborne meant parachutes and paracord. And how could a British guy be in the U.S. Army?

"So what do you say? Head shots? Shall we do it?" Frank said, as every molecule of saliva in my mouth evaporated instantly.

I saw some lights up ahead. Red neon in a small window. It was a bar. I accelerated toward it.

"I have to use the bathroom. I'm going to stop," I said weakly.

"Don't bother," Frank said. "My motor home is parked just up the road. You could go there. Won't be another second."

I kept gunning it and put on the turn signal. "It really can't wait," I said.

"Fine," Frank said as he put down

the camera. "As you Yanks say, 'When ya gotta go, ya gotta go.' "

Maybe I was wrong about him. Was I jumping to conclusions? It didn't matter, I decided. He had turned out to be a lot creepier than I'd first thought.

Frank capped the flask and put it back into the glove compartment as I braked for the turn into the bar's parking lot. When he took his hand back out, he was holding a blunt black gun. He pressed its barrel into one of my nostrils.

"On second thought. Keep driving, skank," he said suddenly in a New York accent. He definitely didn't sound British anymore. In fact, he no longer even sounded gay. "I freakin' insist," he said.

Chapter 46

The Jack Russell started barking from the little space behind the seats as the red lights of the bar disappeared on my left.

"What is this?" I managed to stammer out through my utter shock.

"This? It's a Walther P99," Frank said, waving the ugly gun in front of my eyes. He definitely didn't sound so whimsical anymore. His voice was deeper now, ice-cold.

"Why are you doing this?" I said.

My breath came irregularly. I was on the verge of hyperventilating. I couldn't believe this was happening. Maybe I'd fallen asleep on the side of the road and was dreaming. That's what it felt like.

Because how could this have happened? I'd set out to *pretend* to be abducted.

Now I actually was!

"You know what I hate?" he said, sounding like Robert De Niro. "Cute little things like you who think that all they have to do in life is shake their ass, and the world will beat a path to their door. If I were a woman, I'd hang myself when I hit puberty. I swear to God, I would. You're too disgusting for words."

From out of my terror-induced fugue, I remembered reading somewhere about how victims had to try and humanize themselves. If your abductor thought you were human, it would be harder to hurt you.

"Please don't do this. I'm pregnant. Please let me go."

"Pregnant?" he said. "Does the father know?"

"Are you him?" I said, trying to shift

the attention off myself. "The man in the paper? The one who's responsible for the missing women?"

"What do you think?" he said with a sigh. "The Jump Killer. What a stupid name. Not a single reporter could come up with something better? How about you?"

Pain blossomed in my mouth as he suddenly raked the barrel of the gun hard over my lips and teeth.

"How about instead you shut your face before I break those exquisite cheekbones of yours."

I felt dizzy. The surface of the road seemed to ripple through the windshield. My stomach suddenly clenched into the world's tightest knot.

After a moment, I realized it was full-blown nausea, from Combos and exhaustion and more terror than I'd ever felt in my life. The contents of my stomach started to slosh and churn, demanding immediate release.

I was leaning to my left, about to vomit out the window, when another thought occurred to me. What did I have to lose?

I turned and heaved loudly and violently onto the Jump Killer's lap.

As he howled in disgust, I impulsively reached over and unclipped his seat belt. The engine screamed as I dropped the accelerator to the floor and wrenched the wheel to the right.

Even with the air bag popping, the shoulder belt friction burned into my neck as we hit a telephone pole head-on. The hood of the car folded back into the windshield, shattering it before the momentum of the crash swung the car up and to the right. I heard the world's loudest nails-on-a-chalkboard screech as we skidded along the concrete railing.

Then we flipped over the guardrail backward, and we were falling through the air.

Chapter 47

Stars glittered through the shattered windshield as we free-fell. My skull whacked off the headrest as we hit the water with a booming splash. It felt like I'd been hit from behind with a baseball bat.

It was amazing how quickly the cold, black water poured into the car. Definitely a lot faster than I could think what to do about it.

I tried to open the door, but it was too heavy, and by then the water was up to my neck. I took a last gulp of air as it closed over my head.

I couldn't see anything. The car seemed to twist around and swing forward as we submerged. I wasn't sure if we were upside down.

Along with panic, I was now attacked by a strange, sudden paralysis. Could I find an air pocket? I wondered stupidly. Should I try opening the door again?

I realized the window was open. I tried to pull myself out of it. I couldn't. I was stuck. Then I saw that I was still wearing my seat belt.

Pain bloomed at my right elbow as I desperately tried to unclip myself. It was the Jack Russell. He was biting me under the water. I shoved him away in the dark and finally freed myself. The dog nipped at my boot as I was on my way out. I turned and reached in. My hand wrapped around fur and I dragged him up with me.

I don't know who was gasping louder when we broke the surface, me or the little dog. He tried to bite me again as I pulled him by his collar toward some mangroves growing from underneath the concrete roadbed of the highway to the left.

"Stop it!" I screamed at the dog. "Do that again, and I'll leave you for good!"

He finally seemed to get the message. He made a whimpering sound as he relented and let himself be dragged. In the heavy boots, I was hardly able to keep us both above water.

When I was close enough to the shore to stand, I turned back toward where we'd gone under. There was no sign of the Jump Killer. Did he make it out? God, I hoped not. The whole thing had happened so fast. I think I was still in shock.

The Jack Russell barked and followed at my heels as I headed out of the water through the brush and sand toward the road. I cursed. With its wall angled away from me, it was going to be hard to climb. The top edge of the metal railing was about three feet over my head.

It took me four jumps off a large piece of driftwood to grab on. Because of the angle, I couldn't use my legs. I was hanging there, swinging back and forth, trying fruitlessly to get my huge, heavy-booted leg up onto the top, when there was a splash behind me.

Please be a sea turtle, I prayed.

"Nina? There you are. Wait up," the Jump Killer called from the water in a strangely calm voice.

Chapter 48

"How am I doing, you wanted to know?" he continued, as he sloshed through the water. "Let's see. My collarbone is broken, my face is sliced to ribbons, and one of my eyes is full of glass. Otherwise, I'm as right as rain."

I started to cry as I swung my leg up as hard as I could. I managed to get the toe of my soaked boot onto the metal railing this time. But then it slipped off, and I was dangling there again helplessly as the splashes behind me got louder. I screamed as I tried again. Not even close. I was too terrified.

"Your arms aren't getting tired, are they?" the Jump Killer asked as the splashing became crashing through the brush behind me. "And what are you doing? Don't you know it's not legal to leave the scene of an accident?"

He would catch up to me in a second. My arms felt like wet spaghetti. I had to try again. I swung up. And missed!

"Darn nice try, Nina. You almost had it that time," the Jump Killer said directly beneath me as I swung back down.

I kicked out blindly behind me. My heavy boot heel came into delicious contact with his face. There was a strangled animal scream, and he was on his knees, holding his nose.

With the last of my strength, I changed my grip and did a chin-up to the rail. I hooked my right arm around it. It felt as if I'd torn a stomach muscle as I rolled over it and dropped into the road.

And heard the thunderous whine of an approaching truck.

You have got to be kidding me, was my only thought as I lay there on my belly with the blinding headlights of a truck coming straight at me. I couldn't do anything except watch the lights grow bigger and bigger as the air horn sounded. Its seizing brakes gave a drawn-out metallic chirp-chirp-chirp.

Chapter 49

The truck stopped six feet in front of me with a deafening outrush of the air brakes. From my perch almost underneath the thunderously rumbling vehicle, its grille looked as tall as a skyscraper. It felt like my heart had stopped, too, as well as all of my major brain function.

"Are you out of your goddamn mind!?" someone yelled.

I looked up. Far above me, a middle-aged blond woman's pissed-off face was sticking out of the tractor trailer's passenger window.

She jumped down and dragged me to my feet roughly. All I could do was stand there, staring at her. She was one of those heavy women that people think would be gorgeous if they were skinnier. As if that were relevant. I had post-traumatic stress disorder by this point.

"You stupid, stupid girl," she said, shaking me. "Do you have any idea how lucky you are that my husband didn't kill you? What happened to you? You're soaked. Are you drunk? Drugged out? Is that it?"

I looked back at the concrete wall I'd just climbed and then back at the woman with my mouth open. Where was the Jump Killer? Would he hop out now? Or was he hiding? Running away?

"She's not talking, Mike," the woman called up to the driver. "I think she might be some type of foreign person. Call the police on the CB."

"No, wait," I finally got out.

I wanted to tell her what happened, that I had just run into the Jump Killer, but I realized I couldn't. No way could I have contact with the police. Even after all this, I still had a chance of getting away from Peter.

"No, it's OK," I said. "I broke up with my boyfriend. We'd been swimming a ways back there and when I came back in, he'd, uh, left me. True, I cheated on him last night with his cousin, but still. I'm down here without any money, and I was trying to hitchhike home. I guess I fell asleep," I said.

"Fell asleep? You make a habit of falling asleep on the highway, you're going to wake up in a graveyard, moron. And you're certifiable to be hitchhiking. Couldn't you call your family?"

"My mom doesn't even know I'm here," I said. "Please don't call the police. She'll throw me out if she finds out."

"Where's home?" the woman said.

"Boca Raton," I said off the top of my head.

"Should I call the cops or not, Mary Ann?" the driver called down.

The heavyset woman stared into my eyes fiercely. "Don't bother," she called back up after a second. Then to me she said, "We're going as far as Miami. Would that help you out?"

If by "help out," you mean "save my life," I thought. "Thank you so much," I said.

The woman shook her head. "Well, c'mon," she said, boarding the truck and waving me up.

Mike, the driver, was bald and had a Hemingway-esque curly white beard. His head was down on the wheel, and he was breathing heavily when I entered the cab. And his agitated face was whiter than his beard.

"I'm so sorry, sir," I said to him.

He just shook his head as his wife closed the door.

"Told you this run to the Keys would be interesting, Mike," the woman said. "Keep your eyes peeled for any more youngsters napping in the middle of this goddamn road."

I looked out the window at the water as the truck crunched into gear and we rolled out. I couldn't see anything along the concrete bridge wall. There was no movement in the water, no movement in the brush. The Jump Killer must have been hiding underneath the side of the bridge, I realized. Like a troll, I thought, still dizzy with panic.

After a minute, as the truck began to pick up speed, Mary Ann rummaged in the berth behind her and handed me a towel. Wrapping myself in it, I wriggled up against the passenger door and stared out at the stars sliding past. The lights of the road ahead curved out over the dark water like spots on a connect-the-dots sheet.

What would the next dot be? I wondered. More ruin, no doubt. More horror. More pain.

Because I was cursed, I thought. Wherever I went, death and craziness homed in on me. I seemed to emit a scent that attracted these things.

I tried to figure out why that was. Was it something in my nature? My inherent gullibility?

As we roared around a long curve of the Overseas Highway, out on the water to my right I suddenly saw a small, distant light. It was the tiny running light of a small anchored sailboat.

Or Ramón Peña, I thought as my ten-

ton eyelids began to drop.
soul of the man I had run ov
lowed Peter to sink in the oce
was the reason for my ba
reason why I would always be hounded.
Peter wasn't the only one with blood
on his hands.

I deserved to be haunted, I thought,
and then I finally, gloriously, passed
out.

Book Three

NEW YORK NINA

Chapter 50

I sit in whiteness, getting ready for my wedding. I'm wearing a fluffy white robe and white curlers in my hair. Even the separators between my freshly polished toenails are a chaste virginal white.

I smile as I suddenly notice the white roses that cover the bathroom's entire countertop. They glow almost painfully in the undiluted Florida light that fills the room.

As I put the finishing touches on my mascara in the makeup mirror, there's a pounding on the door.

"Come out with your hands up!" Peter says through a bullhorn. "And those little panties of yours held high!"

I begin to laugh but stop as I hear the coughing sound of a gas engine being started with a rip cord. Is it a lawn mower? I think, turning toward the door.

Immediately bits of wood explode inward, spraying my face, and I see the tip of the chain saw as it cuts a slot in the door. As I watch, the spinning blade disappears, and through the hole a face appears, like Jack Nicholson's in The Shining. I think it's Peter, but it's not. It's the almost Asian face of the Jump Killer.

"How's my fair Nina?" he says, flashing me his white capped teeth.

As I turn to run, I trip on the lip of the tub. I grasp the edge of the shower curtain, but the rings pop off the rail one by one, and I fall backward into warm water. As I scramble up, I see it's not water at all but blood, and in the tub beside me, spooning like a honeymooning cou-

ple, are the dead bodies of Elena Cardenas and Ramón Peña.

Covered in blood, I scream, flailing as I see that half of Ramón Peña's face is missing, the white of his skull stark against the sea of red.

I woke up. Struggling to catch my breath, I looked up into darkness while my heart clubbed the inside of my chest. And I *really* thought I was going to have a heart attack when I saw a dark figure was hovering above me.

"Angel of Death," I spat out.

"Mom?" Emma said, clicking on my bedside lamp.

My eyes burned as she started shaking my shoulder.

"Wake up, Mom," she said. "We both overslept. I can't find my new AE shirt. You know, the nice blue one? Jeez, you're covered in sweat. Are you sick? Don't tell me you've got the swine flu?"

I wish, I felt like telling my daughter as I pulled the sheet over my head. You could get over the swine flu. I mopped my clammy brow on the other side of my pillow.

My recurring nightmares, on the other

hand, were the gift that kept right on giving.

Even after almost twenty years.

"Oh, I know," Emma said. "Too much champagne at my party last night. That's it. You're hungover."

Emma was teasing, of course.

"Ha, ha, wise girl," I said, lifting the cover and suddenly smiling. "Your blue shirt's crisply ironed on a hanger in my closet, Little Miss Sweet Sixteen. And you're welcome for last night's party. It wasn't like it was expensive or anything. I think it was worth having to eat cat food when I'm old, don't you?"

Emma stuck out her tongue. I stuck out mine right back. Emma and I were close, like sisters and best friends put together, only better. We even shared clothes. Which pissed her off. I guess it would piss me off a little, too, to have a mother who could fit into my jeans.

"As if you'll ever be old," Emma said, climbing into the bed and wrapping me in a headlock. "You know how many of my stupid friends' mothers asked if you were my older sister? Even some of Mark's Collegiate buddies were checking you out. It's really not fair. Isn't Snow White supposed to be the fairest one of all? Come on, Evil Queen. Step aside already."

"Never," I said with a cackle.

Again, Emma was teasing. Due to a death-march regimen of treadmilling and starvation, at forty I was just still in the ballpark of merely pretty. Emma, who had inherited Peter's dark, beguiling looks on the other hand, was already nearly six feet tall and a heart-melting beauty.

I wasn't the only one who thought so, either. Every once in a while, she'd get legit offers for modeling from friends of friends. Which I told her that I'd let her do over my dead body, of course.

As much as we were friends, I was very protective of her. Probably overly so. I didn't care. I knew what the world was like, how precarious, how quickly and completely destruction could follow from just one false move.

Emma was going to have a good life, a normal life, a safe life. It was all that mattered.

"The last thing I'd worry about is your

looks, kiddo," I said, knocking on her head with a knuckle. "Now, that brain of yours, well, that's another story."

I ducked as she swung my pillow.

"Shit!" I screamed as I finally glanced at my iPhone charging on the night table and saw the time. "Why didn't you tell me we were so late!?"

Chapter 51

It was pouring rain four hours later when, umbrella-less, I decided to race from my triple-parked taxi toward the crowded Aretsky's Patroon on East 46th Street. Not good. It was only a hundred feet or so, but I got completely and utterly hosed in the monsoon.

Of course, I thought, as I finally squished my way inside. It always rained when you were running late for your very first power lunch with your boss and forgot to check the weather.

To make matters oh so much better, there was a lithe and perfect Nordic hostess behind the podium inside. She acknowledged my sopping presence with a slight lift of her eyebrow. But then she smiled nicely.

"Welcome to Patroon. Name?" she asked.

I stood there as tall and regally as I could, doing my damnedest to pretend that being as wet as a drowned rat was the new black.

"Nina," I said, flicking my ruined hair out of my eyes with a hopefully gracious and professionally competent smile. "My name is Nina Bloom."

I'd lucked out. My boss hadn't arrived yet, so I was able to do some rehab work on my makeup and hair in the ladies' room before I returned to the discreet banquette where I'd been seated.

As I waited, I kicked back for the first time and drank in the vista. Carefully seated inside the modern power-lunch mecca, big-hitter media elites in bespoke tailoring were cutting deals beside Botoxed A-list fashionistas. Among the bottles of San Pellegrino, I spotted Ivanka

Trump and Anderson Cooper chatting it up.

Well, it was more like I studiously ignored Ivanka and Anderson, like we were currently not speaking. I had picked up on one or two things living in Manhattan for the last couple of decades.

After a moment, I smiled and raised my own glass of sparkling water toward the room of power players and took a sip. Given my arrival in New York in 1994 with nothing but the clothes on my back and Emma in my belly, I had good reason to toast myself.

Most of all just for surviving.

I thought about all the craziness of those first few years. The skeevy dive bar around the corner from Madison Square Garden where I worked until I started to show. The place in Chinatown where I got my first fake ID. The shoebox of an apartment in Spanish Harlem that I brought Emma home to after giving birth at Lenox Hill Hospital.

My "big-shot career," as Emma called it, came later. After some extremely creative résumé writing and a New York

Career Institute class and a whole lot of luck, I'd scored my first non-waitressing job as a paralegal at Scott, Maxwell and Bond, one of the most powerful corporate law firms in the city.

I thought working at a law firm would be just a way to make a little more money, but from the get-go I found myself enthusiastically drawn to the work. There was something so exciting about being even a small part of the cases and issues and war room strategizing. After the chaos that had been my life up until that point, I found comfort in the law, its authority, its rationality, its calm and inherent nobleness.

The luckiest thing of all was that after I proved my usefulness in a class action suit, my boss, Tom Sidirov, a legendary litigator and even better person, practically demanded that I go to City College and then Fordham Law School on the firm's dime.

It had taken almost ten years of work and night school, and thousands of logged hours on the New York City subway, but I eventually pulled it off. I became a lawyer. I'd even passed the New York bar exam on my first try.

Over the last three and a half years, my career had steadily started to pick up speed. I wasn't in line to make partner anytime soon, but I had my own cases now, my own clients, even my own personal assistant.

All my hard work at the office and as a mom was starting to reap some pretty plush dividends, I thought, as I sat in the tastefully done restaurant. There weren't supposed to be second acts in American lives, but I was giving it a pretty good go. I was finally starting to come across things I'd never dreamed I ever would again.

Stability. Fun. Dare I even say its name?

Hope.

It seemed that after two decades and a thousand miles, maybe I'd finally run far enough. For a moment there among the high-rent chatter and clacking crockery, I think I actually felt safe.

That's what made what happened next so wrong, so utterly unfair.

Because as I sat there toasting myself, it wasn't just my boss who was on his way.

As I sat cozy and dry and warm and stupidly proud of myself, my rude awakening and reckoning was already hurtling toward me, bigger and badder than ever before.

Chapter 52

"Is this seat taken?" my boss, Tom Sidirov, said five minutes later.

Bald and short, even in his signature Brioni navy chalk stripe, my slight, sixty-plus mentor looked more like a retired bus driver than one of the country's most successful litigators. Which couldn't have tickled the cunning summa cum laude Columbia Law School grad and tenacious former Golden Gloves boxer more.

"When you say lunch, you don't mess around, do you, boss?" I said.

"Well, when it comes to bribing my

protégée," Tom said, twisting an imaginary villain's mustache, "I pull out all the stops."

"*Protégée?*" I said. "Wow, here it comes. I'm almost afraid to ask. What's this urgent new project you wanted to discuss?"

"A multifirm pro bono initiative is starting up," Tom said as he spun his BlackBerry on the tabletop. "I don't know too much about it except that it's called Mission Exonerate, and I'm the partner who was supposed to find the volunteer for it, yesterday. Which I'm praying to Saint Anthony might be you. It starts Monday."

"What about ProGen?" I said.

For the last month, I'd been on a team putting together the contracts and prospectus for a biotech merger. To fall asleep at night recently, instead of counting sheep, I'd go over the alphabet soup of reagents, genomics, proteomics, and cell therapies.

"We'll find someone else to take over your role," Tom said, lifting his gadget and making the sign of the cross at me with it. "I know it's last minute. Hence, the free lunch and my undying gratitude. What do you say?"

As if it were a question. Tom had been like a father to me. Try like a fairy godfather.

"I say yes," I said with a smile.

"*Marone!* How many times I gotta tell you?" he said, reverting to his native Bensonhurst accent as he took an envelope out of his pocket and handed it over. "When you're being bribed, neva eva agree straight offa de bat."

I opened the flap and slid out the two tickets.

And had trouble breathing.

They were double-digit field box seats for tonight's Yankees game. Tonight's Yankees–Red Sox game. The first one of the season. The only bigger Yankee fan than me was Emma.

"Oh, Tom," I said woozily. "Oh, wow. I'm..."

"Hungry?" my fairy god counselor said, winking as he lifted his menu. "Then try the steak frites. Best in the city. Fuggedaboudit."

Chapter 53

You had your good days, Peter Fournier thought from his loge-level seat in the unbelievably opulent and immense new Yankee Stadium.

And then you had your *perfect* days.

"Here we go, Boston! Here we go!" he yelled as loud as he could as Beckett retook the mound.

From the famous façade, to the flat-screen TVs at every turn, to the low bowl-like design that made it seem like you were watching the game from the batting circle, even a die-hard *Sawx* fan like him couldn't deny the billion-dollar ballpark was baseball's version of paradise on earth. Even after they'd dug up Ortiz's jersey.

But to be here in the eighth inning, the Sox up by three and Beckett still on the mound in a *perfect* game, was nothing short of miraculous.

Actually, the true topper was having his family there, his gorgeous wife, Vicki, and his two sons, nine-year-old twins, Michael and Scott, with him. As on all their trips to Disney and last year's incredible European jaunt, Team Fournier was having an unforgettable blast.

The Fournier family had been invited to the game by Tom Reilly and Ed O'Connor, two New York FBI agents Peter had met at the FBI's National Academy course years before. He'd actually had them and their families down for a Boston–New York spring training game in Fort Myers, and now it was payback.

The two big, bearlike Feds sat on either side of the Fourniers with their Yankee-fan families. There was a lot of razzing back and forth, but it was all in good clean fun.

Funny the places life took you, Peter thought, smiling as he shook his head at his twin sons. The second oldest in a destitute family of ten in a South Boston project, Peter had abhorred the idea of ever having a kid.

To be clear, he liked being married just fine. After all, there was nothing more satisfying or fun or clean than having a faithful, monogamous woman in his life. But by age fifty, and now on his third wife, Peter had had the epiphany that he'd actually acquired enough money to completely buffer himself from all the smelly, human unpleasantness of child rearing with a huge house, nannies, and prep schools.

It had worked out even better than planned. He'd never smelled a diaper, let alone changed one. And it was up to him which meaningless ball games or Christmas plays he would attend.

All he needed to concentrate on now was creating as many unforgettable, fun, heartwarming moments as were convenient so his family would give him his space. Like tonight's doozy. Being Daddy was easy.

Beckett started off the eighth with a four-seamer on the black that Jeter just gaped at. Peter squeezed Vicki's hand as their usually sedate son, Michael, jumped out of his seat with excitement, delivering high-fives.

Beckett went up 0 and 2 as Jeter swung and missed a breaking ball.

Peter looked down at Beckett with spine-tingling reverence. What a warrior. Baseball immortality was now within his grasp, and not even fifty thousand screaming New Yorkers could take it away.

One more. C'mon, Josh. One more, baby. Please, Peter prayed.

Beckett threw another off-speed pitch down and away, and Jeter swung and got under it. Youk went all out from first, but it bounced off the top of the Yankee dugout into the crowd.

Damn. Just missed, Peter thought. But at least it was just a foul ball.

A beautiful teenaged girl's face filled the JumboTron in centerfield a moment later. She was holding the ball and hopping up and down like she'd just won the lottery.

There was something familiar about the girl, Peter thought, squinting at the six-story-tall high-def screen. Something in her smile reminded him of his dearly departed mom's high school yearbook picture. Peter had loved that picture and his mom, despite her inability to keep her legs closed.

Peter watched, riveted, as they replayed the girl's one-handed grab.

They even froze the frame.

Then his Heineken fell straight down out of his hand, splattering his ankles.

Because the good-looking blond woman embracing the teen girl reminded him even more of someone else.

His dead wife, Jeanine.

Chapter 54

"Can I borrow those, son?" Peter said calmly, despite his galloping heart.

"Sure, Dad," Scott said, immediately handing over the binoculars that one of the Feds had brought.

Raising the glasses, Peter ignored the thunderous cheer that rose up as Jeter hit a liner into the gap, ruining Beckett's perfect game. He slowly searched into the crowd behind the Yankee dugout, where the foul ball had landed.

He panned over people in suits. Billy Crystal. A bunch of pudgy Yankee fan

goons pointing at a little black girl in a
Boston cap. The new and improved
Rudy, without the comb-over.

He scanned up and down the rows
and sections, one by one, methodically.
Looked through the crowded aisles.

He didn't spot her. Even after five
meticulous minutes. There were too
many people, too many faces. None of
them was Jeanine.

The woman had only looked like her,
and he'd jumped to conclusions, he
decided as he handed back the binoculars to his son. It made sense.

He'd been thinking more and more
about Jeanine over the last year for
some inexplicable reason. He'd even
dreamed about her a few times.

In one of the dreams, he was eating
dinner with her again by the seawall in
their backyard like on their first date. In
another, he had his hands around her
throat, holding her down under the water on an empty beach as she tried to
scratch at him.

All in his head.

When he lowered the binoculars, he

saw that A-Rod was on first and Beckett was heading for the showers.

"Now that just sucks!" his son Scott yelled.

Tom Reilly, the Fed beside them, began to do a little victory dance as he giggled uncontrollably.

You know what's even funnier, Tom? Peter felt like asking his FBI pal. *The way you let me pump you for information about any large upcoming federal drug interdictions. You know what I do with that information and the other information I casually collect from all your asshole buddies at the DEA, Tom? I sell it to the cartels. Have you heard of air traffic controllers? Yeah, I'm like a drug traffic controller. Beckett might have just blown a perfect game, but I made seven figures last year, Tommy Boy. Tax free. Not bad for a hick Florida cop. Tee-hee.*

Peter scruffed his tan son's blond head with a grin.

"Don't worry. It's not the end of the world, Scott," he said. "A man takes disappointment in stride. And what did I tell you about using the S-word?"

"Sorry, Dad," Scott said sheepishly. "I meant to say stinks."

"There you go," Peter said, patting his son gently on his shoulder as he gave Reilly a wink. "Much more appropriate. Always remember, the words we choose reveal our true character."

Chapter 55

It was a quarter to nine on Thursday morning when I stepped into a gleaming black glass office tower at 57th Street and Third Avenue. With a temporary security pass hanging off my lapel, I smiled at the dozen or so other young Global 100 lawyers who sat as fresh and crisp as sharpened pencils in the twenty-third-floor conference room for the multifirm pro bono meeting.

I scanned the impressive corporate firm names on the place cards, some of which actually represented countries. It was heartening to see lawyers about to do some pro bono work.

If, in fact, that really was what we were going to do.

I hoped it was.

Unfortunately, I'd done pro bono initiatives before in which there were a lot of long expense-account lunch meetings and high-minded dialogues but not too much legit legal work that affected anything or anyone.

Whatever the case, the only thing I knew was that I was going to work my ass off for my boss, Tom Sidirov.

For the Derek Jeter foul ball Emma had snagged last night and for the front-row privilege of watching the Bombers turn a Beckett perfect game into a ninth-inning come-from-behind walk-off Cano grand slam?

I was prepared to work forty hours a *day*.

I was gathering up coffee and info folders when I caught a bright flash of red hair in my peripheral vision.

"No way!" I squealed.

"Yes way, José," my pretty porcelain-skinned friend, Mary Ann Pontano, said as we bear-hugged. "Thank God. I just might be able to get through confer-ence hell after all."

I laughed as I hugged her again.

She'd been my first New York friend. She was my next-door neighbor in the crappy apartment I'd gotten on 117th Street in Spanish Harlem two weeks after I'd gotten off the Greyhound at the Port Authority.

Being the only single women and non-Spanish-speaking people in resi-dence, we gravitated toward each other. Especially when we had to do laundry in the *Silence of the Lambs*–style base-ment laundry room. She'd helped me find a waitressing job and a pediatrician for Em. She was actually the one who'd encouraged me to become a paralegal all those years ago.

"It's been way, way too long, Mary Ann," I said.

Mary Ann smiled. She still looked more like an Iraq War news anchorette than a combat Iraq War vet and ex-NYPD cop. She'd parlayed her tough-ness and good looks into a plum inter-national-law-firm investigator job.

"That's fine," Mary Ann said. "I know you greedy, capitalist corporate-lawyer types. Not a minute to spare counting all that filthy lucre. No time for the peasants."

"Well, Mary Ann," I said. "We can't all be keeping it real in the hood up there in Scarsdale with our dentist husband and two toddlers."

"It's Bronxville, OK?" Mary Ann said. "Get it right. Bronxville eats those soccer-mom bitches from Scarsdale alive. Anyway, what are we doing here again?"

"We're here to save some lives, that's what," said a short, friendly-looking man with an unruly mop of black hair, who burst into the conference room with a legal box.

"Welcome to Mission Exonerate NYC, everyone," he said, dropping the box onto the table with a tremendous thud. "Since time is money, I won't waste any. I'm the initiative cofounder and director, Carl Fouhy. You are the brightest legal minds in New York City, I take it. Or at least, New York's currently most dispensable legal minds. Whatever the case, I need you and, more important, the men and women who are right now facing imminent execution need you even more."

He hit the lights as a bright Power-Point board hummed out of the ceiling.

The faces of tough yet defeated-looking men and women began to slideshow.

"You would not believe the amount of witness misidentification and forensic-science misconduct that we've found in some of these capital cases," Fouhy explained. "That's even before getting into some of the flat-out shitty defense lawyering we've uncovered.

"There are cases of counselors failing to investigate witnesses or call experts. Of defense lawyers actually being intoxicated and falling asleep during trial. That's where you folks come in. You will level the playing field for these mostly poor, mostly uneducated men and women."

He lifted the lid of the box, took out thick yellow envelopes, and began to drop them one by one in front of us.

"These are your assigned cases. You can open them momentarily, when you leave. On the first page, you will find the accused's current attorney. We want you to work in conjunction with him. Your job is advisory, to go and do a face-to-face with each defense attorney. See that everything has been covered, the police report, the appeals. We're looking for mistakes, people. Catching a mistake may save someone's life.

"Now, if someone will hit the lights, I'll go over a couple of test cases in which we've overturned executions. We'll review the process and then, basically, you're on your own. Any questions, myself or the initiative's policy advisers, Jane Burkhart and Teddy Simmons, can be reached. Otherwise, I'm confident you guys will figure it out. Improvise and overcome, people. Save a life!"

Chapter 56

"And I thought speed dating was fast," Mary Ann said as we unloaded at Starbucks on Third Avenue half an hour later with Jane Joyce, a lawyer at Mary Ann's firm.

"On your mark, get set, go," I said as we all pulled out our assigned cases.

I flipped through a thick mound of pages. My case concerned a man named Randall King who was on death row for murdering two armored-car guards in a Waterbury, Connecticut, holdup. I showed Mary Ann the mug shot of the bullnecked, malevolent, cornrowed convict.

"Wow, they gave me a bank robber," I said. "Lucky me. This is going to be fun."

"I got a drug dealer who killed his family!" Jane Joyce cried out. "In Texas!"

"You think yours sucks?" Mary Ann said, gaping at her case. "I got a loser they caught on a cold homicide case in South Florida!"

As always, my stomach tightened at the mention of Florida.

"A fricking serial killer, no less," Mary Ann said. "Check this out."

I almost bit through my latte cup. A burning line of coffee sprayed from my nose onto my chin.

In Mary Ann's hand was a photo-copied *Miami Herald* article. She gave it to me.

It had a three-word headline: "Jump Killer Caught?"

Chapter 57

May 17, 2001

JUMP KILLER CAUGHT?

Palm Beach County cold-case detectives placed a state corrections officer into custody for the 1993 murder of a Boca Raton woman Monday night. Police sources confirm that a DNA match led to the arrest of Florida City resident Justin Harris.

Murder victim Tara Foster was still in college in June of 1993 when she was reported missing

after volunteering as an office worker at the Homestead Correctional Institution in Florida City. Her remains were found wrapped in plastic in Everglades National Park a year later.

With DNA evidence originally retrieved from Foster's body, cold-case detectives restarted the investigation this month with an effort to obtain DNA from likely suspects. Because she'd been tied with paracord, the same ligature linked to the infamous Jump Killer disappearances in the early 1990s, cold-case officers cross-referenced original witnesses in the Foster case with former paratroopers.

Justin Harris, a veteran of the 101st Airborne and a guard at the Homestead prison, provided DNA that matched samples found on Foster's clothing.

He is currently being held without bail.

My pulse hammered in my throat, against my temples. The photocopied article in my lap wavered in my vision like something seen through old glass.

As I sat there with Mary Ann and Jane, the traffic beeping outside on Third, the shouted coffee orders, the jet engine whoosh of the milk frother, all began to fade. In their place came a rush of images and sensations I'd thought I'd successfully blocked from my memory.

The Jump Killer's strange dark eyes, the pungent smell of cologne in his car, the ache in my arms as I hung on for dear life as he crashed through the surf behind me.

"Hey, Nina," Mary Ann said, looking at me with worry. "You OK? You look almost as pale as me."

"Fine," I heard myself saying. I braced myself and thumbed to the next page. I found another newspaper article that listed all the women whose deaths the Jump Killer was believed to be responsible for. I scanned the faces until I got to the second one from the bottom.

Above the caption "Victim 20" was a

vaguely familiar face. I guess it should have been, *since it was my high school yearbook picture.*

Sitting there, I felt like you do in that dream where you're back at school, and you have to take that one last test you never studied for. That sour, pit-of-your-stomach, panic-attack realization that the jig is up. The worst thing of all has happened. *You've been found out.*

"Earth to Nina," Mary Ann said. "Hey, if you're so interested, why don't we switch? Connecticut's what? Two hours away at the most. How am I going to arrange everything with my kids if I have to go to Florida? Besides, I've got red hair. Fluorescent bulbs give me blisters. Do ol' Mary Ann a favor. This is a media case as well. Think of the publicity for your firm. You'll make partner."

A media case? It was worse than I thought. Why the hell hadn't I heard about it?

"A media case? Really?" I said.

"Justin Harris? That's right. I heard

about it on Channel Four," Jane said. "Get out of here. You got the Jump Killer case?"

"Yes," Mary Ann said, annoyed. "Do you want to switch?"

"Spend some personal time with a sexually sadistic serial killer? Gee, let me think about that. Uh, no," the tall brunette said.

Mary Ann turned back to me. "Please? For old times' sake?"

That's when I noticed on the cover contact sheet that Harris's lawyer lived in Key West. Fear of Mary Ann recognizing my photograph was replaced instantaneously with fear of death. My mind flashed on a memory. Elena's bullet-riddled, bloody body splayed out on the gas station floor.

Go back to Key West? I thought, failing to banish the image with a sip of latte.

Not after seventeen years. Not after seventy.

If I bumped into Peter, *I'd* be the one receiving the death penalty.

I handed the case file back to her as if it burned my fingers.

"I can't," I said emphatically. "Sorry. Emma's got the SAT coming up."

The lies came as easily as always. I guess I should have felt guilty. I didn't.

"Fine," Mary Ann said. "Fine. Of course, I'd get the short straw. I always get the short straw."

No, I felt like saying to her. I'd just missed it for once.

Chapter 58

I decided to walk back to work. It was one of those bright, iconic New York spring days that make you forget about things like triple-digit parking tickets and transit strikes and construction crane accidents.

But for some strange reason, I wasn't in the mood for thinking about April showers or stopping to smell the Park Avenue tulips.

Back inside my small office on the forty-fourth floor of my Lexington Avenue office building, I closed the door and just stood at the window, staring down at the people scurrying in and out of Grand Central Station. Beyond the Empire State Building to the south, downtown Manhattan sprawled and glinted under the midday sun, intricate and magical, like Monopoly pieces placed on a giant Oriental carpet.

Gazing on it, I thought about the Eighth Avenue pimps and potholes that formed my first vista on my first night in New York and how much I'd accomplished since then.

I continued to stand at the window, hugging myself. At first, I felt sad, then suddenly furious. For all this to get dredged up now, so close to home, just when my life was starting to take off, felt beyond coincidence. It felt intentional.

A media case? I thought. Hadn't I suffered enough? I thought about the life I'd struggled to put together. All the comments and lewd offers I'd received from asshole restaurant managers and customers. The eyebrow raises I'd had to endure from my co-op board for the crime of being a young single mom. All the packed buses and subway cars and work, housework and homework, that never seemed to give me a moment's peace.

Most of all, I thought about all the abject terror that I'd gone through in the middle of the night with Emma those first few months when she was colicky. Night after night, I would rock my swaddled baby, weeping along with her, convinced that I was a day away from failing, losing Emma, being fired, being found out.

That wasn't enough, huh? I thought, staring up at the blue sky. Sacrificing for my daughter, constantly having to look over my shoulder as I worked my fingers to the bone? I haven't paid enough?

Besides, it wasn't like I'd done nothing to try to set things straight. After about a year, when I'd scored a decent studio rental and a solidly paying waitressing job at a SoHo supper club, I saw an article in the *Post* about the Jump Killer. As guilt started to eat away at me one night after I picked up Emma from day care, I took the PATH train out to Hoboken. From an I-95 highway pay phone, I called the New York office of the FBI and gave an answering machine a description of the Jump Killer and his dog and his car.

Over the years, from time to time, I'd think about doing the same thing about Peter, but in the end, I feared that he— with all his law enforcement contacts— might somehow find out. The call would be traced. Peter would know that I wasn't dead and come looking for me and Emma.

I let out a breath as I finally sat at my desk. My brow beaded up with cold sweat as I remembered the Jump Killer's face. The office seemed to fade, and there I was again, homeless and pregnant, running for my life in a pair of secondhand Doc Martens.

After a while, I tried to console myself. Things could be worse. At least I hadn't actually been assigned the Jump Killer case. I'd definitely dodged a bullet there.

What was I getting so upset over? I'd just have to concentrate on my own case, I decided. Keep my head down and my fingers crossed that Mary Ann wouldn't recognize me. This whole thing would blow over like a freak storm.

I lifted Randall King's heavy case file and dropped it on my desk.

I even opened it.

Then I stopped kidding myself.

I shoved the file aside and turned on my computer. I clicked open Internet Explorer and typed "Justin Harris" into the Google search box.

A fraction of a second later, I pushed the hair out of my shocked eyes.

Harris's ten-year-old arrest really was a big media case. There were dozens of newspaper articles. There was even an ongoing segment on the *Today* show about Harris's impending execution.

I didn't really watch the news, but the *Today* show! How the hell had I missed it?

I didn't want to know, was how, I realized. I hadn't checked up on the Jump Killer in seventeen years. I never even once tried to find out what happened to Peter. I knew it was a childish notion, but I thought that if I stopped thinking about all of it, there would be some sort of karmic reciprocity, and everyone I had known would, in turn, stop thinking about me. Subconsciously, I'd made the decision that if I didn't dwell on it, it would be like it never happened.

But it had happened, I thought as I stared sourly at the computer screen. And wouldn't ever stop.

I opened a taped 2006 Fox News story about Harris on YouTube. I was hovering my finger over the mouse's left-click button to play it when my secretary, Gloria "Go-To" Walsh, came in. I immediately minimized the article with a guilty click.

"I thought you had that ProGen prospectus meeting," she said.

"Tom put me on a pro bono case," I told her. "No more ProGen for me."

"Yes!" Gloria said. "Maybe I'll get home before seven this week. Anything interesting?"

No, more like life-threatening, I thought.

"Sort of, Gloria. I'm kind of in the middle of something. I'll let you know, OK?"

I turned up the volume on my computer as she closed the door behind her. Shepard Smith was finishing up an intro about the Jump Killer murders. I took a breath, steeling myself to come face-to-face again with the man who tried to kill me that night.

When a picture of Justin Harris filled the screen, I hit the Pause button, puzzled.

Because the man on the screen wasn't the Jump Killer who'd given me a ride all those years ago on the Overseas Highway.

Wearing an orange jumpsuit above the "Justin Harris" caption was a very sad-looking, very *African American* man.

Chapter 59

I sat there very confused. Breathing slowly, trying to calm myself, I looked everywhere on my desk except the screen. I perused the snazzy gold embossing on a leather-bound copy of *McKinney's New York Civil Practice Law and Rules,* smiled at the framed picture of Emma and me on our Vermont ski trip last January. For a little while, I even watched the minute hand of my gag lawyer's desk clock that broke every hour down into ten six-minute increments, the same way we fun-loving corporate party animals billed our clients.

Then I looked back at the computer screen and winced.

Justin Harris was still there. Nothing had changed in the slightest. He was still black.

Which didn't compute. Harris was definitely not the man who'd tried to kill me the night I hightailed it out of Key West. The terrifying, muscled wacko who'd put a gun up my nose was definitely Caucasian, or a mixture of Asian American and white.

Staring at the goateed black man, I came up with the most probable scenario. The one that the Mission Exonerate people kept on harping about: *The Florida authorities had convicted and were about to execute an innocent man.*

With a queasy feeling in my stomach, I clicked on the link for the most recent *Miami Herald* article. After I read its first paragraph, I kicked back my rolling office chair and clicked my forehead onto the varnished edge of my desk.

The execution was going to take place on April 29? Which was next Friday! Justin Harris was going to die in nine days.

Unless I did something about it.

I spent some time staring down at the industrial Berber carpet between my pumps as I took it in. Then I began to moan.

I was the only person who could.

I would have to come forward. It wasn't fair. I'd spent so many hard years keeping the lid shut on the can of worms I called my life. Coming forward would mean exposing every one of my dirty little secrets once and for all, up to and including my part in Ramón Peña's death.

I'd lose my job, everything I'd struggled and scraped for.

And what about Emma? Her life would be flattened. Good-bye, dream MOMA internship. Good-bye, Brown. Not to mention: Good-bye, her trust in me. How was that going to work?

That's when I made the mistake of peeking back up at the screen. Justin Harris's sad, deer-in-the-headlights gaze seemed to look directly into my soul.

It wasn't a choice. A man's life was at stake. I would have to come clean.

Chapter 60

They say that a lawyer who represents herself has a fool for a client.

That described me to a tee.

For the next hour, I used my astute legal mind to go over my current situation. I started off by compiling a detailed damage assessment on a legal pad. I began scratching down notes under happy headings like "Friends I'd Lose" (pretty much all of them). "Likely Legal Ramifications" (firm would fire me and I'd lose my license to practice law). Then I wrote, "Statute of Limitations for Manslaughter"(?) and "Emma" (in family services?).

I had my reading glasses on the edge of my nose and was flipping through my trusty *McKinney's* when I suddenly pushed the glasses up on my forehead and slammed the law book shut.

Because there was actually another option.

It was nuts. Absolutely insane. Not to mention an outrageously long shot. Of course it was. Insanity and long shots went together in my life like Ben and Jerry.

What if I did switch cases with my friend Mary Ann? I thought. What if *I* took Harris's case?

I could stay on top of it. Maybe I could even figure out a way to free Harris without dismantling my life and especially Emma's. Harris didn't do it, right? I knew that. Therefore, there had to be something in his case, some overlooked detail, that proved it. It was just a matter of finding it and bringing it before the court.

"Down in Key West" came a tiny dissenting voice.

Right. I knew there was a rub. I'd have to consult with Harris's lawyer, who lived in the last place I wanted to go.

Just the thought of setting foot in that beautiful, dangerous place again made me want to swallow a handful of Xanax.

I sat there for a little while on the horns of my dilemma.

Choice A: finally face up to my buried past.

Choice B: lie my ass off and try to continue the con that was my life.

It was no choice at all.

I'd have to figure it out, I decided. Key West was a big town. Sort of. I could just lie low. Maybe Peter wasn't even living in the area after seventeen years.

I lifted my cell phone. It felt like it suddenly weighed twenty pounds. I spun down to Mary Ann's number before I could change my mind.

"What?" Mary Ann said sharply.

"I've been thinking. Let's trade cases," I said.

"For real?" she said ecstatically now. "Are you sure?"

I wasn't sure of anything, but I had to do it anyway.

"Say yes before I change my mind," I said.

"Yes," Mary Ann said. "See? I knew you were a good friend. I'll help Emma with her SAT, whatever you need, I promise. Just remember, no backsies."

"No backsies," I agreed, biting the inside of my cheek.

Chapter 61

As I did with each of my long-shot plans, I arranged my newest one with gusto.

By the next morning, I'd managed to nail down everything. The flight to Key West, the hotel, the car to the airport. Emma was happily surprised to find out she'd be spending the next week at her best friend Gabby's town house in Brooklyn. The only thing left to do was swing by my office on the way to Kennedy to pick up Harris's case file, which Mary Ann had messengered over.

Then all I had left to do was try not to get killed by Peter as I saved a man from execution.

In a week's time.

"Piece of cake," I mumbled as I rolled my bag into the kitchen.

Em was listening to her iPod and drumming a pencil against her open trig book in front of a bowl of Cap'n Crunch. I stole a spoonful as I e-mailed Harris's lawyer, a man named Charles Baylor, to tell him I was coming down.

I winced when I turned on the kitchen laptop and opened Internet Explorer. In "History," I found searches for "Bloom Family" and even "County Wicklow," the place I'd said Emma's fictional dad was from.

Great! Another headache. What timing. As if my in-box weren't currently full of disaster. The tape I'd made before Emma's party had only whetted her appetite for more, I realized. More juggling. I was getting it from all sides at once. Leave my secret identity alone! I felt like yelling.

"Mom, I've been meaning to ask

you," Emma said, taking back the spoon. "Why don't I look more like my dad?"

That was one of my biggest worries. That Emma might notice that Aidan Beck was fair instead of black Irish like Peter.

"I have no idea," I said cheerfully, making it up as I went along. "I do know you have his good nature and his laugh."

Emma, no dummy, frowned at my utter bullshit. "Why do I get the feeling that you don't want me to find out about him?" she said.

I had to struggle to keep from pulling my hair out. "Do I give you that impression?" I said.

"Whatev," Emma mumbled, fat tears suddenly springing into her big blue eyes.

I knew that Em was just being a sixteen-year-old girl, a ball of hormone-charged emotion. But I couldn't let her do this. I couldn't afford it, and neither could she. What the heck was I supposed to say? Sorry to have to tell you this, kid, but your dad's a psychopathic killer, and I'm a pathological liar?

Instead, I used my secret weapon.

I dropped my keys loudly on the countertop, collapsed onto the island stool, and started crying myself. "I wish I could make your life make more sense, but I can't," I said, sobbing.

"I'm sorry, Mom," Em finally said, coming around to embrace me. "You don't think I know what you've done for me, but I really do. I'll stop freaking you out with all this stuff."

"No, I'm sorry. You could look up your Irish roots, just not right now, OK? You have college prep and so many other things on your plate. When I get back, we'll rent *The Quiet Man*. And eat Lucky Charms for breakfast. I hear they're magically delicious."

My iPhone rang as Emma hugged me again. It was a number I didn't recognize. Terrific. What now?

"Hello?"

"Hi, this is Carl Fouhy from Exonerate NYC. Is this Nina Bloom?"

"Yes, Carl. What's up?"

"Since you've got the Justin Harris case now, I thought it would be a good idea for you to meet Harris's mother." Mary Ann must have called him, I surmised. No backsies indeed. "What's your schedule looking like?"

"Real tight, Carl. I'm actually on the ten o'clock flight to Florida," I said.

"Could you come by Rockefeller Center before you leave? Justin's case is making big news now. The *Today* show is doing a piece on it this morning, and we're actually out here right now, protesting. Trying to get some national publicity."

The *Today* show? Publicity? That would really help my fly-below-the-radar strategy.

A fist-sized ball of fear suddenly clenched in my stomach. I knew I shouldn't have done this. Taking this case on had been a mistake.

"Nina? You still there? I know it's a crunch, but I feel it's really imperative that you meet."

I couldn't think of an excuse. I'd have to figure it out. If I was asked to get anywhere near a camera, I'd just refuse and walk away. Run away, if it came to that.

"Um, OK, I guess," I said, checking my watch. "But only for a minute. Give me half an hour."

Chapter 62

"And four, three, two," said some wimpy bald guy all in black and wearing a headset. He pointed at the massive high-tech television studio camera beside him as its red light came on.

"And we're back," Al Roker said, reading off the teleprompter screen mounted beneath the saucer-sized bluish lens of the camera. "We're concluding our three-part series today on Florida's Jump Killer execution by talking to a family member of one of the alleged victims."

Sitting on the couch across from

America's weatherman, wearing jeans and a light blue cashmere sweater, Peter Fournier smiled. Behind him outside the Rockefeller Plaza studio window, a crowd of people were waving signs. This was the reason Peter had traveled up from Key West to New York for the weekend.

"Peter Fournier's wife was only twenty-three years old," Roker continued, "when she was believed to have crossed paths with Justin Harris. Mr. Fournier, a Key West, Florida, police officer, is the head of the victims' rights group for the Jump Killer's victims. Good morning, Mr. Fournier. Has Harris actually admitted to murdering your young wife, Jeanine?"

"No," Peter said sadly. "He has not, Al. He maintains his innocence not only in the case of my wife's death, but even of the Foster girl, for which he was convicted."

Peter took a breath as the glossy eye of the camera stayed on him.

"That's why I, and all the other families, are gratified that the execution is finally going to take place next week.

This man needs to pay for his crimes, and on Friday night, God willing, that's exactly what he'll do."

Al nodded. "I can't imagine your pain, but it's long been debated whether capital punishment actually helps the victim's family. What's your take on that?"

"Seventeen years ago, this person abducted my wife and killed her, and he doesn't even have the semblance of humanity to tell me where he dumped her body so I can have a proper funeral," Peter said calmly. "What do I do with that, Al? Forgive and forget? My pain and the pain of all of the victims' families will never go away. Dante said that hell is the place where all forgotten things go. That's exactly where I want to put Harris. I just want him to be forgotten by me, by the other families, and by every other human being on this planet."

"What are your plans now?" Al wanted to know.

"I, and the other family members in our organization, have learned that death penalty opponents are scheduling protests, so we will be front-row center to make sure that our voice, and the voices of the people that Harris truly disenfranchised, are heard."

"Thank you, Mr. Fournier. I wish you well, sir," Al said. "Up next is Meredith with some money-saving travel tips."

Chapter 63

My airport car let me out in front of Rockefeller Center on the corner of Fifth and 50th and kept going. I'd asked the driver to go ahead to my Lexington Avenue office building to pick up the Harris case file and wait for me there. After my aggravating meet and greet with Harris's mom, I would hustle over to my office and, by some miracle, make my flight.

I spotted Fouhy standing in the crowd in front of the 10 Rock Center window where they taped the *Today* show.

Beside him, a large black woman

wearing a YES WE DID ball cap was holding a large handwritten sign:

FREE JUSTIN HARRIS!

DON'T KILL MY SON!

"Mrs. Harris. Hi, I'm Nina Bloom," I
said, coming through the crowd.

Mrs. Harris almost knocked me down
as she barreled into me, wrapping her
arms around me in a full embrace. She
pressed her smiling face against my
cheek. She seemed enthusiastic,
strangely upbeat despite her son's pre-
dicament.

"Oh, she's a good one. I can feel it,
Mr. Fouhy," she said in a honey-smooth
Southern accent, her soft brown eyes
staring hard into mine. "You're going to
save my Justin."

"I'm going to, um, try," I said, eyeing
Fouhy for help.

"Try won't do, Ms. Bloom," Mrs. Harris said, rapidly shaking her head at
me. "Try won't do. You are going to do
it, and that's an end to it. It's going to
end with you. There's no other choice."

She released me and rummaged
through the brimming Duane Reade
bag beside her and showed me a pic-

ture. It was of a teenaged Justin in a drum major high school uniform. There was another one of him on a stage playing with the rest of an all-black marching band.

"That was at Carnegie Hall for a Wynton Marsalis tribute." She laughed as she stared at the photo. "All them lessons and practicin'. The neighbors used to call the police twice a month. That was the proudest moment of my life."

Then she placed something cold and metal into my hand. At first I thought it was a coin, but it was a military medal, a bronze octagon with a green, white, and blue ribbon.

"Justin earned this medal when he responded to a helicopter accident during his Ranger training. Last time I checked, serial killers don't go around pulling bodies from burning wreckage. You know, I used to believe in the system. That the truth would come out. But every day, it just got worse. I wish I knew the words to express how wrong this is, the legal terms and such. You're going to have to do it for me, Ms. Bloom."

Mrs. Harris let out a breath, trying to keep herself composed.

"That's why I needed to meet you. To try to make you feel what I know. So you can know Justin like I know Justin. He didn't do it. Justin isn't a monster. It's all lies. All of it. Justin was my best child, my nicest boy. His brother was the mean one. His brother would tussle with him. But Justin would never strike him back. He's incapable of hurting anyone."

"Ms. Bloom is going to do everything she can, Mrs. Harris. Now she really has a plane to catch," Carl Fouhy said gently.

"Wait, please," Mrs. Harris said, without taking her eyes off me. "Do you have a child, Ms. Bloom?"

"A daughter," I said.

"What's her name?" she said with a smile.

"Emma," I said, smiling back.

"What would you do if people had Emma and were about to kill her?"

"Everything I could," I answered immediately.

Mrs. Harris let out a loud breath.

"Good," she said. She nodded. "Justin is in good hands. My prayers have been answered. My baby is safe now."

I tried to hand back Justin's medal. Mrs. Harris shook her head.

"No. You hold on to that," she said as a tear, a single tear, slid over the soft brown curve of her cheek. "Don't lose it, now."

I stared at the medal, then at Fouhy. I could see why he'd wanted me to come. The son of a bitch wanted me motivated, emotionally involved, not just going through the motions. He wanted me to see that Mrs. Harris was flesh and blood, a good, warm person and a desperate, loving mother who would do anything not to lose her child.

Mission accomplished, I thought, my own eyes wet as I walked away.

Chapter 64

It was five to nine when Peter Fournier walked out the tunnel-like NBC studio exit onto West 50th Street beside Rockefeller Center.

"Baby, you did so good!" his wife, Vicki, cooed when he opened his ringing cell. "I still can't believe it. It's like I'm dreaming. You having a chat with Al Roker, like he's your best buddy. I would have passed out. Let me put the boys on."

"Dad, you rocked!" Scott said.

"Yes. That's right. My dad is Mr. Cool!" Mike yelled in the background.

"Thanks, guys. I love you, too. I'll tell you all about it when I get back to the hotel," Peter said.

Peter smiled as he closed his cell. He had done well. He thought he might be nervous about going on live national TV, but once the red camera light came on, he'd felt perfectly fine, like himself, calm, in charge. He'd always suspected that he'd be good on TV. Now he knew. In another life, he could have been an actor, a talk show host. He had the looks, the charm.

Was it narcissistic if you knew you actually *were* the biggest swinging dick in the room? he wondered. Any room? Every room?

Flying under the radar was his usual game plan, but in this case he'd taken a calculated risk because there was business involved.

One of the victims' group members, Arty Tivolli, was an elderly multimillionaire hotel chain owner from Palm Beach. After befriending the silver-haired gent with bottomless pockets, Peter had persuaded him to take a serious look at bidding on Key West's only run-down golf course and turning it into a massive luxury resort.

For the last year, he'd been working with Arty's company, the Tivolli Group, introducing them around to the "right" city council and zoning board members. If all went as planned, Peter's slice of the proceedings would be massive, a seven-figure windfall. It would be the most money he'd ever made in his life. Well, at least legally.

So in actuality, his *Today* show appearance had exactly squat to do with his desire to steal Matt Lauer's job or to mourn his dearly departed other half, Jeanine. His victim group activism and nationally televised righteous indignation at Justin Harris were all for Arty, who had lost his only daughter to the Jump Killer in 1991.

Peter, still jazzed, looked out at midtown Manhattan's swirling chaos of delivery trucks backing up and double-parked taxis honking. It was morning rush now, and rock concert–sized crowds of businesspeople and hard hats hustled past him up and down the cavernous side street.

What absolute suckers, he thought. Get to work, you ball-less serfs. Step to it!

Though his cell phone camera stunk, he decided to take some pictures with it anyway to show the kids. He snapped a shot of the famous television studio's door, a passing mounted cop, a bike messenger across the street smoking a cigarette.

He was about to take a shot of a pigeon pecking at a doughnut in the gutter when a blond woman flashed out from the east corner of the building by Rockefeller Center. There was something so New York about the tall head turner: her creamy thigh, her get-the-fuck-out-of-my-way pace, her just-so salon-colored platinum hair.

Then she turned to her right to check the approaching traffic, and Peter's serene smile faded as he lowered the phone.

All he could do was watch in silence as his dead wife, Jeanine, stepped across the street.

Chapter 65

"Dammit," I said, checking the time on my iPhone as I cornered onto Fifth Avenue. I needed to be on my way to the airport already. My driver, waiting at my office, was going to have to floor it and maybe eat some red lights on our way out to JFK if I was going to make my flight.

I thought about calling and having him come back around onto Fifth to pick me up, but then I decided against it. Midtown morning rush hour was so insanely gridlocked and unpredictable, it was actually quicker for me to go to him on foot.

I was picking up the pace, crossing to the east side of the street, when my iPhone jingled its incoming text alert.

I glanced at the screen, fearing another delay, but then let out a breath when I saw that the message was from Em.

Who else? I could almost see her there on her early free period in the Brearley library illegally texting. Her books open in front of her, her phone under the table.

I thumbed the View button on the touchscreen.

"Willlllsonnnnnn!!" her text read.

Despite my full-blown hurry, I smiled. Then I laughed out loud. It was a reference to the stupidest and our hands-down-favorite part of the movie *Cast Away*, in which Tom Hanks, a plane crash survivor, nonsensically befriends a Wilson volleyball.

It was also our way of saying hi. All day long, Emma and I texted each other silly inside jokes like that.

There was another jingle as another text came in.

"Worst 80s band?" Em wanted to know. "REO Speedwagon?"

Since I'd actually been there, I had to disagree: "Close," I texted back as I walked. It was a glacial process for someone over the age of sixteen. "Culture Club. Their hit song was 'Do You Really Want to Hurt Me.' The answer was yes. Google 'Boy George' if you don't believe me."

"Fine," Em texted back in a finger snap. "Movie quote throwdown! *Toy Story*. *'That's not flying. That's falling with style.'*"

"What does a space ranger actually do?" I texted her back pretty quickly this time. Em would be proud.

Then I pocketed my phone as a sudden lump caught in my throat. After a moment, I started crying. As I walked, I started sobbing uncontrollably right there in front of Fifth Avenue's tourist shops and luggage stores and overpriced pizzerias.

Because I suddenly realized, Em actually wouldn't be proud of me.

What would Em think of me when everything came out? I wondered, snorting into the lapel of my faux Burberry coat. When she found out that I'd been lying to her ever since she could walk? That I was an impostor? That someone had died because of me?

Who was I kidding here? The idea that I could exonerate Harris in a week while keeping the house of cards that was my life from quickly becoming a game of 52 pickup was a tall order even for someone with my extensive creative skills. I'd dodged a bullet at Rockefeller Center, but it was just the beginning, I knew. The deeper I went into this, the more I would be at risk. What the hell was I doing? I had one mother of a skeleton in my closet, and here I was about to put the key in the lock and turn.

My phone text jingled again.

"There's a snake in my boots," Em had typed.

There's a snake in your family, I thought, shaking my head at the phone.

Chapter 66

Peter moved smoothly with the morning rush hour crowd on Fifth Avenue, a
half block behind Jeanine.

He couldn't decide what surprised
him more. The fact that Jeanine was
actually alive or how incredible she still
looked. She was what now? Forty? Yet,
look at her—stylish, confident, model
thin, regal. Audrey Hepburn in *Breakfast at Tiffany's*.

Despite the fact that he'd only glanced
at her, Peter *knew* it was her, didn't
have the slightest doubt. He knew now

that he'd seen her at the Yankees game as well.

The unlikeliness of coincidences didn't matter to him. He paid close attention to things and made it a point to remember everything and everyone. Especially faces. The way he operated, you forgot a face at the peril of your life.

He was fifty, yet his senses and instincts were as sharp as ever. Bravo, Jeanine, he thought, as he trailed her. Not too many people walking around on this earth could brag about putting one over on Peter Fournier.

In fact, Jeanine, Peter reflected, *besides you, there's nobody at all.*

He ran to catch up as she turned the next left around a corner. Dead-ending the shadowed side street two blocks to the east was a massive, dirty old building: Grand Central Terminal. He and his family had visited it on their first day up here.

Tunnels, he thought. *Darkness, speeding trains, crowds. A place where accidents happened. Or random acts of violence.*

He had his small police backup Glock in his ankle holster, but since the station was crawling with antiterror cops, there was no way he could use it. That left the illegal spring-loaded blackjack he kept snug in the small of his back, ever since his days on the Boston PD, or his belt buckle knife. The knife, then. He could have it out and in and back as quick as a coin trick. Open the femoral in her leg and keep going. He began to visualize it. Don't even make eye contact. Flank her, stab, and saw.

He relished what he had to do now about as much as a carpenter relished using a hammer to hit a nail. There was no glee. There was just brutal necessity, covering his margins, business. He was no animal. He was just one of the rare breed of men who were born unafraid to wield violence as the efficient tool that it was.

A soft, aching warmth filled his chest as he remembered the outrageous romantic times he had shared with Jeanine. The way she looked coming out of the Gulf with the water sluicing off her tan, incredible body. The bullhorn outside the bathroom was a classic. The cut-your-throat creases she used to iron into his uniform shirts.

No question, of all his dead wives, she was by far his favorite.

Heading down the slightly sloping street toward Grand Central, Peter shook his head sadly at his runaway wife.

"Oh, Mermaid, we had ourselves some times, didn't we?" he whispered, keeping his eyes centered on the back of her fancy ivory spring coat.

What a shame.

Chapter 67

I was only mildly melting down by the time I came off Vanderbilt into Grand Central. I'd managed to stop crying at least by the time I hit the west marble staircase above the main concourse.

It never failed to amaze. Cream-colored marble everywhere, the famous tsunami-sized windows, the constellation mural on the massive green ceiling.

Walking through its old-world elegance in my business clothes, I always felt instantly classy, a true New Yorker.

I'd often pretend I was in an old movie, Eva Marie Saint in *North by Northwest*.

Thirty seconds later, I was across the massive cathedral-like space in the long corridor that led toward Lexington Avenue. The mall was lined with businesses. I passed a jewelry store, a boutique, a shoeshine stand, a Starbucks.

I dodged all the way to the left as a fresh batch of people started spilling into the corridor and up the stairway that connected to the Lexington Avenue subway lines.

But not far enough, apparently. I winced in pain as some Wall Street jackass in a pin-striped suit rushing past stepped on my right foot.

My toes felt severed. I stopped against the wall in the crowded passageway and slipped off my open-toe pump to count my toenails.

"Excuse you," I yelled, pissed and in pain.

But I suddenly wasn't angry anymore. The pain in my foot faded, instantly forgotten.

At the mouth of the swirling corridor was a tall man. He was handsome and had short salt-and-pepper hair and blue eyes. He stood like a rock in the stream of the crowd, and he was staring at me.

I ripped my eyes away and stuffed my foot back into my shoe. Hobbled and blind with fear, I pointed myself forward toward the exit and broke into a full-out finish-line sprint.

It couldn't be. It shouldn't be.

But it was.

Peter had found me at last.

Chapter 68

Shit, Peter thought, flattening himself against the wall next to a pay phone. He'd been following too close. Jeanine had stopped. She'd looked back. Had she seen him? It was hard to tell with the trillion-people march going on in the passageway between them. It was a definite possibility.

He could have whipped himself. The last thing Jeanine would have been expecting after all this time was a visit from him. The element of surprise was critical. But he'd crowded her and blown the whole thing.

What the hell had gotten into him? What happened to that cold patience and reserve he was so proud of?

Too late to cry about it. He needed to move.

He counted to three and then chanced a look back up the wide concourse. He thought she might have headed down the subway entrance on the right, but then he thought he caught a flash of ivory going out through the distant exit door.

What the...? She was leaving? he thought, as he started to run. She'd only cut through the station? So she wasn't getting on a train?

"Yo, slow down!" someone scolded him.

Peter turned. In the doorway of a camera store was an NYPD cop decked out in full antiterrorist gear, bomb vest, M16. There was a no-nonsense expression on his face as he looked Peter over. He didn't need that kind of scrutiny. Not now. Instead of giving the cop the finger like he wanted, Peter slowed immediately, nodding to his fellow peace officer with an apologetic wave.

He squinted when he came out onto bright Lexington Avenue. He looked up and down the block, across the wide street clogged with delivery trucks and buses and yellow taxis. He looked up at the Chrysler Building, right in front of him now.

There was no white jacket in either direction. Audrey Hepburn had left the damn building. Nothing. He'd taken his eyes off her for five seconds.

That was the problem with this rat race city! he thought, infuriated. Too many damn holes for the rats to hide in! She must have seen him.

Jeanine had disappeared.

Chapter 69

That didn't just happen.

Inside the wall-to-wall-crowded Grand Central Starbucks, I stood at the milk and sugar stand by the window.

Bathed in sweat, I tried to keep myself from hyperventilating.

Peter? Here? Now? How was that possible?

I didn't know. I was having trouble breathing, let alone thinking.

When I wasn't looking out over Lexington Avenue, I had my head craned around at the shop's side window and side door, which opened onto the train station's corridor. If Peter came in, my plan was to run screaming through the door back into the train station's main concourse and try to flag down one of the many antiterror cops. I shivered like a cornered rabbit.

I hadn't even gotten down to Key West, and already I was playing a game of hide-and-seek, with my life as the prize.

Maybe I was just being paranoid, I thought, scanning the passing faces beyond the plateglass window. Couldn't it have been somebody who just looked like Peter? I was heading down to Key West now, after all. Peter was certainly at the forefront of my mind, not to mention embedded in my subconscious. Maybe my overstressed brain had jumped to the wrong conclusion.

Then again, maybe not!

I needed to act. I looked across Lexington. I could actually see my town car, idling outside my office building. I quickly fumbled open my bag. I took out the card that the driver, a very pleasant West Indian man who called himself Mr. Ken, had given me.

"Hi, um, Mr. Ken?" I said. "This is Nina Bloom. Were you able to get my package from my office?"

"It's right here in the front seat beside me," he said.

"Great. Do you see the Starbucks on the west side of Lex in front of you? I'm right here by the window. Would you come over and get me?"

"On my way," he said.

"Thanks, Mr. Ken," I said to him in person when I bolted across the sidewalk and dove into the car ten seconds later. And thank God for cell phones, I thought.

I locked the door before I scrunched down low in the seat.

Mr. Ken raised an eyebrow at me in the rearview mirror.

"Did you forget your coffee, Ms. Bloom?" he said in his lilting accent.

"Oh, I already drank it, thanks," I lied, glancing out the window, panicked. "If we could head out to JFK now, Mr. Ken, that would be really great."

I scrunched down even farther in the seat. I didn't breathe again until Mr. Ken hit the gas.

Chapter 70

On the corner of 42nd Street and Lexington, Peter stood scanning faces. He looked frantically up the unbelievably crowded street in front of Grand Central. Nothing. No ivory jacket. Not across the street or anywhere. He'd screwed up. His rat had found her hole.

What a bust! He'd had her, and then he'd lost her again.

As he stood there fuming, a memory bubbled up. It was of his first and only bow hunting trip with his dad in New Hampshire when he was seven. He was in the forest taking a leak when an enormous black bear appeared ten feet in front of him. Before he could yell out, there was a thwap from his dad's compound bow, and the shaft of an arrow popped out of one of the bear's eyes. The animal dropped like a tipped-over piece of furniture.

His father climbed down from the blind and knelt over the fallen monster, inhaling loudly as he wafted the blood aroma into his face like a chef over a pot. Peter had almost wet himself when his dad suddenly grabbed him and shoved his face down toward the blood-splattered bear until they were nose to black-and-bloody nose.

"This life, you either get the bear," the crazy drunken bastard had said in his French Canadian accent, "or the bear gets you. Your choice, yes?"

Exactly, Peter thought.

At least he knew Jeanine lived in New York City, knew that she worked somewhere around here. Hell, knowing that she was still alive was enough. Catching up with her wasn't an if anymore, it was a when.

His phone rang. He glanced at the screen. His wife, Vicki.

Horns honked as he stared up at the endless windows, his rage cooling now, replaced by his hunter's natural, cold patience.

"Don't worry, I'm going to get that bear somehow, Pop," Peter said as he lifted his phone. "Always have. Always will."

Book Four

THE PRODIGAL WIFE RETURNS

Chapter 71

I didn't know what time it was when I woke with a start, spilling Justin Harris's court transcripts.

The plane that I was now on was a tiny fifty-seater. I'd had an hour layover in Atlanta before getting on the disconcertingly small aircraft.

After I put Harris's folder away, I looked out the tiny window, wondering how close we were. There was nothing but water underneath us now, as silver and bright as tinfoil under the harsh Southern sunlight.

As I was staring at the light, the butterflies in my stomach woke up and got right back to work.

It was Florida light. Key West light.

Was I safe now? Hadn't I left Peter back in New York? I didn't know.

I looked up as the cabin speaker tolled out a musical bong, and the stewardess announced that we were about fifteen minutes out. Across the aisle, a decent-looking, fair-skinned man of about fifty smiled at me. He wore Bermuda shorts and a gray NYU gym shirt and had wavy strawberry blond hair.

He was Australian and quite drunk. I knew these things because he'd tried to hit on me by the gate in Atlanta. Under other circumstances, I probably would have let him. I certainly could have used a drink.

"To paradise," Crocodile Dundee said with a goofy theatrical flourish as he raised his plastic cup to me. I smiled politely before looking away.

More like Paradise Lost for me, I thought, staring back out the window. I made out the line of a large structure beneath us.

I closed my eyes, my stomach suddenly seizing up, my teeth and ears aching with tension. Clammy sweat stuck my shirt to my back as the coffin wall of the fifty-seater plane suddenly felt like it was bearing down on me, burying me alive.

The structure I'd spotted was the Overseas Highway. The same Overseas Highway where the Jump Killer had almost murdered me nearly two decades before. As if that weren't heart attack–inducing enough, as the plane descended, the white hot Florida light began sparking off fishing boat after fishing boat, each one a carbon copy of the Stingray Peter sailed.

I shouldn't have come here, I thought, instantly overcome with terror. This was stupid. I was stupid. I'd escaped from hell. Why was I going back?

"Oh, I'm so sorry, honey," a Southern voice cooed in my ear. It was the stewardess, a short, sturdy blond woman in her early fifties. She held my hand. "I can see it in your face. Don't worry. Everybody gets airsick sometimes. Even me. Is there anything I can do for you?"

Turn the plane around, I felt like telling her. But was that even safe? Did I have anywhere to hide now?

As she snapped open a vomit bag, I heard the landing gear hum down. I felt its jolt beneath my feet as it locked into place.

Then black stars lit across the inside of my closed eyelids as I threw up. With an embarrassingly loud and drawn-out retching sound, I returned the airline's complimentary honey-roasted peanuts and Diet Coke. When I glanced across the aisle again, my Aussie buddy was intently studying his in-flight magazine.

Terrific, I thought, wiping my mouth with a napkin.

Way to hit the ground running.

Chapter 72

Having splashed some water on my face, I felt slightly better as I came down the rolling stairs of the tiny jet onto the airport tarmac. The small Key West airport looked the same as it always had: namely, as laid-back and weathered as its baggage handlers. You could actually see the crystal blue water sparkling beyond the runway's chain-link fence, lulling and beautiful and beckoning.

I tore my eyes off it as I followed the line of smiling, ready-to-party young businesspeople. This wasn't a vacation for me. It was more like a suicide mission. Get in and get the heck out, I told myself.

"Miss?" said an NBA-sized black guy in aviator shades and a green tennis visor, tapping me on the elbow on the airport's sidewalk.

Christ, did he recognize me? I thought. "What?" I snapped at him.

"Do you need a taxi to your hotel?" he said warily as he pointed at the car behind him.

We stopped at the Hyatt five minutes later. After I paid and tipped the driver, I hurried into the lobby as if the parking lot were a sniper zone.

The large black female concierge gave me an easy smile when I came in. "Nina Bloom?" she said when I showed her my credit card. "Oh, yes. I just got off the phone with someone about you."

What?!

"Your firm just upgraded your room," she said. "They must like you. You've been transferred to one of our penthouse suites."

The first time I felt that I'd breathed all day was after I'd tipped the bellboy and had the door securely locked behind me.

It really was a beautiful suite. South Beach chic. White leather furniture, black quartz countertops, neon bright modern art. Outside the sliding glass doors, a queen-sized white chaise with my name on it lay on a private, Mexican-tiled roof deck.

There was also a huge gift basket on the countertop. Tropical flowers, Godiva boxes. Even an orange and green magnum of Veuve Clicquot champagne.

"Thanks for doing the right thing, kid. Go get 'em!" my boss had written in the message.

Well, at least I was making someone happy.

I read in one of the hotel magazines about the upcoming Conch Republic (as Key West jokingly called itself) Independence Celebration. There was a bed race down Duval Street and, of course, lots of drinking. Maybe that was a good thing. Hopefully, the whole police department, including Peter, would be more than busy with the greater influx of tourists than normal.

I plopped down on a low, white leather couch and called Emma.

"I made it," I said. "I'm so tired."

"Sure you are, Mom," Emma said. "I feel for you. Enjoy your *business* trip to Key West. Try not to throw your back out limbo-ing the night away."

I shook my head. She didn't understand. She had no idea how much I wanted out of this place, how much I wanted to go straight to the airport and head home.

"You better not do any partying with that Gabby, either, Miss Wiseacre. I love you, Wilson. I'll call you tomorrow."

After I hung up, I put in a call to Harris's attorney, Charles Baylor, whose office I would be visiting tomorrow. No answer. What else was new? I was going to take a shower, but then I saw the sky. The sun was going down, and the sky was turning a ridiculously intense electric blue.

I shook my head again as I remembered partying in Mallory Square that last sunset on spring break. Dancing and singing to Bob Marley, I'd actually thought I could be happy and carefree forever.

I'd thought wrong.

Despite the memory, and my usual

policy of not mixing business with pleasure, I decided to bring the bubbly bottle out onto the roof deck with a water
glass. Because if anyone on earth
needed a drink at that moment, it was
me.

On second thought, I left the water
glass inside and headed for the white
chaise, the champagne bottle's foil trail-
ing behind me.

Chapter 73

Charles Baylor's office was on Terry Lane, a block south of Hemingway's house in Old Town. Nine a.m. sharp on Friday morning, holding a box of Dunkin' Donuts in one hand and a box of coffee in the other, I rang his bell with my elbow.

As I waited, I heard a screaming saw at the rear of the house. On the porch, a rusty bicycle sat next to some beat-up diving tanks. What the hell kind of law office was this? When the saw stopped, I put down the coffee and whammed on the door with my fist.

A bleary-eyed, tan, shirtless guy wearing a green bandanna, goggles, and an air mask opened the door a minute later. He wiped his hands on his sole visible item of clothing, his cutoff jeans.

"Yeah?" he said.

"I'm looking for Charles Baylor. The attorney?" I said.

"He's not here at the moment," the guy said, grinning like an idiot as he pulled down the mask. "I'm Charlie Baylor, the carpenter. Maybe I can help you out?"

I restrained myself from rolling my eyes. Nice to meet you, too, wiseass, I thought. "I'm Nina Bloom from Scott, Maxwell and Bond. They put me on to assist in the Justin Harris case. I left you about a dozen messages."

"Well, bless my banjo," Baylor said in an exaggerated hick accent. "You must be Miss New York City here to learn the hillbilly beach bum some lawrin'. I got every one of yours and the righteous Mission Exonerate's calls, all right. You didn't get my e-mail? 'Thanks, but no thanks.' My client is in competent hands. You should check your BlackBerry. My message heading, I believe, was 'Go Find a Tree to Hug.' Guess you'll have to drink all that coffee yourself. Shame. See you around."

Could this guy be a bigger prick? I thought, as he started to close the door in my face. I drop-kicked the doughnut box into the gap to stop it.

I'd come down here for a lot of reasons. Messing around wasn't one of them.

" 'Competent hands,' huh?" I yelled as he looked down at the crushed doughnuts in pained shock. "What are you building back there, Mr. Baylor? Harris's coffin?"

He pulled off his bandanna and ran a hand through his sandy hair. He looked to be in his early forties, but his lean, brown, weather-beaten face was still boyish somehow. He looked more like a landscaper than a lawyer. One with eyes the color of the sky I'd seen from my balcony last night, but that was beside the point.

"Harris's coffin?" he said with a grin. "That's cold, woman. Damned if I'm not starting to like you. Please call me Charlie. When are they changing your firm's name to Scott, Maxwell and Soulless Bitch?"

I held eye contact with him, then smiled for the first time myself. "Invite me in, and we can go over it, Charlie."

Chapter 74

Half of the lawyer's house was beautiful: golden, varnished Dade pine floors; a completely refurbished curving banister and stairway; a white-on-white marble cook's kitchen out of *Architectural Digest*. The other, gutted half, with its shattered plaster walls and garbage-brimming joint compound buckets, had a striking resemblance to a crack house.

Luckily, I was quickly escorted through the construction site into an artfully finished oak-paneled office behind the kitchen.

Charlie dropped the salvaged doughnut box onto his immaculate desk and took a Heineken keg can from a mini-fridge.

"Out of orange juice?" I said, making a show of checking my watch.

"In Key West, this *is* orange juice," Charlie said, popping the beer can's top and taking a slug.

I almost passed out when I noticed the framed Harvard Law diploma on the wall, a little magna cum laude banner bridged across its lower right-hand corner.

"Impressive, isn't it?" he said, rocking back and forth in his chair. "I missed summa by like point-oh-six or some such. I really wanted to go to Yale, but their rugby team flat out blew that year." He took a long sip, burped, and helped himself to a crushed Boston Kreme.

"What are you doing down here?" I said.

"Some people claim that there's a woman to blame," he sang with his mouth full. "But I know—"

"Please shut up," I said.

"Fine," he said, chewing. "Like everybody else, I guess things went south until there was no more south left to go. This is actually my granddaddy's place. He was a Texas oilman. He actually won it in a poker game at the age of seventy. Family legend has it he came down, took one look around, and telegraphed back, 'If all works out, I'll never be sober again.'"

"Touching story," I said.

"Anyway," Charlie said. "A few years ago, I inherited it and his dusty toolbox. After I bring this baby back to its former glory, I'm not sure what I'm going to do. I got a friend who works for HGTV, said I'd be a shoo-in for one of those hunky carpenter dudes. How much money they make, you think?"

"You're too old," I said.

He finished his doughnut with another slug of beer and made a growling sound. "Don't tell anyone, but I'm also actually taking a stab at being the next John Grisham or Ernest Hemingway. You been to Papa's house yet? Did you know some of the cats there have six toes?"

"Did you know Hemingway blew his head off with a shotgun?" I said quickly.

"This is a lot of fun and everything, but we need to go over Harris's case. I got the brief, but I'd like to hear in your own words, in a nutshell, where it went wrong."

"In a nutshell," Charlie said. "OK, let's see. It all went wrong probably right around the time the cops said, 'Hey, Harris, you have the right to an attorney,' and Harris didn't say, 'Where's the phone?'"

He leaned back in his swivel chair, balancing the can on his bare chest.

"Harris was his own worst nightmare. First he tells the cops he didn't know Foster. Lie numero uno. Then, faced with the DNA results, he claims he remembers having consensual sex with her at the prison where he worked and she was a volunteer. He said the coed scholarship musician was 'quite the little freak,' quote unquote. That she liked to slap and scratch him and for him to cuff her up before they did it in the janitor's closet.

"Which is exactly what he said happened when she came in to volunteer that morning before she went missing.

He claimed after he went off shift that day, he was with another woman, his fiancée, the whole day at the Miami Seaquarium. But when police questioned his alibi, the fiancée completely denied it."

"Crap," I said.

"On a pointy stick," he said. "That's why my white-shoe firm handed the case to me when his first lawyer was disbarred for bilking his real estate clients. See, like you, I was once moronic enough to believe in Harris, too. Enough at least to take it to trial."

"What happened in court?"

"It came down to the jury not buying that a poor black prison guard could possibly have consensual sex with an angelic white college student who volunteered there. Foster's mother sat in the front row, and she cringed and cried whenever the notion of her daughter and Harris being together came up. The jury wasn't too hot on the idea either. Slam dunk. Capital murder."

Charlie yawned and licked some custard off his finger.

"I left my firm a year later. Couldn't

stop thinking about it, I guess. So there you have it. In a nutshell. Trying to dig Harris out of his hole cost me pretty much everything. How you figure you're going to get it done in a week?"

"I don't know," I said standing, "but I'm going to do something that maybe you haven't thought of this year."

"Yeah, what's that?" Charlie said, sitting up.

"I'm going to fucking try," I said.

Chapter 75

It was four in the afternoon by the time my chartered plane brought me up to Raiford, where Harris was being held on death row.

Raiford, in North Florida near Jacksonville, was about as far from Key West as you can get without leaving the state. Charlie had suggested to Harris that a local attorney might be more practical, but Harris had refused to get someone else.

It was Charlie or no one, Harris had said. Which made me wonder about Harris's judgment.

I passed a small group of young protesters sitting on cars parked in the brown grass across from the maximum security prison. A waiflike teen in a vintage flowered dress waved a sign at me that said, DOWN WITH THE DEATH PENALTY. FREE JUSTIN HARRIS!

"Doing my best," I mumbled as I approached the razor-wire fence of the prison parking lot.

With its king palms, hedged grounds, and whitewashed mission architecture, the entrance of Raiford looked more like a nineteenth-century resort than a prison.

But I nearly forgot that impression forever the moment I stepped inside and took in the stark concrete-and-steel interior decoration. I was buzzed in and felt as much as heard the clack as a door bolt shot home behind my back. It was the first time I'd ever been inside a prison. Movies didn't do justice to the demoralizing horror.

From somewhere and everywhere came indeterminate shouts, overly loud televisions, flushing toilets, steel on steel.

I thought about that night on the beach so long ago. About Ramón Peña. About the fate I'd dodged.

Or had I? I wondered. Every time I thought I'd gotten away from it, it seemed to pop up again, like a will-o'-the-wisp in reverse.

After being admitted and having my bag searched, I was escorted by a mute, broad-backed Hispanic guard down a bleak cement hallway. I had to wait twenty minutes before Justin Harris hobbled into the death row visitor area in wrist-to-leg shackles. The guard with him actually cuffed him, like a wild beast, to a raised iron ring in the floor beside the table.

And the guard didn't go far. He stood watching us intently from the other side of a large wired-glass window.

I looked at Justin Harris for the first time. He was heavier than his Fox News picture. He was a big man, gone to fat, his massive shoulders and arms and chest crumpled toward the floor as if something at his center had caved in. He sat there breathing raspily as he stared at me blankly. I noticed a raised, bluish bump on his cropped head.

"Where's Charlie?" he finally said. "I thought they said my lawyer was here."

"I'm Nina Bloom. I work at a law firm in New York, and I was assigned to help out Charlie on your case. What happened to your head?"

"This?" he said, pointing at the bruise with a goofy grin. "I bumped it water-skiing."

I let out a breath as I held eye contact with him. He had a week to live, and he was being a wiseass? Was Harris actually nuts? I wondered.

"I know you didn't do this, Justin," I said quietly. "I'm here to help."

Anger flashed in Harris's suddenly wide eyes. His chains jingled as he sat up. "Oh, really. How do you know I didn't do it? Because I'm black, and you voted for Obama? Listen, I fought for this country with honor with the Army Rangers in the first Iraq War, and now they're closing down Gitmo. Maybe you and your ACLU pals should skip me and try springing a terrorist."

"I know you believe in this country,

Justin," I said even quieter now, as I took his medal out of my bag.

"Who gave you that?" he said, outraged.

"Your mother. I'm here for her as well as you."

He stared at the medal. He took a breath, held it. He shook his head, quickly closing his eyelids before a tear could escape.

"They executed Ted Bundy here. Did you know that?" he said matter-of-factly. "The electric chair is down the hall. They said there's a new portable one I could choose if I want. Or I can go the needle route. Problem is, they botched one a few years back when they missed the vein. Left foot-long chemical burns up both of the guy's arms."

"I'm going to get you out of here, Justin," I said.

He huffed out a breath, then looked at me for a long beat. Finally, he smiled at me. A genuine smile for the first time. He had straight teeth, dimples. For a split second, I saw the resemblance to the young, grinning drum major on the Carnegie Hall stage.

"I'm sorry about the Obama crack. I didn't mean it," he said, squeezing his hands together as if in prayer. "I understand what you're trying to do, Miss Bloom. I admire it. Trying to help out desperate people is a nice thing. You really seem like a nice person, and I thank you for believing in me. But the governor of Florida isn't going to grant me a stay. I got myself into this mess, and I'm resigned to suffer the consequences. I lived my life. It didn't turn out so hot. Now it's going to end."

"Look at me," I said passionately. "I'm not talking about a stay. I'm going to get you out of here, Justin. I know your DNA was from consensual sex with Tara Foster and that your fiancée lied about you. I'm going to straighten the whole thing out. Can you remember anything at all that can prove your alibi?"

"It's been really nice talking to you, Nina, but I need to get back to my reading now," Justin said, knocking on the wired glass.

As the guard was taking him away, Justin turned back. "Wait, there actually is one thing," he said.

"What? What is it?" I said, sitting up.

"If you hear from my mom, tell her I love her, and that I'm OK, and that I don't want to see her at the execution, OK?"

I nodded and let out a breath as I watched Justin be led away.

Chapter 76

Charlie was on the front porch of his Key West bungalow, playing an electric steel guitar, when I arrived at his house at around nine on Saturday morning. He actually had an amplifier and everything. His eyes were closed as he maneuvered the glass slide over the strings, really getting into the jangling blues tune he was playing.

He opened his bloodshot eyes immediately when I stormed up the stairs and yanked the amplifier's plug.

"I see that writing isn't the only occupation that you share with Papa

Hemingway," I said as I kicked the half-empty box of Heineken keg cans between his feet. Had he been drinking all night? Or just all morning?

"How's Justin? Still as optimistic as ever?" Charlie said, finally looking up at me after a slow sip of breakfast beer. "Did you know the *Today* show called me to see if I wanted to go on and plead Justin's case? I asked Justin, and he went crazy. He wouldn't let me do it. He doesn't want to be defended. He's sick of living in prison, sick of living, period. How do I fight for the life of a man who so obviously wants to die?"

Charlie really was playing the blues, I realized. He looked depressed as well as drunk. It was obvious that Justin wasn't the only one who was listening to the ticking of a dwindling clock. Charlie was blaming himself for Justin's fate. He felt that he'd let the man down.

Worst of all, like Justin, he seemed to think the whole thing was over. I had to change that.

"Justin is hopeless, as hopeless as his lawyer," I said, waving Harris's thick case file along with the printer sheets from the research I'd done at my hotel the night before. "Which has to change right now. We need to turn this around, Charlie. We need to go over this case with a fine-tooth comb. What about justice?"

Charlie tipped up his can and dropped the empty on the porch floor.

"Ours is a world where justice is accidental and innocence no protection. Someone said that. Euripides? Smart fuck, whoever he was," Charlie said as he cracked open another beer.

I went over and snatched it out of his hand and threw it off the porch before I sat down next to him.

"Did you know that at the time of Harris's arrest," I said, showing him my papers, "the local West Palm news showed his picture and broadcast his perp walk? Several local newspaper editorials called for swift justice before the trial even began. A motion to move the trial upstate to a neutral venue by his first lawyer was dismissed out of hand. You and I both know Harris was ramrodded."

"I hit on those points at his direct appeal and at the writ of certiorari we sent to the state supreme court, but no sale," Charlie said. "I was at that trial, sweet peach. I actually held the envelope that had Foster's underwear and Harris's DNA. I killed myself on that case. I did everything possible. I brought in the phone-book-sized record of all the men in South Florida who have been in Airborne units to show how circumstantial the state's evidence was, but they didn't want to hear it. Harris getting capital punishment is what got me to hang up my briefcase. I'm against the death penalty."

"But he didn't do this!" I yelled.

"But so what!" Charlie yelled back.

This was crazy. I'd come down here and risked everything to help out an innocent man, and I was getting resistance from both him and his lawyer.

I struggled to think up a way to inspire Charlie. I needed him on board. I couldn't do this alone. At least not without revealing the dangerous lie that was my life.

"And maybe he did do it. How do

you know? Were you there?" Charlie said.

"I just know," I said.

"I get it," the Southern beach bum lawyer said as he began tuning his steel guitar. "You're a *psychic* bitchy New York lawyer."

"Haven't you ever believed in anything?" I said. "Believed in something not for any reason, but just because you believed in it with every square inch of your body? That's how I feel about this case."

Charlie lifted a new can to his lips. He let out a breath before he lowered it. "And if you only believe, then fairies will sparkle magic dust on Justin's jail cell door and make it disappear," he said, angrily putting down the guitar. "Fine. You win. I guess you should go in and put on some coffee while I take a look at the old file yet again. Gee, this is going to be fun, dredging up my life's worst failure for the thousandth time."

I smiled as I walked past him toward his front door.

"New York City pain in my ass," he mumbled as he opened the folder I'd brought. "Milk with two sugars, you hear me? And one of those doughnuts and...and I hate you, Nina, whatever the hell your name is."

"I love you, too, Charlie," I whispered to myself as I found the kitchen.

Chapter 77

Charlie and I spent the rest of that Saturday working our asses off. On a beat-up leather couch in Charlie's office, we went over Harris's trial transcript line by line. Later Charlie, humming, sitting behind his desk, spun a rugby ball as he drank coffee, nodding as he read to himself.

Charlie really had done one hell of a job, I soon realized, as I turned the trial transcript and appeal pages. Pointed out inconsistencies. Objected to every cheap emotional trick the DA tried to pull. But the cards were stacked against

Harris. The judge, more than the DA, seemed to want to convict Harris.

The worst of it was the excessive victim-impact testimony the judge had allowed during the sentencing portion of Harris's trial. A total of sixteen family members, friends, and classmates gave over three hours' worth of sobbing, heart-wrenching, emotional testimony as to the damage done by the loss of Foster. No wonder the jury had voted unanimously for the death penalty.

By the afternoon, we'd both pretty much gone over everything. We even got down on the Oriental carpet and arranged Foster's original 1994 homicide case file, compiled when her body was originally found, beside the 2001 file, begun when the case was reopened.

I stood there, rubbing my eyes. All the photos, evidence lists, time lines, alibis, and lab reports seemed like one giant postmodern art installation. One that was making my brain ache as I tried to make heads or tails of it.

I knew I needed to try everything to come up with a way to clear Harris, but after a while, even I was starting to lose hope. I yawned, fighting exhaustion. We needed something. Anything.

"Look at this girl, would you?" Charlie said, sadly shaking his head as he waved his hand over the list of Jump Killer victims. It felt like I'd just had a shot of espresso when I realized he was pointing at my picture.

"What a beautiful young woman," he said, suddenly looking at me. "She remind you of anyone?"

I stared back at him, wide-eyed.

He snapped his fingers. "Renée Zellweger," he said. "A young Renée Zellweger."

Renée Zellweger? I thought, relieved but suddenly frowning. Renée was OK, but how about a young Gisele Bündchen?

I jumped back as Charlie suddenly threw the rugby ball against the wall, almost knocking down his Harvard diploma.

"I got it!" he said, pacing back and forth. "I could slap myself. How could I be so stupid? Why the hell didn't I see this before?"

"What? What?" I said, standing.

"The hairs. Where the hell are the hairs?"

"What are you talking about, Charlie?"

Charlie knelt down and pointed to the evidence list from the 1994 file.

"Right here. Look. There were three hairs found on Foster's body underneath the paracord ligature she was bound with," he said, pointing at the original file.

"But here," he said, indicating the 2001 lab report, "there's no mention of them. They test the semen found on the girl's panties, but not the hairs. Why not?"

"They forgot?" I offered.

"Maybe," Charlie said as he lifted his phone. "Or maybe they tested them and then deep-sixed the results when they came up inconclusive. Maybe the cops and DA conveniently left out the lab report when it didn't match."

"Who are you calling?" I said.

"The airport," Charlie said. "We need to be on the first flight up to Boca tomorrow morning to get our hands on those hair samples in the old case file. We need to have them tested. Maybe you should head back to your hotel and get some rest. I know I need some. The cops up in Boca are a real pain in the butt. We're going to need to kick ass. Speaking of ass-kicking, I want to thank you for kicking mine."

"Anytime," I said. "That's what I'm here for."

Chapter 78

I hardly recognized Charlie when he picked me up in an airport taxi wearing a crisp blue serge suit.

"You own shoes? Wingtips? I'm in shock," I said.

"I shaved and even took a shower," he said as he lifted his bulging briefcase. "But if you tell anyone, I'll categorically deny it."

Our plane was on time, and so were we when we arrived at ten sharp at the Boca Raton PD station, about 150 miles to the north. We had an appointment to meet with the detectives who originally arrested Justin Harris, but we had to sit in the department's lobby for the better part of an hour before Person Crimes Unit Detectives Roberta Cantele and Brian Cogle buzzed us in.

Instead of going back to their office area, we were seated in an interview room by the front door, as if we were suspects.

"What's this about?" Cogle, a tall detective with a white goatee and a huge gut under his Cuban shirt, wanted to know.

"Didn't the DA tell you?" Charlie said. "We need to take a look at Tara Foster's original case file. The evidence envelopes, the whole nine."

"Why?" Cantele said.

"Because Justin Harris is about to be executed in five days, and we want to make sure it isn't a mistake," Charlie said.

"You goddamn defense liars, uh, I mean lawyers, never quit, do you?" Cogle said. "Are you aware that one of Harris's victims was the wife of Peter Fournier, Key West's chief of police?

She was, like, twenty years old. That doesn't chill you?"

Peter was the police chief now? I tried not to pass out. That was unbelievable. Not to mention terrifying. As if I didn't feel paranoid enough coming down here.

"I know Fournier," Charlie said. "My taxes pay his salary, unfortunately. I saw his dumb ass on the *Today* show on Thursday spouting all his victims' rights, fry Justin, Jump Killer crap to Al Roker. I have no doubt his wife was killed by the Jump Killer. The problem is, and I know it's a hard one for you guys to follow, Justin Harris isn't the Jump Killer."

It felt like the wind had been knocked out of me.

Peter had been on the *Today* show? On Thursday?

I really had seen him in Grand Central Terminal!

Chapter 79

"Harris is the mistake," Cogle shot back. "And his murderous ass is going to get corrected come Friday. This is bullshit. You already had all the appeals you're going to get. Everything is in order."

"You wouldn't just be saying that because it'll be your job if we find something, would you?" Charlie said, taking out his cell. "You're not actually going to make me call the DA again, are you?"

"Fine," Cogle said, leaving.

"This is a wild goose chase, isn't it?" Detective Cantele said, drumming her fingers against the cheap office table as we sat there, waiting. "It's gotta suck knowing your boy is going down, and you couldn't stop it, huh, Baylor?"

Why don't you shut up, bitch, I wanted to say to the cop as Cogle came in with a bulky white evidence box.

Charlie threw open the lid and quickly flipped through the file folders. He lifted out a bag with a faded pair of panties in them and shoved them back into the box.

"Where are the hair samples?" he yelled at Cogle.

"Hair samples?" Cogle said, scratching his tilted head. "What do you mean?"

Charlie pointed at the evidence manifest.

"Right here. Evidence Sample D2. Hair sample found beneath the ligature."

Cogle hummed as he slowly flipped through the file folders. Finally he stopped and shrugged elaborately.

"What do you know? Must have gotten lost," he finally said. "Maybe a rat ate them or they evaporated. We are talking seventeen years, right? Was that all, or do you two need to use the rest-room before you leave?"

Back out in the baking parking lot, Charlie seemed to have trouble open-ing our rental car. He suddenly threw the keys as hard as he could across the lot, then sat down on the concrete car stop beside it.

I sat down next to him, stewing in my own depressing thoughts.

Peter knew I was alive.

That was bad. About the worst thing possible. Was he still in New York? I thought about calling Emma and telling her to get out of the apartment, but then I remembered she was at her friend's in Brooklyn.

I wondered if I should go straight home and grab my daughter. I'd run once before. I could do it again. Throw a dart at a map and just go. Even if Peter was onto me, at least he didn't know about Emma.

I shouldn't have been surprised that Peter was chief of police now. He'd al-ways been ambitious. But representing the Jump Killer victims' advocate group? What a goddamn bullshit artist. He must have been thrilled all those years, thinking I was dead without having to kill me himself.

"The police destroyed that evidence, Nina," Charlie finally said. "They're laughing at us. They don't care that an innocent man is about to die. No one does. That's it, Nina. That's all she wrote. We're done. Justin's done. It's over. We have to accept the inevitable."

I sat there thinking about that. Maybe Charlie was right. Maybe I should just let Charlie and Justin figure it out. Every man, woman, and child for themselves.

But right there, among the cop cars, with tar sticking to my four-inch heels, my anger tipped the scales against my fear. I was tired of running. Tired of Peter. Tired of what I had become.

I wasn't going to run. I wasn't going to hide. I *was* going to do the *right* thing.

"Nothing's inevitable," I said as I finally stood. I held out my hand and helped Charlie back to his feet as well. "They won this battle. Now let's go and win the war."

Chapter 80

After we found the rental's keys (Charlie had flung them under one of the Boca PD cruisers), we drove to the parking lot of a nearby Burger King, where I proceeded to go through Charlie's messy files like I was possessed.

Alone and penniless, I had managed to raise a daughter in New York City with nothing but sheer will. I was pissed off now. I was going to straighten out Justin's case if it killed me.

"What are you looking for now?" Charlie cried.

I pulled out a sheet of copy paper on

which Charlie had typed, "HARRIS'S ALIBI INFO!" in big, bold letters across the top.

"This," I said.

I read that Harris's ex-fiancée's name was Fabiana Desmarais. She was a Haitian immigrant who lived in Princeton, Florida, a few miles north of the Homestead Correctional Institution.

"How far away is Princeton from here?" I said. "We need to speak to Fabiana."

"Wait one second," Charlie said. "I tried that before the first habeas corpus appeal three years ago. Not only wouldn't Fabiana's mother let me speak to her, but she actually sicced her dog on me, a half-starved boxer with a bad attitude."

"Hey, maybe you rub dogs the same way you rub people, Charlie," I said. "I'd like a shot at her."

"Oh, right," he said. "We'll use your secret weapon: charm. I forgot about the universal love all people have for pushy New York broads."

We took the Florida Turnpike and about an hour and a half later, we zigzagged through some side streets until we pulled up in front of a sign that said HOMESTEAD MOBILE HOMES.

"No!" I said as we pulled up at Fabiana's address. Beyond a rusty mailbox was an obviously deserted double-wide trailer with broken windows.

"I'm the manager. Can I help you?" called a very dark black man beneath the retractable awning of another trailer across the street.

As we stepped up, I saw that he was sitting on a faded wooden grapefruit crate and that he was working a paper or something in his dark, nimble fingers.

"We're looking for Fabiana Desmarais," I said.

"You cops?" the man said without looking up.

"No, we're lawyers," I said.

"I'd tell you even if you were cops," the old man said with a yellow grin. "Fabiana and her snooty mother took off in the middle of the night about two years ago. No forwarding address."

"You wouldn't happen to have her

social security number on file?" Charlie said, glancing at the rusted trailer.

"Since she owed me six months' rent, I actually tried all that skip trace stuff. Number they both gave me was fake. Maybe they went back to Haiti like the old battle-ax of a mother kept threatening. Said America was an uncultured cesspool. America! I used to say to her, 'How many illegal American immigrants they got paddling shark-infested waters into Haiti on tire rafts last time you checked?'"

"Oh, well. Thanks for your time," Charlie said.

"You know what Fabiana's mother reminds me of? This," the old man said, holding up the piece of paper he'd been working. It was an origami cobra. He made a hissing sound as he twirled its tail between his fingers.

"Nice," Charlie said. "Thanks again."

"Well, at least we didn't get bit," Charlie said as we got back into the hot car. "Are you finished now, or do you need some more face time with the origami man?"

I scrubbed at my forehead with my

fingers. "We need to speak to Justin again."

"Up in Raiford?" Charlie said. "You were just up there."

"If he doesn't give us anything, then it'll be on him," I said.

Chapter 81

It was coming on three by the time our chartered Cessna twin-prop arrived in Raiford on Tuesday. All this flying was costing a fortune, but an innocent man's life was at stake—and I was billing everything to my Global 100 firm. Charlie called and made arrangements with the warden as we were driving past the growing crowd of protesters outside the prison grounds.

Harris looked stunned as Charlie and I met him in the lawyer visiting room.

"Back again so soon?" he said to me.

"Hate to interrupt your reading," I said, tossing him a bag of mini pretzels.

"Hey, thanks. They're my favorite," he said, actually sounding pleased. He ripped open the bag with his shackled hands, dumped the pretzels onto the interview table, and ate one.

"OK," I said. "I got you something, Justin. Now you have to give us something. We need to speak to Fabiana, but she's no longer living in Princeton. She left and didn't leave any forwarding info. Do you have any clue where she might have gone?"

"You kidding me?" he said with his mouth full. "I haven't spoken to Fabiana since she threw the engagement ring I bought her in my face a decade and a half ago. That bitch wants me dead, and she's going to get her way. You're digging a dry hole."

"You know what I'm sick of, Justin?" I said, suddenly smashing one of the pretzels on the table with my fist. "You and your attitude. You don't want me to try to save your life? That's not macho, that's just stupid. Or just come out and say it. Have the guts to say, 'I did it! I killed Tara Foster!'"

He gaped at me with his open mouth for a moment before he closed it. "But I didn't," he said, spitting crumbs.

I held my hand to my ear. "Holy moly! Did I just hear someone actually defend himself?"

"Who's running the show here, Charlie?" Harris said.

"Isn't that obvious?" Charlie said, eyeballing me.

"Fine. Try her cousin Maddie," Harris said. "She was the one who actually introduced us."

"Maddie what," I said, thumbing my iPhone.

"Maddie Pelletier," Harris said. "She's a teacher at the high school in Key West now. She was always pretty cool to me. She even writes sometimes."

I thumbed the phone book app. "I got a Madeline Pelletier on Fogarty Avenue."

"That's her," Justin said.

I stood. "We have to go, Justin," I said. "But we'll be back."

"Yeah, for the execution," Harris mumbled.

"No, dumbass," I said, pointing at the barred gate. "To open that door and let your mother hug you again."

Chapter 82

"Hey, who wants a beer brat?" Peter yelled, smiling, as he snapped barbecue tongs in front of his smoking grill.

With the festive smell of charring jerk chicken and chorizo sausage, the cries of running children and Neil Diamond playing softly from his backyard speakers, the barbecue seemed more like a birthday party or a christening than an event for the surviving family of serial killer victims.

It was an eclectic group: black, white, brown, rich, poor, even a gay Protestant minister. Death didn't discriminate. Peter knew that firsthand.

The barbecue was actually one of several events planned for the group this week. Tomorrow, a chartered bus and plane from Miami would take all of them to the governor's mansion in Tallahassee for a sit-down and some more press coverage, Peter hoped. Then it was over to Raiford on Friday for an all-day camp-out vigil before Harris's midnight execution. An exhausting schedule for these poor folks but one that he hoped would provide some closure.

Knowing that Jeanine was actually still alive disqualified Peter's membership in the group, but, hey, who was he to burst everyone's bubble with a technicality?

Besides, she'd be deader than grunge music once he went back up to New York and hunted her down after the execution.

He was flipping some peppers and onions when the minister formed a prayer circle around the pool.

"In the name of the Father and of the Son and of the Holy Spirit," Peter said along with everyone as he took his place between his beaming wife, Vicki, and the minister.

Across from them, his new best friend, Arty Tivolli, the multimillionaire, smiled approvingly.

The closing on the golf course was scheduled for a week after the execution. Peter would be splitting the six percent commission with the broker. In two weeks' time, if all went well, he'd be handed a check for three and a half million dollars.

And it all would go well. He of all people would see to that.

An hour later as everyone was lining up along the seawall in lawn chairs to watch the sun set, Peter's cell rang.

"Hey, Peter. How's it going? It's Brian Cogle from the Boca PD."

"Of course, Bri. What's up?" Peter said to the crusty old cop. He knew everybody who was anybody in South Florida law enforcement. It was all about the networking.

"Just wanted to let you know that we got a visit from Harris's mouthpiece, that son of a bitch Charlie Baylor. He was asking about the hairs."

"Those, huh?" Peter said, frowning. Baylor was such an asshole.

"There was a woman with him, too. A lawyer. He got some help."

Shit, Peter thought. That was all he needed to upset the apple cart. Some eleventh-hour crusade. If Justin Harris was given a stay, who knew how pissy Tivolli would get. Now was not the time for the unexpected. Harris needed to be in a pine box by next week.

"Any chance your boy at the lab who squelched the hairs will squeal?" Peter said. "If there's any friction, I'd be willing to make it worth his while."

"Pete, c'mon. Don't insult me," Cogle said. "I got it under control. The lab rat is my geeky little brother-in-law. I'm his son's godfather. Besides, he'd get canned. Not a chance."

"Good," Peter said. "Like I told you before, Brian, getting rid of them was the right thing. Showing that there was a second person at the crime scene would have complicated the whole case and gotten that son of a bitch off. You did the right thing, brother. I'll never forget it."

"Don't even mention it. Had it been my wife, I know you'd do the same for me," Cogle said. "You going up to demonstrate at the execution?"

Behind Peter, the gathered crowd began to ooh and aah as the sun began to descend over the gulf. Peter squinted out at the water as the sky turned the color of a new penny.

"Wouldn't miss it for the world, Brian," Peter said.

Chapter 83

We had to drive up to Jacksonville to get a direct flight back to Key West, so it was almost nine p.m. by the time we spilled out of a puddle jumper back at the Key West airport.

We had our cabdriver take us directly to Madeline Pelletier's house on Fogarty Avenue, not far from Key West High School. The front yard of the small stucco house she lived in was strewn with toys.

"Yes?" said the pretty, petite teen-aged black girl who answered the door.

"Can we speak to Maddie Pelletier?" Charlie said.

"Mom," the girl called back into the house. "It's white people."

"Hello," said a not much older version of the girl who'd answered the door a minute later. "I'm Maddie. Can I help you?"

"Hi, Maddie. Sorry to bother you so late. We're lawyers representing Justin Harris. Could we speak to you?"

"Oh, wow. Poor Justin," she said, shaking her head. "I pray for him. What can I do for you?"

"Well, we actually need to speak to your cousin Fabiana," I said. "But we can't seem to find her."

"Do you think Fabiana can help Justin?"

"Justin claims that he and Fabiana were on an all-day date at the Miami Seaquarium the day he was accused of killing that girl," Charlie said.

"But Fabiana said it was a lie," Maddie said.

"We know," I said. "But we have some new information and just need to ask her some questions. We really need to speak to her."

"That's what helped the jury to convict Justin?" Maddie said with a stunned look on her face. "I had no idea. If I didn't know any better, I'd say her mother is behind this somehow." Maddie shook her head. "I'm not sure what to do. My aunt Isabelle, Fabiana's mother, is a very old-school Haitian, very suspicious of everything. She stopped speaking to me for years after she found out that I introduced Fabiana to Justin at a bar. She'll go crazy if she finds out I sent you."

"She won't find out from us," Charlie said.

"Aunt Isabelle runs a pretty successful Haitian restaurant near South Beach in Miami. It's called the Rooster's Perch. She and Fabiana live in Little Haiti. Hold the door. I'll get the address for you."

Charlie and I stared at each other as we waited.

"Is this what I think it is?" Charlie said. "Are we actually making some progress?"

"Shhh," I said. "Hold your breath. We don't have the address yet."

Chapter 84

After agreeing that neither one of us could physically set foot on another airplane until morning, Charlie and I decided on dinner instead.

"I'll behave, too. I'll drink only light rum," Charlie said as our taxi let us out on crowded Duval Street.

We sat in a booth at Jack Flats. The place had an awesome, long, beat-up wooden bar and old black-and-white photographs of cigar factory workers who had populated the island in the late nineteenth and early twentieth centuries. Outside the open stall-like doors,

Duval was the same as ever. Think a drunken Greenwich Village block party in New York, with flip-flops. Only it was even crazier now that the Independence Celebration was in full swing.

I stared, amazed, at the Yanks-Rays game playing above the crowded bar beside a neon Dolphins helmet. I'd been so busy in the last few crazy days, I'd almost forgotten that there was a sport called baseball. I needed to call Emma as well. I decided I'd text her once I got back to my hotel.

"Don't tell me. You're a Yankees fan, too," Charlie said as I clapped at a Posada double. "Could you try just a tiny bit more not to make me hate you even more?"

"Not a chance," I said before finishing my beer and standing. "Watch my seat, and I counted my wings, by the way, Harvard boy."

The first thing I noticed as I headed back to our table a few minutes later was that there was a police car at the curb in front of the open doors. The second was that there was somebody in my seat.

When I realized *who* that somebody was, I stopped in midstride in the middle of the bar as if I'd hit an invisible wall.

Chapter 85

I stood there. The people at the bar and the multiple ball games on the TVs above them suddenly seemed out of rhythm, somehow both too slow and too fast. The sound from the bar's speakers, which had been playing the classic rock song "A Whiter Shade of Pale," alternately blasted and dipped, as if a child were playing with the volume knob. The cigar factory workers now sent me malignant stares from the vintage photographs. So did a stocky waitress, jostling past me, as I stood in the middle of the crowded room, my lungs and heart seizing.

Peter sat in the booth with Charlie less than ten feet away on my right. He was wearing his dark blue police uniform, his thick, chiseled arms as deeply tanned as I remembered them. It was as if he hadn't aged at all.

I couldn't take my eyes off the butt of his gun on his Sam Browne belt. In a moment, he would turn and see me, I thought. In a moment, he would stand and draw and fire his gun into my face. People or no people, the fact that almost two decades had passed meant nothing. Killing was what Peter did.

I was suddenly extremely aware of my heartbeat. I could feel the systole and diastole of my heart clenching and releasing as I waited for Peter to catch me out of the corner of his eye.

But after one second and then two, miraculously he didn't turn. After a third moment, my paralysis lessened, and I was suddenly able to move. I mustered up the last iota of my will to live. I backpedaled, turned, and squeezed into a place along the crowded bar.

"So you're still trying to pull some tricks up in Boca," Peter said to Charlie at my back, as I eavesdropped. "I mean, you seem like a decent lush, Baylor. Why represent a piece of garbage like Harris? Controversial client like that is bound to stir up people's emotions. I'd hate to see you become a victim of a violent crime."

"Is that a threat?" Charlie said.

"Just some friendly advice," Peter said. "Your own personal public service announcement from Key West's chief of police."

"Don't you have any drunks to beat up?" Charlie said.

"Fresh out," Peter said. "But if you're free, we could head outside."

"Be happy to," Charlie said. "You keep the badge, I get the gun."

"You're real funny, Counselor, but what's not funny is that you're trying to protect the man who killed my wife from his just reward."

I swallowed. Peter was referring to me, I realized.

"It doesn't matter," Peter said. "No matter what you do, Friday night, your precious client is walking into that chamber, and they're going to carry him out in a bag."

"We'll see about that, won't we?" Charlie said calmly.

"Yes, we certainly will," Peter said.

I heard Peter stand. Would he come to the bar and order a drink? Was he behind me? Before I could muster up the courage to turn around, I felt a hand at my back.

"There you are," Charlie said.

I couldn't have been more relieved.

"Who was that cop?" I managed to spit out.

"Chief of Police Peter Fournier. Must have heard it through the grapevine that we were looking at Tara Foster's file."

I blinked down at the floor, trying to absorb that.

"Some people say he's dirty, but whenever any complaints arise, he always ends up smelling like a rose. You have to see him, with his perfect Barbie doll wife and two perfect little Stepford kids, like he's Mr. All-American Dad. Then he comes in here just now with that high-wattage Tom Cruise smile of his and threatens me. Sick puppy."

Peter had a wife and kids now?! I wasn't sure how I felt about that. I'd be sure to go over it when my heart started beating again.

"You want another beer?" Charlie said.

"Yes," I said. "And a shot of whiskey."

"There you go, Nina. Get into that Key West vibe. I didn't know you had it in you," Charlie said with a wink. "But then I call us a taxi. We need to rest up for tomorrow. We have only another three days. I have a feeling this one is going to be a race to the finish line, don't you?"

Chapter 86

I immediately hit the shower when I got back to my hotel room. With my hands flat against the glass tile wall, I stood directly under the spray in the suite's spa-like bathroom for almost an hour, my eyes closed as the hot needles pinged off my face and skin.

I was hoping the heat and the rush of the water might clear my mind, deliver some much-needed calm, but as the minutes passed, I knew it was fruitless.

I couldn't stop thinking about how

dangerously close I'd come to Peter, but after a while, I realized there actually were some positives. One, Peter was back in Key West, away from Emma. Two, if Peter didn't ask Charlie about me that meant Peter didn't seem to know that I wasn't in New York. And three, he didn't know that I was helping Charlie.

But I had to keep things that way. Going out for dinner and drinks on Duval Street was about as reckless a move as I could have made. All Peter had to do was turn, give the slightest of glances over his shoulder, and he would have seen me again.

Freeing Justin was my priority, but I had to be smarter. I also needed to wrap this up as soon as possible. Every moment I stayed down here, I was playing with my life.

Finally, reluctantly, I squeaked off the faucet and squeezed out my hair. After I dried and wrapped myself in a couple of fresh towels, I pulled on the fluffy bathrobe that was hanging on the inside of the bathroom door. I went into the bedroom and set the alarm clock for five so I could get up early to do my hair.

I was going to call Emma back in New York, but then I realized how late it was and decided to just text my daughter good-night instead. Too exhausted to get into my pj's, I sat for a moment on the side of the bed.

Beyond the open doorway of the bedroom, the living room curtains were wafting gently in the breeze from the rooftop patio slider. Between them a slight sliver of the moon glowed over the still silver plain of the water.

Could Charlie see it, too? I wondered. I couldn't deny how I was starting to feel about him. He was funny, intelligent, not hard to look at, though the breakfast beers would have to go.

I turned off the light and lay back on the pillows, already half asleep, when I had a much less romantic thought. Without turning, I glanced over at the billowing living room curtains, furling now in the dark like a full sail.

But how could the curtains be blow-ing in the breeze? I thought.

When I'd locked my balcony door before my shower?

Chapter 87

For the next two solid minutes, I lay there in the dark, my heart rapping like a set of brass knuckles at the inside of my chest, silence sizzling in my ears.

But there has to be a good reason was the thought that scrolled through my unraveling mind like a continuous news crawl.

Then my molars clicked together involuntarily as a faint scraping sound came from just beyond the open bedroom door.

Something in my chest started to flutter when I heard it again. It came from the left, as if someone standing in the suite's kitchen had shifted his weight.

Not just any someone either, I suddenly thought.

I guess Peter hadn't missed seeing me at the bar after all.

I knew I couldn't just stay there, that I needed to get up, hide, run, do something. But I didn't move. I couldn't. Animal fear pressed down on my chest like a lead blanket, making me weak, pinning me to the bed.

After a long, careful, silent breath, I lifted my hand as if to prove to myself that I could, in fact, move.

Good, I thought stupidly.

Now I needed to do the same thing *with my feet.*

I reached out as I slowly sat up, my right hand brushing along the top of the bedside radio alarm clock. I was standing, my eyes glued to the dark doorway, when I had an idea. I bent down slowly, unplugged the heavy clock, and brought it with me to the side of the open bedroom door.

As I arrived, a dark figure moved

smoothly and silently through the bed-room doorway.

At first, I didn't believe it.

This isn't happening, I thought, sud-denly frozen and senseless again. *How could this be happening? I'm dreaming this.*

Then a switch tripped somewhere in the primordial part of my brain, and I snapped out of my daze and swung the clunky alarm clock by its cord two-handed as hard as I could.

There was an unexpectedly loud shat-tering sound followed by a heavy thump as the figure immediately went down. I'd swung high and assumed I'd hit Peter in the head, but I didn't stick around to find out. I dropped what was left of the clock and ran in a blind panic out of the bedroom.

In two strides, I was through the suite's living room, my hand wrapped around the front doorknob, turning and pulling in one motion.

Then my arm almost came out of its socket as the door jerked to a stop only a quarter of the way open.

Hysterical, I tried the door two more

times before I realized the slide lock was still engaged. Moaning and literally shaking with terror, I forced myself to methodically close the door, flip the lock free, and then try the knob again.

That did it. I ran out into the blindingly bright hallway and burst through the closest stairwell door to my left. My bare feet slapped painfully off the concrete as I half ran, half fell down the stairs.

As I made the next lower landing, I paused. Huffing and puffing, I tried to quell my rioting mind and figure out what to do next. Should I go into the hallway and knock on some doors? Go down to the lobby? That's when the stairwell door above me blew open like it had been torn off its hinges.

Heavy footsteps began to hammer down the stairs as I turned and ripped open the lower floor's door. Shedding towels, with my robe flying wide, I ran half-naked now down the new hallway. Every molecule of my being was focused on one thing: pumping my legs up and down as fast as they would go, moving away from the sound behind me.

As I turned the next corner, I spotted a red metal box on the wall. A loud clanging started immediately as I yanked the fire alarm on the run. Doors opened up and down the hallway. A groggy teenager's eyes almost popped out of his head as he saw me streak past him at about thirty miles an hour.

I hit the next stairwell door and took this newest set of stairs two by two all the way to the ground floor. I crossed the empty lobby in nothing flat and headed for the hotel driveway. Standing in the drive's turnaround, the night manager was on his cell phone and looking up at the building.

I thought about stopping and asking for his help, but even he would be no protection from Peter, I realized. I spotted a taxi stopped at the light on the corner and bolted for it.

The traffic light turned from red to green when I was still about twenty feet away.

I wasn't going to make it, I thought as I ran barefoot, wheezing and covered in sweat, into the street. I winced, waiting for the feel of a bullet in my back, to fall sprawling on the asphalt. In my hysterical mind, it was already over. I could actually see Peter coming over and smiling his easy smile as he placed a gun to my forehead.

But instead, the cab suddenly stopped short and I jumped in. I broke a nail ripping open the handle of its rear door.

"In a rush, are we?" the young Asian wiseass of a driver said as I collapsed across the rear seat.

"Drive," I gasped. "Drive, drive. Please just drive."

Chapter 88

I made the taxi driver promise to wait for me as I pounded on Charlie's front door.

He finally opened it, wearing a pair of Texas A&M boxer shorts.

"What the hell?" Charlie said. "Nina?"

I smoothed my still wet hair as I stood in my bathrobe, staring at him. I hadn't thought this far in advance. What could I say? How could I explain what had just happened?

He reached out and grabbed my elbow, sudden concern in his eyes.

"Nina, are you OK? Are you hurt?"

I was about to tell him that there was a fire at the hotel. Why not? What was another lie on top of nearly two decades' worth?

I was more surprised than anyone about what happened next. Maybe it was the fact that I'd come unglued with shock and wasn't thinking straight. Or that I'd been working so hard over the last week under such enormous stress.

I stepped over the threshold and crashed into Charlie like he was a tackling sled. I wrapped my arms around him like he was my last hope. Probably because he was.

He seemed baffled, to put it mildly. But that shocker wasn't anything compared to what came out of my mouth a second later.

"My name isn't Nina," I said in his ear. "Oh, Charlie. You have to help me. Please."

Chapter 89

Charlie stared at me, blown away, for a few moments before he brought me back into his office and sat me down. After he paid for the taxi, he put a half-full water glass of Johnnie Walker in my hand and one in his own, sat slowly himself, and let out a breath. After several more beats, he yelled, "What?!"

I stared at him for a few seconds, biting my lip. How could I do this? I thought. How could I open up after so many years, so many lies? I'd been keeping my secrets for too long. How could I reveal them now?

At first, I scrambled to think of a way to minimize the utter outrageousness of my insane life story. But after a minute, I realized how impossible that was.

Harris's case file was sprawled out on Charlie's desk. I stood and retrieved the sheet with the photographs of the suspected Jump Killer victims.

"Look, Charlie," I said, tapping my high school yearbook picture twice. "This isn't a young Renée Zellweger. It's me. My name is Jeanine. Jeanine Fournier. I used to be married to Peter Fournier, the Key West chief of police."

Then for the next half hour, as Charlie sat there blinking, I explained myself. Or at least tried to. When I got to the part about my faked abduction, he held up his hand.

"So you're telling me that Fournier, the chief of police, is not only a bad cop, but, in fact, a psychopath?" Charlie said.

I nodded vigorously. "That's why I faked my death. Peter's first wife tried to leave him through regular channels. I didn't feel like being stalked and gunned down."

Then I told him the part about the Jump Killer and my new life and identity up in New York with Emma.

"When my firm volunteered me for the pro bono initiative, and I found out about Justin," I explained, "I knew I had to come back down here to help. I knew Justin was innocent because the psycho who picked me up hitchhiking and tried to kill me the night I left was white."

Charlie closed his eyes and began to rub them. He opened his mouth to say something, then closed it again.

"Are you really a lawyer at least?" he finally spat out.

"I went to Fordham Law at night. I even passed the bar. My plan here was to get Justin off, but keep my life secret and safe and intact. But that's out the window now. Peter was in my room tonight. He must have seen me at the bar when he was talking to you. I'd call the cops, but Peter is the cops. What am I going to do?"

Charlie lifted his drink and stared at it, thinking. Then he finally finished it.

"Well, from one lawyer to another, here's my best advice, off the top of my head," he said. "You need to get on a plane and get as far away from Fournier as possible until we can figure out a way to deal with him. You need to go back to New York."

Chapter 90

"Go back to New York?" I said. "What about Justin? I had contact with the real Jump Killer! That's pertinent to Justin's case, isn't it? I'm probably the only person who's ever seen the Jump Killer and lived. Don't I need to testify?"

"It's not that simple," Charlie said. "In order to get a stay of execution with this little time left, you have to go through the Florida Office of Executive Clemency. We're going to get only one shot at convincing the board to look at any new evidence. As it stands now, Justin's fiancée recanting her damaging testimony is still the best possible scenario. She's the only one who has vital exculpatory evidence that speaks directly to the case. The members on the board would be forced to consider it."

"But—" I started.

Charlie silenced me with a palm. "Your, uh, new revelations, on the other hand, are essentially this: you came into contact with a white man who seemed to be the Jump Killer. It's certainly thought-provoking, but there's not enough legal red meat there. In fact, it might be seen as so fantastical that I wouldn't be surprised if the governor dismissed it as a desperate stunt. Fabiana's testimony is it, our only shot."

"But we haven't even found her yet," I pointed out. "Let alone convinced her to tell the truth. And what if we don't? Then what do we have? Nothing. Fantastical as it is, my testimony is at least something."

"Maybe," Charlie said. "But it'll be really hard for you to testify if you're dead. You're not thinking straight. Didn't you just say that Fournier was in your room? You getting out of Key West isn't a choice."

I sat there staring at him. He had a point. I definitely was in danger. Now more than ever. But after meeting Justin, I knew I couldn't run again.

"I need to see this through," I finally said. "Whatever happens, I'm not leaving until I've done everything I can do for Justin. I'm staying."

Charlie stared at me, exasperated. He drummed his fingers on the desk.

"Mission Exonerate? Mission Impossible is more like it," he said. "Fine. I'm not going to deny that I do need your help. For Justin's sake, I guess we don't have a choice. But until this is over, we stick together. Agreed?"

"Agreed," I said, letting out a breath.

I couldn't believe it. I was still here. I had actually told someone my secrets, and I hadn't burst into flames.

Not all of my secrets, I reminded myself. I had yet to mention Ramón Peña, but I guess it was a start.

"I can't tell you how much this means to me, Charlie," I said. "For me, for my daughter. I've been holding this inside for so long. I've never told anyone. I'm so sorry I lied to you."

Charlie lifted the phone. "I should have known you were trouble the second you crushed your doughnuts in my door, Nina. Or do I have to call you Jeanine now? Never mind. What's the number for your hotel? That bathrobe is probably too casual even by Miami standards. If we're still going to go up there to find Justin's ex-fiancée, I have a funny feeling you're going to need your bags."

Chapter 91

Early the next morning, Charlie and I were in Miami. It was around nine when we rolled up in front of the address Fabiana's cousin gave us, a tiny stucco house in the northeast Miami neighborhood known as Little Haiti.

I looked anxiously down the block at the bars on all the neighboring windows, the chain-linked front yards cluttered with garbage and barking dogs. Loud Caribbean hip-hop blasted as a bunch of muscular kids in gangbanger do-rags sat on a battered gray leather sectional on the corner, giving new meaning to the word *loitering*.

"Wait in the car," Charlie said, opening his door. "With the doors locked."

"No way," I said, following him out. "You're not leaving me out here."

We hurried up the cracked concrete path to Fabiana's tiny house and rang her doorbell.

"Fabiana!" Charlie called, giving the door a couple of quick pounds for good measure.

A minute later, one of the larger corner "kids" rolled past on a BMX trick bike, alternately sizing us up and glancing at our rental.

"There doesn't seem to be anyone home," I said quickly as the kid rolled back toward his posse. "Why don't we check for Fabiana at her mom's restaurant?"

"That's funny. I was just thinking the same thing," Charlie said as we raced each other back to the car.

After Little Haiti, Fabiana's mother's restaurant, the Rooster's Perch, was a happy surprise. It was half an hour away in South Beach, a block west of the trendy art deco hotels of Ocean Drive and the beach. Behind the eatery's battered wooden sidewalk tables, a wall mural depicted cattle and chickens under palm trees, smiling black kids in plaid school uniforms, dark women in colorful dresses carrying wash.

"We do not open until lunch," said a very dark old woman who was cutting open a bundle of tablecloths at the bar just inside the door when we walked in. She wore an expensive cream-colored dress, pearls, and a suspicious, sullen expression.

"Let me guess. You're Isabelle," Charlie said.

"Who are you? How do you know my name? What do you want here?" the woman said, her eyes gleaming as she came immediately around the bar.

Now I understood what the trailer park manager meant when he compared her to his paper cobra.

"We're here to speak with Fabiana," Charlie said.

"There is no one here by that name," the old woman said, pointing at the door with her knife. "Leave, I tell you. Now."

"It's OK, Mama," said a younger black woman in an apron who suddenly appeared in the swinging kitchen door- way.

Charlie and I looked at each other in happy surprise.

"It is not OK!" Isabelle insisted as she turned.

The younger woman barked some- thing in French. The old woman's eyes went wide before she reluctantly stepped out of our way.

"I am Fabiana Desmarais," the young woman finally said as she waved us into the kitchen. "How can I help you?"

Chapter 92

Fabiana was petite with very light blue eyes and cinnamon-colored skin. Though she was almost in her fifties, she looked maybe half that. She wore a simple, wide-necked peasant blouse with a fuchsia cotton skirt that seemed much cheaper than her mother's.

Behind her, several quartered chickens sat on a cutting board beside a pile of Scotch bonnet peppers. From an industrial-sized bubbling pot on the stove came the strong but comforting smell of chicken broth. Immediately hungry, I had to resist the urge to ask for a bowl.

"Hi, Fabiana. I'm Nina, and this is Charlie," I said, taking the lead. "We're really sorry to bother you, but we're here about Justin Harris."

A look of fear wafted through Fabiana's blue eyes. Her mouth opened in a tiny O. "What about him?" she said, collecting herself after a moment.

"You mean you don't know?" I said.

She shook her head. "Know what?" she said.

"Justin Harris is going to be executed, Fabiana," Charlie said. "In two days, he's going to receive the death penalty for killing that girl, Tara Foster."

Fabiana pinched her chin as she stared wide-eyed at the tiled floor. "Are you from the police?" she said.

"No, we're here to help Justin," I said. "We're his lawyers. We want to save him. But we need everyone to tell the truth once and for all so that he will not have to pay for a crime he didn't commit."

Fabiana walked over to a stainless-steel counter where a large mortar and pestle sat. "I loved Justin," she said as she began violently grinding a pile of spices. "He was a good man, always a gentleman. He had a car. He would take me everywhere. I never knew that the world could be so wonderful. He said he was going to marry me. He said he was going to take me away from Mama.

"Then the police said that he had done a bad thing with that white woman. That he had done nasty things to her at his job. He lied. He was no gentleman. Mama was right. I could never love such a man."

"But he was with you on the day the girl was abducted, Fabiana. We know that he was. You went to the Miami Seaquarium together."

"That never happened," she said as she dropped the pestle. "On that day, I was with my church group. Mama will tell you. Justin was mistaken. I must get back to work."

"Wait," I said, grabbing her wrist. "What Justin did with Tara Foster was wrong. To treat you in such a manner was unconscionable. But he shouldn't have to die for it. If he was with you on that day, then everyone needs to know.

Or you'll be the one who is responsible for his death."

Fabiana shook her head. "I have nothing more to say. You must leave now. I must get back to work."

"Yes," Queen Isabelle said, coming through the swinging door. "Leave now."

"Fine," Charlie said, putting his hand into his jacket pocket. "You know the South Beach Marriott?"

"The hotel around the corner?" Fabiana said, puzzled. "Yes. What about it?"

Charlie handed her his card with a room number scrawled on the back. "Well, we're going to be there for the next two days. If you want to come by, you can watch the coverage of your ex-boyfriend's execution with us."

"But you said you were his lawyers. Won't you be there to help him?" Fabiana said, confused.

"It's out of our hands, Fabiana. You're the only one who can help Justin now," Charlie said as we left.

Chapter 93

"Room service?" Charlie said into our phone at the Marriott ten minutes later. "Please send up two turkey clubs and a pitcher of—"

I kicked Charlie in the back of the knee with my pump.

"Um, lemonade," he finished, hanging up.

I dropped my laptop and briefcase in a heap by the couch. I walked across the suite and drew the drapes. Reeling with disappointment and exhaustion, I shook my head at the too bright Florida sky, the too bright glittering ocean.

My return to Florida wasn't going as I had hoped. I'd wanted to avoid Peter, but I failed. I was continuing to lie to someone I was starting to have feelings for. And now, after we'd finally found Fabiana, she was refusing to help Justin. Talk about cruel and unusual punishment. What the hell were we going to do now?

Behind me, Charlie kicked off his shoes and lay down on the couch.

"Do you think Fabiana will take the bait?" I said.

"Do I know?" Charlie said, closing his eyes. "Depends on how much she hates Justin, I guess. Hell hath no fury like a woman scorned, right? It's looking like Justin must have scorned the living crap out of Miss Desmarais. Is it actually possible for a woman to hate a man to death?"

"You'd be surprised," I said grimly. "How long do we wait?"

Charlie let out a tired breath. "Two, three hours at the most," he said. "If she doesn't show, then we won't have any other choice. We'll have to go with Plan B."

"Which is?" I said.

"We still go up to meet with the clemency board in Tallahassee, but instead of Fabiana recanting her testimony, you're going to have to tell the board your bizarre life story instead. It's gonna suck, and it probably won't even work, but it's like you said. Other than that, we don't have a damn thing."

I pieced through that excruciating scenario. I'd had trouble enough telling my secrets to Charlie. How exactly was I going to give them up to the governor of Florida?

A long hour later, after my third game of solitaire, I was heading out onto the balcony to give Emma a call when there was a soft knock on the door.

"Lunch. Finally," Charlie mumbled from where he lay dozing on the couch.

"No, please don't get up. I got it, really," I snapped as I crossed to the door.

My mood definitely lifted when I opened it.

It wasn't room service.

I stepped back and let Fabiana in.

Chapter 94

"Thank you so much for coming, Fabiana," I said. "I promise that when you testify that—"

"I haven't changed my mind. I'm not testifying. I came to give you this," she said, taking a sheet of newspaper out of her pocket.

I unfolded it. It was a yellowed page of classified ads from the *Miami Herald.* I held my breath after I spotted the date in the corner. It was from June 19, 1993. From reading and rereading the case and trial transcripts, I knew that was the day after Tara Foster had been abducted.

"What is this, Fabiana?" I said, quickly scanning the classifieds.

Fabiana took it out of my hand and turned it over. My eyes fell immediately to the photograph at the bottom. A group of people were sitting in some stands by a pool with a woman in a wet suit and some dolphins.

"Floridians beat yesterday's heat at the Miami Seaquarium," said the caption.

"Justin and I are in the picture," Fabiana said. "Right there in the front row. You were right. I lied."

I peered at the photograph more closely. It was true. You could just make out Justin and Fabiana sitting in the front row.

"Charlie!" I yelled, handing him the page. "You're not going to believe this. Look!"

He took the newspaper page out of my hands, looked at the picture, looked at the date.

"Yes!" he said with a triumphant grin. "Finally, a break!"

"All you need to do is show this to the authorities, and my lie will be exposed," Fabiana said. "Then they can set Justin free, yes?"

"Actually, well, no, Fabiana," Charlie said. "It's not that simple. This is extremely helpful, but you need to come to Tallahassee with us and bring this forward yourself. You'll have to give your testimony as well."

"I'm absolutely not willing to do that," Fabiana said coldly.

"Why not?" Charlie said.

"Nina?" Fabiana said, looking at me. "Can I speak to you alone?"

I eyeballed Charlie to get going.

"Fine. I'll be out in the hall, I guess."

"Don't judge me," Fabiana said after Charlie left.

I shook my head. "Of course not, Fabiana."

"Seventeen years ago, Justin made me pregnant. He told me that he couldn't afford a baby and a wife, but that if I...got rid of the baby, he would eventually marry me. He even bought me a ring. So I agreed. I didn't want to kill my baby, but in the end I decided I didn't want to lose Justin more. It was three months later that I found out through a friend that he was cheating on me. Not with just one woman, but with several."

Ouch, I thought. Justin really had scorned the living crap out of her.

"When the detective told me years later that Justin had admitted to having sex with Tara Foster in the prison, it brought back all that horror and hatred and pain. So I lied. I wanted to hurt Justin as much as he had hurt me. The last thing I want to do now, after all these years, is tell my dirty little story to the whole wide world. You can understand that, can't you? I'll probably be in some trouble myself for lying."

"That's true, Fabiana. But there's no other way. You don't have to get into specifics about why you lied. All you need to do is explain that you did lie and that Justin was with you the whole day."

"Can't you do it for me?" Fabiana said, closing her eyes.

"It doesn't work that way, Fabiana. I know it'll be painful to testify, but how do you think you'll feel if you don't come forward and Justin is executed? Seventeen years is a long time to hold on to your pain. It's time to let yours go."

Fabiana let out a breath. "You'll be there?"

"Of course," I said.

"OK," she said. "I guess I don't have a choice. I'll do it."

Chapter 95

Just before dinner, on the second-to-last day of his life, Justin Harris lay on his cot with a book open in his large hands. It was a cheesy old paperback about a brilliant and bulky detective named Nero Wolfe.

"News flash, fatso," Justin mumbled as he tossed the book under his bunk. "In the real world, the killer gets away with it."

He sat up immediately as boots squeaked and metal clicked out in front of his death-watch cell adjacent to the execution chamber.

"Harris, visitor," the day captain, Johannson, said, opening the gate.

Visitor? he thought as Johannson cuffed him. Must be that irritating new lady lawyer, he guessed, smoothing his orange jumpsuit.

The white execution chamber Johannson brought him past could have been a large doctor's examination room, except for the singular black velvet curtain covering one wall and the leather restraints on the gurney.

"Oh, yeah, by the way, Harris, since you were a guard, all of us got together and chipped in on a little gift," Johannson said, showing him a box. "We thought maybe if you got bored, you'd like to see a movie tonight."

Harris glanced down at the box. *Dead Man Walking*. "Nice of you guys," he said, cheerily refusing to let these bastards or anyone else get to him. "Some of Sean Penn's best work right there. Too bad I don't have a DVD player, though."

"You won't need one where you're going, lowlife," the guard cooed in his ear.

"Yeah, you deserve it, you sick freak," called out Jimmy Litz, one of his neighbors down the row. Litz had dropped a cinderblock off an overpass and then, pretending to help the victim, a twenty-three-year-old Jacksonville housewife, raped and killed her instead.

"Well, I guess we all can't live up to your moral standards," Harris said with a smile.

Yup, it was the lady lawyer, he told himself as he turned the corner and saw her and Charlie in the visitor room. Then he saw the second woman in the room, and the stone-hard set of his face buckled.

It was Fabiana. No. Not her, he thought. He could face anything. Tomorrow, even. But not her.

He turned to Johannson, fighting back his emotions. "Take me back to my cell."

He had turned around in the corridor when there was a loud bang behind him.

It was Fabiana. She was at the wired glass. She bashed it again with her fist. "It's OK, Justin," she yelled, with tears in her eyes. "I forgive you. I made a mistake. I'm sorry. Please don't go. Please talk to me."

Justin turned again and stood there in the corridor, biting his lip as he stared at her. This woman he had hurt beyond reckoning was saying she was sorry to him?

Charlie and Nina were grinning from ear to ear.

"We got news. Good news. You're going to like this, Justin. I promise," Charlie called.

"What's it going to be, Harris?" Johannson said, annoyed.

"I guess I got some visiting to do," Harris finally said.

Chapter 96

At nine thirty the next morning, Charlie, Fabiana, and I arrived, crisp and scrubbed and combed, at the state capitol in Tallahassee.

The last thing to do was the most important. We needed to deliver Fabiana to our ten o'clock meeting with the executive clemency board.

All in all, Fabiana seemed nervous but ready. The emotional meeting between her and Justin at the prison the night before had made them both feel better, I thought.

Maybe confession really was good

for the soul. Who knew? Maybe I'd look into it myself at some point.

We were crossing the street toward the capitol's plaza when we noticed the commotion. People holding signs were filing off a tour bus. About two dozen people were walking across the manicured capitol grounds or had already taken up position in front of the modern capitol building's main entrance.

"What's this? A tea party?" I said.

Then I saw the signs.

MEET YOUR MAKER, JUSTIN HARRIS! one said.

An attractive brunette in jeans and an American flag T-shirt waved a banner that said, NA, NA, NA, NA. HEY, HEY, GOOD-BYE, JUSTIN!

"You gotta be kidding me," Charlie said as a news van pulled in behind the bus. A reporter got out with a beefy guy in a Braves cap and a shoulder cam.

"Pro–*death* penalty people are here!?" Fabiana said.

"Damn it," I said to Charlie. "That's all we need. The circus is starting, and it looks like we're in the center ring."

"And that's not the worst of it, not by a long shot," Charlie said, pointing toward the bus.

I stopped in midstride as I saw where he was pointing.

I felt numb.

Peter was standing by the bus door, all smiles as he helped people off.

Chapter 97

I swallowed, suddenly feeling weak, as the blood drained from my face.

I felt like running back to the car, or at least diving behind a parked one. All Peter would have to do was turn up the block and see me.

The only positive my seizing mind could latch on to was the fact that he wasn't in uniform, wearing his gun. Then that slight hope was torn away as I remembered he most definitely could be strapping an off-duty concealed weapon.

I let out a breath and a tiny thankful

moan as Peter turned his back to us. A minute later, he took up position directly in front of the capitol's lobby doors with the group of protesters.

"That son of a bitch," Charlie said, shaking his head. "It doesn't matter. We have to deliver Fabiana to the clemency board, Peter or no Peter. We'll split up. You guys hang back by these trees until I distract him, then you go straight into the lobby.

"If anyone tries to stop you, kick them in the balls and keep going. Our contact from the clemency board, Mr. Sim, said he'd be waiting in the lobby to take us up. I'll make it if I can, but if I don't, you're going to have to start without me."

"Distract him?" I said. "How? What are you going to do?"

"Oh, I'll think of something. Be ready now," Charlie said as he began to jog down the block toward the crowded plaza.

"Hey, Fournier! What the hell is this?" Charlie screamed immediately as he entered the plaza.

I put my head down as Fabiana and

I moved along the stand of trees that lined the plaza's sidewalk.

"What does it look like I'm doing, Baylor?" Peter called back.

"Making a jackass out of yourself, as usual," Charlie said, taking a sign from a protester's hand and tossing it onto a grassy knoll beside the capitol's steps.

"Go home, all of you!" Charlie yelled at them with his hands over his head, his face clenched with theatrical rage. "My client is innocent, but if it were up to you, you'd kill him yourselves. What is this, some kind of lynch mob? This is disgusting. You make me sick!"

The gathered crowd looked at Charlie in complete astonishment. Except for the news crew. They looked like kids on Christmas morning. The beefy guy immediately took his camera off a tripod, put it up onto his shoulder, and turned it on.

"You've finally gone crazy, haven't you, Baylor?" Peter said, stepping toward Charlie. The crowd slowly followed him, unblocking the front doors.

Charlie's plan was working. At least

so far. I still had about forty yards of open plaza to cross.

"Finally lost it, huh, Counselor?" Peter continued to yell in the dead silence. "This is unstable even for you. Let me guess. You're drunk."

"I'll show you unstable," Charlie yelled back, throwing his briefcase at Peter and raising his fists as he ran toward him. He really did seem like a complete lunatic. When Charlie said he was going to create a diversion, he wasn't kidding.

Fabiana and I walked hurriedly across the plaza as Charlie and Peter rushed at each other and pandemonium broke out. No one even came close to noticing us as Peter swung at Charlie. The crowd made an ooh sound as Charlie ducked at the last second. But then a big, burly guy holding a JUSTIN HARRIS MUST DIE sign punched Charlie in the side of the head, sending him spinning.

"What? You can't fight one-on-one, Fournier?" Charlie said as he sent the burly guy tumbling back with a shove.

"Miss Desmarais?" said a soft-looking Asian man in a tan suit as we finally made it into the end zone of the capitol's cavernous lobby. "I'm Assistant Commissioner of Agriculture Dennis Sim. Where is Mr. Baylor, and what the heck is going on out there?"

"He's, uh, been delayed," I said. "I'm Mr. Baylor's assistant, Nina Bloom. If you'll take us up, we're ready to meet with the board."

Chapter 98

Two hours later, I sat in the capitol's wood-paneled second-floor corridor, checking the time on my iPhone every minute or so. It was either that or pull my hair out.

Because this was it.

Do or die.

Literally.

For the last excruciating hour, Charlie and I had been sitting on a long bench outside of the board's meeting room, like bad children in front of the principal's office. Inside, Fabiana was delivering her testimony to the executive clemency board. We'd already turned over the newspaper article to the parole investigator. The only question now was as simple as it was significant.

Had it been enough?

"She'll do fine," Charlie said with an aggravating calm as I spun my phone on the bench. He had a small cut under his left eye and a smushed right ear from the scuffle with Peter and the crowd. He'd probably gotten on YouTube by now as well for his taped "don't Tase me, bro" moment in front of the capitol plaza crowd.

"I should tell them," I said. "I should march right in there and tell them about Peter. About everything. What if this doesn't work?"

"But it will," Charlie said as the door opened.

Assistant Commissioner Sim appeared with Fabiana.

I took a deep breath.

"What's the verdict?" Charlie said.

"The board will weigh the evidence now," Sim said.

"What? More waiting?" I said.

"It's not like we have a lot of time here, Mr. Sim," Charlie said.

"That's all I can say for now. Thank you for coming," Mr. Sim said as he closed the door.

"What does that mean?" Fabiana said. "We have to keep waiting?"

"I need to tell them," I said, stepping past Charlie toward the door.

Charlie got in front of me.

"No," he whispered fiercely in my ear. "You don't. You're a victim here, too. Did you ask that son of a bitch Fournier to be a monster to you? You came down and actually risked your life to help Justin, and that's exactly what you've done. But you can't do everything. None of us can. We've done everything possible. We've petitioned the courts and petitioned the governor. It's out of our hands now and in theirs."

"But—"

"But nothing. I just went toe-to-toe with your ex-hubby. Do you really want to mess with me? Let's head over to the jail."

Chapter 99

The witness room for the execution chamber looked like a community theater that Friday night. There were two rows of cheap red chairs, black walls, a black curtain. But beyond the curtain, instead of a lit stage, was the brightly lit window of the death chamber.

Placed directly in the center of it, like some kind of malevolent modern art piece, was an empty gurney. It was fitted with thick leather ankle and wrist straps, a cross awaiting the crucifixion. The digital clock on the wall behind it showed 10:27 p.m.

At around nine, the warden, Tom Mitchner, had come in and given a short explanation about what would happen. At five to midnight, Justin would be brought in and strapped to the gurney. A witnessing doctor would oversee the proceeding as two intravenous tubes were extended and placed into Justin's left and right arms. At the stroke of midnight three drugs would enter Justin's bloodstream in succession: sodium thiopental to render him unconscious; pancuronium bromide, a muscle relaxant to stop his breathing; and potassium chloride to stop his heart.

A reporter from the *Miami Herald* and one from the Associated Press spoke softly at the back of the room. Tara Foster's mother, as well as the rest of her extended family, had declined to come. Fabiana sat in the front row, talking and holding hands with Justin's mother.

My hand was cinched onto Charlie's.

"I don't know if I can do this," I said to him, my eyes on the gurney. "It's too much. Way too much. Why haven't they stopped this? What are they waiting for? These bastards are still going to go through with it, Charlie. How is that possible? How can they?"

"Have faith," was all Charlie would say, seemingly more to himself than to me.

Eleven came. Then eleven thirty.

"What's up, Charlie?" I said.

"Have—"

"Faith?" I said. "I don't know if I can."

It was eleven fifty when the door opened, and a pale, heavy man in a gray suit appeared. It was Warden Mitchner.

I stared at him breathlessly, waiting to hear that it was over.

"It's time now," the tired-looking official said somberly. "They're bringing in Mr. Harris."

I had trouble focusing as they did just that. Justin stood ramrod straight, shoulders back, eyes steady and forward like the dress parade soldier that he once had been. He was flanked by two guards, as well as a white-jacketed orderly and a gaunt middle-aged woman in a navy pantsuit who I assumed was the doctor. Justin didn't even flinch as his mother stood and put her hand on the glass. He just walked obediently over to the gurney and sat, spreading out his arms as he stared up intently, like a magician about to perform a particularly difficult trick.

In the silence, the orderly's footfalls sounded, like the slow raps of a snare drum, as he stepped across the death chamber. When he stepped back a minute later, the IVs were in Justin's arms.

The clock on the wall kept right on going. When it clicked forward to eleven fifty-nine, one of the reporters cupped a hand over his mouth like he was about to throw up. Tilted back in the gurney, Justin kept his eyes pinned to a point directly above the glass viewing window.

The room was still. Then the clock flashed.

It was twelve.

The injections started. A yellowish liquid suddenly appeared in the IV tubing and started to flow toward Justin's forearms. All I could do was follow its path.

There was a collective intake of breath

as the liquid entered Justin's blood-stream and he closed his eyes.

"No," I whispered.

Then my vision swam, and I doubled over.

Chapter 100

I was still doubled over, in the midst of nearly passing out, when a deafeningly loud buzzer sounded in the execution chamber.

The orderly inside ran behind the partition as the witnessing doctor raced toward Justin. A thin stream of yellow liquid and blood splattered onto the floor as the doctor tore the IVs free. The orderly returned and motioned to the guards. After a moment, Justin was quickly rolled out of the room on the gurney with the guards and the doctor in tow.

"What the hell?!" Charlie said, running up and hammering on the glass.

The door to the viewing room flew open thirty seconds later.

It was Warden Mitchner.

"It's OK," he said, wheezing. The tall, flabby man was sweating, red-faced. "The first drug was just the painkiller. They didn't drop the second plunger. Justin received only the painkiller. He's going to be OK."

Both reporters jumped up and began yelling at the same time.

"This isn't happening," Charlie said beside me. "This state runs executions about as well as its elections."

"Please. We'll have order here now. I just received this from Governor Scott Stroud," the warden said, lifting a sheet of paper.

" 'Today I have decided to stay the execution of Justin Harris, an inmate on Florida's death row for six months,' " Mitchner read. " 'I have done this to allow the district attorney and investigators involved in this case to gather and properly analyze any and all new information that has come to the attention of the clemency board. After a careful and close review, and conferring with the state attorney general and the parole board, I am not satisfied that it is proper that the execution should proceed until such new information is disseminated and reviewed.'"

The warden let out a breath. "That's it," he said.

Charlie sat heavily in one of the folding chairs. His head dropped down between his knees.

"Just tell me how Justin's OK again," he said, looking up at the warden.

"The doctor on call says his pulse is fine. He just needs to sleep it off. They're bringing him to the infirmary."

Charlie let out a breath, then sat up, wiping at the tears in his eyes. I came over and hugged him.

"Then we did it?" he whispered as if he could hardly believe it. "We actually did it?"

After a minute, we joined Fabiana and Justin's mother in a standing embrace as the reporters spoke excitedly into their cell phones.

"See, I knew you would help Justin,

Miss Bloom," Mrs. Harris said to me as she kissed my hand, then my cheek. "I never doubted it for a second."

"Me, too, Miss Bloom," Charlie said winking from over her shoulder. "I knew you could pull it off."

Book Five

THE TRUTH WILL SET YOU FREE. OR WILL IT?

Chapter 101

A violet-tinged shadow rose up the cabin wall of the small American Eagle jet like a tide as we made the final descent for Key West the next afternoon. Beside me, Charlie started to snore as the landing gear hummed down beneath our feet.

Now that Justin had been given a stay, I wanted nothing more than to be landing in New York. But after we visited a groggy Justin in the infirmary that morning, Charlie had called his law school buddy FBI Special Agent Robert Holden and told him about Peter.

Holden was already waiting for me at Charlie's house to formally interview me and open Peter's case. Getting back to my life, unfortunately, would have to wait.

I unburdened my troubled soul in Charlie's office for a second time.

Agent Holden, a tall, black, former college basketball player, sat across from me taking extensive notes on a yellow legal tablet as I told him about Peter's first wife, Elena's shooting, my faked death.

When I was done, Holden looked at me, poker-faced, expressionless. Whether he thought I was crazy or heroic or a liar, there was no way to tell. He capped his red Mont Blanc pen and tucked it into the inside pocket of his charcoal suit coat.

"Would you be willing to repeat what you just told me in open court?"

I thought about that. What would happen when my bizarre story of faking my death and changing my identity came out? It would probably mean my job, some of my friends. I decided that losing it all was worth getting my life back, becoming whole again.

"Yes, of course," I said. "So what do you think? Is there a case against Peter after all these years?"

"We'll have to see," Holden said. "There's no statute of limitations for murder. The most interesting angle from where I'm sitting is Peter's corruption as the chief of police. We can start by going after him for Hobbs Act public official violations and see where that leads us. I'm definitely satisfied enough to open an investigation on him forthwith. Because of the threat to you, after I leave here, I'm going to recommend to my boss that he send a team down and that we place Fournier under immediate surveillance. When will you be heading back to New York?"

"Tomorrow," Charlie said, coming into the office, clinking a couple of Coronas together. "We still have some serious celebrating to do."

"Well, take it easy and keep an eye on her until she gets on that plane, Charlie," Holden said. "I'll keep you guys updated."

As the FBI agent stood, I wondered yet again if I should bring up that one pesky little detail concerning Ramón Peña. Try to get ahead of it before it undoubtedly came out.

Yet I kept my mouth shut as Holden went out the front door.

"To you," Charlie said, handing me a beer. "I'm proud of you. You've been holding that in for seventeen years. That took guts."

Guts, lack of scruples. Whatev, as Emma liked to say.

I threw the lime wedge garnish into the office wastepaper basket and took a long hit off the beer. It was crisp, delicious, as cold as an ice cream headache, and after another hit it was empty.

"My plane leaves in twelve hours," I said, wiping my mouth with the back of my hand. "We don't have time to fruit the beer, Baylor."

Chapter 102

It was six o'clock when we arrived in Mallory Square for the sunset celebration. The kooky Key West sunset party hadn't changed a bit. It was the same uplifting reggae music I remembered, the same happy dancing fools splashing beer all over themselves and one another, the same seductive champagne-colored light.

The original plan had been just to chill back at Charlie's house, but about an hour before, Agent Holden had called. He'd said that they'd put Peter under surveillance and that they had tailed him up to a boat show in Key Largo, where he'd checked into a hotel with his wife and two kids. Which meant that Key West was ours at least for the night.

Charlie held my hand as he guided me through the street performers and sunburned drunken tourists. He said he had a surprise lined up. I let him walk me out of the square and down a few narrow blocks. We finally arrived at the water at Schooner's Pier, a restaurant and private marina.

I closed my eyes and sighed as a sea breeze lifted my hair.

I actually deserved to celebrate a little. I had helped get Justin a stay of execution. I'd even made some progress in cleaning up my own life in the past week. There was still the ghost of spring break past haunting me, but what were you going to do? Despite the still unresolved issue that was my life, I officially decided to give my guilt a well-deserved night off.

"Is this where it happens? Your big surprise?" I said to Charlie.

"You'll see," Charlie said, taking my hand again.

Instead of taking me into the restaurant as I expected, Charlie walked me down the wooden dock. We stopped in front of a massive two-decked luxury motor yacht.

"After you," he said with a courtly wave toward its boarding ramp.

"What...what are we doing?" I said, gaping at the white Ferrari-sleek lines of the majestic ship. The black-tinted windows on the captain's bridge made it look like it was wearing shades.

"It belongs to a client of mine, Bill Spence. He owes me a favor," Charlie said as he tugged me up the ramp. "He runs an upscale sunset dinner cruise. Even at a hundred and eighty a pop, it's usually pretty crowded, but I got us the whole shebang. She's all ours. At least for the next three hours."

"What?" I said, ecstatic.

"Wait here," Charlie called as he stepped through a doorway off the first deck.

He came back two minutes later, smiling, as he grabbed my hand and pulled me forward. We passed a Jacuzzi and a tiki bar before arriving at the railing of the bow, where an intimate table for two sat waiting.

Charlie handed me a champagne flute and pulled a bottle out of a silver ice bucket.

"Our host is putting the finishing touches on our dinner," he told me as he filled my glass with bubbly. "He said to enjoy a toast as he takes us out. The first course is coming up."

"First course?" I said in surprise.

"Now, now. Enough chitchat. This is a surprise," Charlie said, winking.

Chapter 103

Twenty minutes later, the Mallory Square crowd roared at us like we were celebrities, as the luxury yacht swooshed us past them toward the setting sun.

The captain let off the ship's air horn. When we turned, we could just make out his large silhouette waving to us from behind the bridge's tinted glass windshield. Charlie hugged me as we waved back with raised champagne flutes.

"Take it off, hottie! Work it!" a handsome black guy standing on the shore railing yelled between cupped hands.

"Come on, Nina. Accommodate the man," Charlie said.

"Um, I don't think he was talking to me, hottie," I said, bursting into giggles.

Charlie laughed, too, as he took a handful of cards out of his jacket pocket. They were the business cards he'd received from media people during his press conference outside the prison after Justin's stay. He finished his champagne and started thumbing numbers into his cell phone.

"Whoo-hoo! Look at me, momma. What do we have here? Producer for Larry King. A *Vanity Fair* guy. Heck, I've got Geraldo on speed dial now," he said. "Screw HGTV. Maybe I'll score one of those mock trial shows. How does Judge Charlie strike you? Hello, fifteen minutes. What took you so long?"

I smiled as the bow cut through the Tiffany blue waves. The wind was absolutely wrecking my hair, but I didn't give a hoot. We were heading directly at the reddening sun now. I was almost back in the human race.

I finished my champagne and poured another. I tipped the glass to my lips.

To me, I thought.

I was lowering my flute when I suddenly felt dizzy. I blinked, rubbed my eyes. No! Don't tell me I was getting seasick.

"Probably should take it easy until the first course, huh?" I said.

Then I felt *really* dizzy, extremely light-headed. I blinked as my vision blurred.

"Charlie?" I said, putting out my hand toward the ship's rail to steady myself.

I turned as there was a loud thud.

Charlie had fallen out of his chair. He was facedown on the varnished teak deck, his cell phone by his hand, his business cards fluttering like leaves.

When I leaned forward out of my chair to see what was wrong, I lost my balance and pitched out of my seat onto the deck as well. I tried to get up on my knees, but I was suddenly weak, unsteady. I lay back down on my stomach, struggling to catch my breath.

I craned my neck around and looked up at the bridge's tinted window. The captain was gone. Before I could figure out any of this, the door to the bridge opened a moment later. There was a jingle and a click-click-click sound, and then a cute little dog appeared on the deck. It was a Jack Russell.

Chapter 104

I wasn't sure if it was ten minutes or ten hours later when my eyes snapped open in the dark.

I was on my back. I lay there, blinking and breathing rapidly, as my weak, disoriented mind struggled to remain conscious.

My face felt like someone had used it as a hammer. My stomach was one large, acidic sour knot. The taste in my dry mouth was vaguely medicinal. My entire body felt strange and puffy, as if I were wrapped in a cotton ball cocoon.

Accident? was my first coherent thought.

Then the below-deck cabin I was in tilted and creaked, and my eyes went wide as I remembered everything. An aha moment straight from hell.

I remembered Charlie, facedown on the deck beside me. The champagne had been doctored, I realized.

"No," I said weakly. I tried to move my right arm. I turned my wrist maybe a centimeter before it rolled back like a too heavy log. I was still drugged. Was it anesthesia?

I was trying to move my other arm when I heard something in the distance: a hollow thump followed by a tremendous splash.

I closed my eyes as panic bloomed in the pit of my stomach. It began to rise into my throat like the numbers on a thermometer in a blast oven when I heard the close sound of heavy footsteps above.

Think! I urged myself. I tried to. But there was nothing except the dark. Nothing but the accelerating beat of my heart. Finally, a wave of temptingly sweet exhaustion passed through me like a last hope.

Of course, I thought. I needed to go back to sleep. Figure it out later, much later.

I heard the opening of a door, some-one coming down the stairs.

Stop it! Wake up! some other part of me thought.

Stand up! I frantically began to beg myself.

The other lazy part was having none of it. I free-fell back toward the safe oblivion of sleep with a sigh, as if that would save me.

A moment later, my eyes bolted open as the reek of ammonia scoured my nostrils like a serrated knife.

"Haven't I seen you someplace be-fore?" the Jump Killer said as he lifted me into his arms.

Chapter 105

The jump killer carried me into a bright room that looked like a library. There were dark, varnished, oak-paneled walls; leather-bound books on shelves; an expensive wooden globe; a cigar humidor; a fully stocked bar. Above the bar, a signed collector's baseball bat was lit like a painting in a gallery.

But instead of furniture, in the room's exact center was a massive four-poster bed. The incongruity of it reminded me of the gurney they'd strapped Justin Harris to in the death chamber. That wasn't the only similarity, I realized.

From all four posts dangled dark metal circles. Handcuffs, I realized, as I was dropped onto the bed.

"Welcome to the Jungle Room," the Jump Killer said. "This is where all the magic happens."

I noticed what I was wearing for the first time as my wrists and then my ankles were cuffed. I stared down at myself and began to weep.

I was in some kind of see-through bra and underwear, a garter belt, stockings. My arms and legs had been moisturized with a sickeningly sweet cherry-scented lotion. I realized then that I was wearing makeup. Gobs of it were greased onto my cheeks, smeared on my lips, caking my eyes.

"Please," I said through my slimy lips. "Please don't...don't kill me."

"That's funny. That's exactly what Tara Foster said all those years ago. Right before I strangled her to death with her bra," the Jump Killer said, folding his meaty arms. "Maybe if you'd been smart and let Harris take the fall for it, you wouldn't be in this pickle."

That's when I noticed there was another door in the room's corner. From behind it suddenly came Mexican pop music, loud, frenzied racing horns. There was the clop of stamping feet, excited voices, drunken laughter. The Mexican music was cut short to howls and then a rap song started up and there was more stomping and howling.

"What is this? Who are they?" I said.

"They're drug dealers," the Jump Killer said. "Top Mexican cartel guys. Real big shots. I get their women for them. Don't worry. You're going to get to know them all very soon, very intimately."

My mind whited out for a moment. Sizzling fuzz filled my head like a lost TV signal.

"I'm not a prostitute!" I cried.

"They don't want a prostitute, silly," he said. "This is a special celebration. These boys just closed a huge deal for very, very big money. They risked their lives, their freedom, and came out on top. They're ready to party till you drop. In your case, party till they get sick of raping you and drop you dead in the water."

There it was. The most horrible thing of all. It explained why there were so many disappearances, why some of the missing women's bodies were never found.

"You wouldn't believe the amount of money these guys spend. Not that I don't deserve every penny, with all the cleanup. Sometimes I think some of these fellas must be half Mayan or Aztec because after they're done, you'd think it was a human sacrifice in here with all the blood. I have to wash the goddang *sangre* off of the ceiling." The Jump Killer smiled.

"I'm getting your attention now. I can see it in your face. You're a little long in the tooth for them, but I'm offering you as a special, a half-price appetizer. Those are my orders, and I'm not going to screw them up this time. After all, they came straight from the big man himself."

Orders?

"What are you talking about?" I mumbled. "From who?"

The Jump Killer started laughing then. "You still don't know what the hell is going on, do you? Even now. Of course not. Precious little Jeanine always kept in the dark."

What!?

"My orders come from Peter, Jeanine. Remember him? Your husband? My best friend. There is no Jump Killer. There never was one. There's just Peter. Peter and me."

Chapter 106

The hilarity next door hit a fever pitch as the old-school rap classic "Wild Thing" by Tone-Loc started up. The volume suddenly blasted twice as loud as I lay there staring up at the coffered ceiling.

"You know Peter used to talk about you all the time," the Jump Killer said, sitting in the chair by the side of the bed and checking his watch. "The silly things you guys used to do together. He really thought you were a good kid. I wanted to meet you, but of course Peter said no way. I think he might have really even loved you. That's why I was so surprised when he asked me to kill you."

I looked at his face. He was still smiling.

"You never figured this out?" he said, shaking his head. "Peter hired me to kill you, Jeanine, while he was off on his fishing trip. Make you disappear. Sell you to our drug-running friends like all the others. I was going to do it, too, when I saw you leave the house.

"I followed you around all goddamn day, watched you cut yourself on the beach, watched you dye your hair. I didn't know what the hell you were doing until you hit the Overseas Highway and I realized you were exiting stage left. That's when I pulled up and gave you a lift. But then you pulled that trick with the Mercedes and you got away. At first, I didn't know what to do. But it looked like you weren't coming back anyway, so I just lied and said I killed you."

The cotton ball effect of the drug began to wear off and was replaced by a dull head-to-toe ache. I moved my right arm. It went a foot before the handcuff got painfully taut against my wrists. I stared at the bed's heavy wooden posts inside the steel cuffs. They were scratched and worn from use, as if chewed. I gagged as I realized it was from women rattling them as they struggled.

When I looked back, the Jump Killer was picking at something in his perfectly capped teeth with his pinkie.

"I should have told Peter the truth, but frankly I was afraid to," he said. "You think I'm bad? Peter's like the Tony Soprano of Key West, except without the sense of humor." The Jump Killer shrugged. "But he never showed you that side, did he? With me, it was always death threats and slapping me around for forgetting something, but not you. With you, it was always flowers and rainbows and love notes."

He stood and yawned.

"See, Jeanine, women, even wives, come and go, but friends are forever. Best friends, anyway. We were in the Rangers together. When he needed someone to watch his back, I was the one he called. I'll admit that he really wasn't too happy with me when he saw you in New York. But he finally relented and gave me a second chance to take you out. I almost had you at your hotel room, too."

The Jump Killer walked to the door and opened it.

"Don't worry, though. I'm not going to blow it this time. When these boys are finished with you, before your burial at sea, I'm going to put two bullets in the back of your head to make sure you stay dead. Once and for all."

Chapter 107

The door closed. A quotation popped into my head as the electric guitar riffed between hip-hop bass thumps next door.

The hard way is the only way.

Whether it was from a writer or the Bible, I couldn't quite recall. All I remembered was that I never understood it. Why would someone choose for things to be hard?

But as I lay there, my face drenched with tears, an ironlike fear clenching every sinew of my body, I finally knew what it meant.

It meant there were no shortcuts. You had to pay for things. Sometimes, it was your job to go down no matter how unfair things were. Meeting Peter had allowed me to avoid my fate for killing Ramón Peña, at least up until now. Today I was going to pay for that crime with interest.

I remembered how shocked I'd been when I'd seen how resigned to die Justin Harris had been. I wasn't shocked anymore.

Someone knocked on the door.

But instead of stiffening with a soldierly stoicism like Justin, I went into a full-body twinge of revulsion and horror. My tendons felt like they were about to pop.

"Hola!" said a jolly whisper as the door opened.

The man who stepped in looked more French than Mexican. He was swarthy and tall and lean with long, lustrous shoulder-length black hair. A cigar jutted from his stubbled jaw. In his tailored pinstripe suit coat, an open-throated banker's shirt, and nice jeans, he looked European, a sophisticate, a rich ne'er-do-well dandy ready for a night on the town.

When he took off his suit coat, I saw that he wore a pearl-handled automatic in a shoulder rig. He smiled at me from around his cigar as he selected a bottle and glass from the bar and poured himself a tall drink of whiskey. He pointed to the drink and then at me in a gallant gesture, wondering if I wanted one.

The handcuffs started click-clacking off the wood as I started to shake.

He shrugged his shoulders in an oh-well gesture. Then he puffed elaborately on his cigar, blew smoke up at the cof-fered ceiling, and approached the bed.

He was sitting at the foot, pulling off one of his cowboy boots, when there was a noise over the loud music.

It was the wail of an air horn above deck.

Next door, the volume quit as men shushed one another, listening.

"This is the United States Coast Guard!" came the order from a bull-horn. "No one move!"

Two gunshots blasted one right after

the other above us. There was a surprised yell in Spanish followed quickly by a splash.

"Don't move! We will shoot! Don't move!" the bullhorn speaker said.

There was some more gunfire, and the long-haired man at the end of the bed looked up in shock as running footsteps passed directly overhead.

One boot on, one boot off, his cigar in his mouth and his automatic out, he clopped to the door. He opened it. Then I screamed as he pulled the trigger.

There were more shots and yelling as someone returned fire. A hunk of paneled wood blew out of the wall beside the drug dealer's head. Then the gun suddenly fell from his hand. The expression on the man's face was one of curiosity as he looked down at his blood-soaked banker's shirt. Then there was another violent, earsplitting bang and then another and he fell, sparks from his cigar flying up as he crashed forward onto his face.

I was crying as young men dressed in blue and carrying rifles rushed into the room. After another moment, Charlie, soaking wet, was smiling down at me. He wasn't dead somehow.

I tried to say something, but found that I couldn't. It seemed like I was in shock.

Charlie tried to pull me off the bed until he saw the handcuffs. Then he took the baseball bat off the wall and began breaking the bedposts one by one.

Chapter 108

"OK, one more time from the top," Scott Dippel, the commanding officer of the coast guard ship, said, clicking his pen in one of the now docked cutter's staterooms.

I was wearing some borrowed USCG sweats and my hair was still wet from, by far, the best shower I'd ever taken in my life. Charlie sat next to me. He was holding a bag of frozen green beans against the lump on his head that he received when he planted his face on the deck.

"Yes, please. From the tippy top,

considering we have two men dead and three Mexican nationals in custody," added FBI Agent Holden. He'd come aboard immediately when we returned to the coast guard's base.

The Jump Killer, or whoever he was, had been shot dead. Trying to escape in the drug dealers' boat, he had fired on the coast guard ship. The coast guard guys returned the favor with their fifty-caliber machine gun.

As I was taken aboard, I actually saw his blown-apart body, floating face-down in the water, under the ship's floodlight. I didn't need any grief counseling. If anything, my only regret was that I hadn't been able to do it myself.

"Slowly now," Dippel said. "Who was the big guy we shot?"

"Captain Bill Spence," Charlie said. "He's a client of mine, or he was. He drugged us and threw me overboard. I woke up in the water on my back with two gallons of salt water in my stomach. I saw the yacht's running lights and dog-paddled toward them for what seemed like three hours. The go-fast speedboat pulled alongside when I was about a couple of hundred feet away. When the Mexican guys boarded the yacht, it took everything I had to drag myself onto their boat, and I used its radio to call you."

The tall red-haired sailor clicked his pen again. "And the Hispanic men are?"

"Mexican drug dealers," I said. "Spence abducted women and brought them out to sea and sold them to drug runners who raped and killed them at their sick parties. Which was exactly what would have happened to me if Charlie hadn't called you."

"How do you know all this?" Agent Holden wanted to know.

"Spence told me!" I yelled. "Don't you understand? I wasn't kidding when I said I knew that Justin Harris didn't kill Tara Foster. Spence was the Jump Killer. He was the man who tried to abduct me all those years ago. He's been abducting and selling women since *Miami Vice* was popular. Not only that, he said the chief of police was involved. Peter Fournier was his partner. In fact, he said Peter ran the drug trade in Key West."

"That one I can't understand," Dippel said. "Peter Fournier? I know him. I've eaten at his house. Our kids are on the same baseball team. That can't be right."

"You think you feel stupid? I married the man," I said. "Spence also said Peter had hired him to kill me before I got away."

"It all actually makes sense now," Charlie said, shifting the frozen beans to his other hand. "The captain became my client and good buddy right around the time it came out in the local paper that I was representing Justin. He would ask about the case all the time. And I thought he was just a crime buff or something. He was the one who actually offered the free cruise for us to celebrate!"

Holden frowned. "What a goddamn mess," he said. "This is what you call taking it easy, Baylor?"

Agent Holden left the room to make some calls. An hour later, at around four a.m., he came back in and told us we could leave.

"Your story seems to pan out so far.

I checked the registration on the yacht. Peter is actually listed as one of the owners. I also just got off the phone with my agent in charge. We're putting round-the-clock surveillance on Fournier. Until we grab him, I want you out of here, Miss Bloom, or Fournier, or whatever the hell your name is. I want you to get checked out at the hospital and then get on the first flight out of here this morning, and don't think this is all over. We'll be keeping an eye on you. And you, Charlie. You can bet your ass I'll be in touch."

Chapter 109

We skipped the hospital and went straight to the airport, stopping only to swing by Charlie's house so I could get changed and grab my bags.

The sun was rising behind the smudged Plexiglas window of the airport waiting area when Agent Holden called Charlie on his cell an hour later. Charlie excused himself to take the call.

"Holden just got to Spence's house with the state CSI team," Charlie said, clicking his phone shut as he came back inside. "Hopefully, they'll find evidence that'll link that psycho son of a bitch to Tara Foster's murder as well as to the disappearances of all those other women. He said the place looks like a landfill, so it'll probably take awhile."

Charlie shook his bruised purple head. "What a night, huh? Do I know how to party or what?" he said as they called my plane.

"Charlie, listen. I need to tell you something," I said. "I left something out."

"No," Charlie said. "Please. Not more."

"It's going to come out, and I want you to hear it from me first. It's about how I met Peter." I took a breath. I felt a weight shift inside me, the weight of so many years of holding it all in.

"Seventeen years ago, when I was on spring break, I'd been drinking and got behind the wheel, and I accidentally killed a man. Peter was the first cop on scene. He helped me. He got rid of the body."

"What?" Charlie said.

"Yes, Charlie. That's how we met. That's probably why I married him. He protected me from going to jail. I'm just like him, Charlie. Corrupt. You need to stay the hell away from me. Everyone does. My whole life is just one big lie. I guess it always has been."

Charlie stared at me. He winced, looking away. I could see tears in his eyes, pure hurt. It killed me to see him like that. He opened his mouth to say something, then he closed it again.

"Charlie," I said, starting to cry myself.

"I'm leaving," he said a moment later.

And that's just what he did, without another look back.

Chapter 110

I sometimes have trouble sleeping on planes, but not this time. I slept all the way to Atlanta, and after I switched planes I put my head back and went out like a light switch again. I didn't wake up until we were touching down in New York.

I was in my apartment an hour later, showered and in my own bathrobe and fuzzy slippers, when my wall phone rang.

Please let it be Charlie, I prayed, answering it.

"I just heard!" my boss, Tom Sidirov,

yelled triumphantly. "You pulled it off! You actually saved a guy on death row. Home run! Grand slam! Come in right now. We'll go to lunch. I need to hear all about it."

"I'd love to, Tom," I said. "But I just got off the plane. How about tomorrow? I'm zonked."

"Of course, of course. Rest up for the TV cameras. I already called the PR guys. The firm's going to milk this thing for all it's worth. I'm so proud of you. I've been gloating to all the other partners all morning. We'll do a victory lap tomorrow. I knew you could do this, kid."

After I hung up, I wondered how jazzed Tom was going to be when he found out that I'd been lying to the firm, that I'd killed a man in a drunk-driving accident and covered it up, and that my name wasn't Nina Bloom.

Oh, well. I'd find out soon enough.

Then I heard the lobby buzzer in the kitchen.

"Who is it?" I said, pressing the Talk button.

"It's me, Mom," said Emma.

"Emma!" I yelled. Well, at least I had someone who'd stand by me.

"Baby, I missed you so much!" I said.

"Mom, c'mon," Emma said. "Buzz me in already."

I pressed the Door Open button and unlocked my apartment's front door before I went back into the bedroom. I was unzipping my suitcase when I noticed the message indicator on my cell. Someone had called while I was in the shower.

"Listen, Nina," Charlie said, sounding out of breath.

Thank God. Charlie did want to speak to me again.

I heard the front door open.

"Hey, Em!" I called behind me. "Hold on. I'm in the bedroom. I'll be right there."

"The FBI tracked Fournier to a hotel room up in Key Largo. When they went to arrest him half an hour ago, they found something horrifying. His wife and two young sons were dead, shot execution-style in the back of the head. Fournier wasn't there. No one has seen him. They think he's been gone for at least twenty-four hours. The FBI is putting out an APB on him right now. Whatever you do, don't go back to your apartment. Call me pronto. I need to know that you're OK."

That's when I heard Emma outside my bedroom door.

"Mom?"

"Em, listen, pack a bag now. I'll explain to you in a second. I have to—" I started, dialing frantically.

"No, Mom. Whatever it is, it can wait," Emma said, a strange, angry edge in her voice. "There's someone I think you should meet."

"What?" I said.

I turned around. The iPhone spilled out of my trembling fingers and bounced off my glass-and-metal bedside table with a loud crack before somersaulting onto the Oriental carpet and landing facedown.

I shook my head slowly, my unmoving eyes wide, bugging as if they were being pushed out from their sockets.

Emma was in the doorway staring at me.

There was a man behind her wearing

a Boston Red Sox baseball cap, an Adidas warm-up jacket, camo pants, and shiny black combat boots.

"Mermaid!" Peter said with a tip of his cap as he stepped into the room.

Chapter 111

"How could you?" Emma cried at me. Her voice was angry, hurt. Her face was damp from crying. She was upset. At me?

"You've been lying to me my entire life. How could you be so selfish?" she yelled. She took out a picture of twin boys. "These are my stepbrothers. I do have a family. You're sick, Mom. You're a sick person."

"Emma, please," I said, my mouth going dry.

"Stop it! Stop lying!" she screamed. "Why didn't you ever tell me that I had a father? That he was alive. I went out to lunch today, and there he was outside of school. Waiting for *me*. One look in his eyes, and I knew he was my father before he even opened his mouth. There was no Kevin Bloom. What did you do? Hire an actor?"

"Emma, you don't understand," I said.

"Yes, I do. Peter told me everything. How you used to be married down in Florida. How you ran away and abandoned him. How could you be so cruel?"

I ignored her. My gaze was on Peter behind her as he put his hand into his pocket.

He produced a large black semiautomatic pistol and waved it at me with a smile. He put it back into his pocket as he placed a shushing finger to his lips.

I cupped my hands over my mouth and nose and shook my head slowly at first but then faster and faster. This couldn't be happening. Nightmares couldn't come true.

"Please," I said to him, finally placing my hands together in a begging gesture. "Peter, she has nothing to do with this."

His smile never wavered.

Peter suddenly grabbed Emma by the back of her head and rammed her face into a cloth that he took out of his other pocket.

"No!" I screamed, running forward.

"Yes!" Peter screamed back as he kicked me in my stomach with his heavy police tactical boot. Breath whooshed out of me as I was knocked back on my butt to the floor.

Chapter 112

I helplessly watched Emma struggle in Peter's arms. There was nothing I could do as she glared at me in horror and confusion.

A moment later, her eyes rolled back into her head as she went slack. Peter let her slide onto the hardwood floor in front of me. Her chest was barely moving. She was out cold.

"Much better," Peter said, taking a roll of duct tape from his jacket pocket. "I thought my boys were annoying. Does she ever shut up?"

He duct-taped my hands behind my

back before he dragged me into the living room and handcuffed my ankle to the radiator.

"Nice place, Jeanine," Peter said, sitting down on the couch across from me. He removed the gun from his jacket and placed it, along with the duct tape, on the cushion beside him before he put his feet up on the coffee table.

"I love all the hardwood. We should have done that picture frame molding in our dining room, don't you think? What's this couch? Pottery Barn? I like a lady who treats herself right. What about the modern painting over the fireplace? Let me guess. Crate and Barrel? I mean, how *Sex and the City* can you get?"

I stared down at the floor.

He put his arms over the back of the couch and let out a breath.

"Hold up. What's this?" he said, suddenly jumping up and grabbing a Yankees hat off the TV stand.

He looked at me with disgust before he sent it flying, like a Frisbee, over my head.

"Not bad enough ya had to abandon

ya ol' hubby?" he said, reverting to a perfect Southie accent. "Ya had to go and become a Skankee fan, too!"

His eyes went wide and wild as he suddenly lifted the gun off the couch. He came over and pressed it to my forehead, dug it right between my eyes.

"Remember on the beach all those years ago," he said quietly. "I saved you, gave you everything. A house. A life in paradise. This is how you pay me back? Lies. Faking your death? You're fucked up, you know that?"

"I don't care what you do to me," I said. "I'll do anything you want. Just please let her go."

He shook his head. "That's the best you can do? You'll do anything I want anyway. Request denied. Emma stays with Daddy. You should have thought about our precious bundle of joy before you came back down to Florida and set my whole entire world on fire."

He racked the slide of the automatic.

"I knew I should have killed you myself," he said.

"You killed your first wife. And your baby," I whispered. "You killed Elena and Teo and that gas station guy. Your new wife, your kids."

"Yes, I did, Jeanine," Peter said. "And now for my next act, ladies and germs. I'm going to kill my second wife as slowly and painfully as possible."

Chapter 113

Peter tossed the gun back onto the couch and undid my cuffed ankle. He pulled me up by my hair and brought me into the bathroom.

He stoppered the tub drain and turned on the hot tap. He pulled a rubber kitchen glove out of his back pocket and put it over his right hand. When the steaming water reached the top of the tub, he turned off the knob and tossed in some scented bath powder that was sitting on the tub's edge.

"Smell that. Nice, huh?" he said. "Ocean breeze? No, calla lily. Now, for a little experiment. Let's see if mermaids really can breathe under water."

He wrapped his gloved hand around my hair and dunked me, headfirst, under the water. It was burning hot. I tried to struggle, but his hand was like an iron bar pinning me to the tub bottom. He started scraping my forehead against the enamel, as if I were a Scrubbing Bubble. A minute passed. Then two. I was about to open my mouth when he ripped me back up into the world.

I made an animal moaning sound as I sucked air, my face on fire.

"Wheee," Peter said. "Doesn't this remind you of something? See, I remember your worst fear, Jeanine. Drowning. Remember the story you told me when you were at the beach with your dad when you were a kid and got caught in a rip current? How you actually stopped struggling and were sinking when Daddy came to your rescue. But guess what, Jeanine? Daddy's not here. Daddy's dead. I'm your daddy now."

My head went back under the scalding water. I held my breath until it felt like my eyes were about to pop, until my skull felt like it was being filled with acid.

I was about to give in and swallow to get it over with when he pulled me back up a second time. When my ears emptied of water, I realized that Peter was laughing. Not a creepy mad-scientist laugh, but a kind of unable-to-catch-your-breath, uncontrollable fit of hilarity. As if instead of torturing me to death, he was watching an Eddie Murphy DVD.

"I'm sorry," he said, wiping at his eyes after a second. "Forgive me. I always promised myself not to take enjoyment from stuff like this, but this one time I'm making an exception. I knew coming back would be worth it. Oh, and before I forget. After we've had our fun, our little daughter is heading down to Mexico with me. I'm going to sell her to the highest bidder. Her fate is on you, Jeanine. I just thought it was important for you to know that. Husbands and wives shouldn't keep things from each other."

He burst into laughter again, snorting as he fought to contain himself.

"Now, come on. What are you waiting for? Dunk for those apples," he said as he slammed me under again.

Chapter 114

Peter was wrenching my head out of the water for maybe the fourth or fifth time when I had the hallucination. I must have been deprived of oxygen because all of a sudden, I thought I saw Emma in the doorway behind Peter.

She looked like an angel. There was something over her head. Wings?

No, I realized. It was the glass-and-metal table from my bedroom. She had it reared back like a baseball bat.

At the last second, Peter turned.

But it was too late.

An elongated, rattling explosion of shattering glass rang off the tile walls as Emma crashed it onto his skull like a sledgehammer.

Peter's eyes rolled back into his head as he went over and down, spurting blood. Burned and feeling dizzy, my palms getting cut by broken glass, I wriggled over his legs on my hands and knees out of the bathroom. I made it as far as the living room when Emma knelt down beside me and cut my taped wrists free with kitchen shears.

"Run," I said hoarsely. I gained my feet. "Door. Go. Police. Run!"

"Leaving so soon? Without giving Daddy a kiss?" Peter said behind us.

I turned slowly and froze. I had trouble registering what I was seeing.

The glass table had injured Peter. Grievously. His left ear was hanging off, flopping against his jaw, dangling by a string of skin. More skin had been shorn from the side of his head, from his temple to his jawline, the exposed pink tissue like bloody bubble gum.

Peter reached up and grabbed his damaged ear between his thumb and forefinger. He grunted and, with a quick hard tug, tore it free. It made a small, wet, ripping sound, as if he were removing a Band-Aid. He frowned as he looked down at the detached ear. He shook his head before he laid it carefully on the picture shelf on the wall by his shoulder.

"Someone," he said, nodding to himself with conviction, "is going to have to pay for that."

Then he smiled, his blue eyes flashing like neon, like a gas burner cranked up all the way.

"Bitches, bitches, bitches!" he said in his Southie accent. "All the same. Can't live with ya. Can't kill ya."

The razor-sharp kitchen scissors were on the floor at his feet. He stooped and picked them up.

"No, wait. Spoke too soon," he said, snip-snapping them open and closed like a barber about to get to work. "Actually, I can."

Chapter 115

Emma and I stood in the living room like statues, kids caught in a game of freeze tag.

"Daddy doesn't like bad little girls," Peter said, grabbing Emma by her wrist with his free hand. He pivoted on his heel as he leaned back and swung her like a rag doll. There was a shattering sound as she crashed face forward into our glass bookcase. It teetered and fell over on top of her, raining down books as she hit the carpet.

That's when I saw it. Peter's gun was where he'd left it, on the couch next to the tape. It was my only chance. I spun, my feet sending fallen books flying, as I dove for the couch.

The gun bounced with a double thud off the carpet. I grabbed it, my finger curling around the trigger as I swung around. But I wasn't in time.

Peter slammed into me, knocking the gun out of my hand as he pile-drived the back of my skull into the hardwood.

I felt as if my head had been split open, as if I'd been hit with a hatchet. I forgot the pain as Peter wrapped his hands around my neck.

I made an involuntary gurgling sound as he started squeezing. More books went flying as I kicked and flailed my arms. My vision dimmed as my oxygen was cut off.

Peter interlaced his fingers around the back of my neck and dug his thumbs into my windpipe, as if he were trying to pry it open.

I'd lost all hope for myself when the tightening at my throat eased up suddenly.

"Don't go yet, Jeanine. Time for one last round of truth or dare," Peter whispered in my ear. "I go first. Truth. Remember Ramón Peña? That night on the beach? Yeah, well, you didn't actually kill him."

He licked my earlobe and gave it a playful bite.

"That was all me," he said.

Chapter 116

Gasping, my throat on fire, I stared at Peter's smile.

"That's right," he said with a nod. "Peña was an informant who was going to rat us out to the Feds. I was actually chasing him over the beach, planning to kill him, when I heard you drag-racing down the beach road. As he ran to the sidewalk to wave you down, I shot him three times with a suppressed gun. Next thing I know, he falls into the street in front of your spinning car. There was no way you could have avoided him."

I shook my head, my eyes slits of disbelief and pain.

Peter nodded. "At first, I thought I was going to have to kill you, too, until I smelled alcohol on your breath and came up with a quick plan. I never got a chance to thank you for giving him a lift back to my house. Great job, Jeanine."

As Peter's hands went around my throat again, something happened. A cold ball of pure hatred formed behind my eyes. It traveled down my left arm into my hand, where it formed itself into a claw.

I swung up stiff-armed and buried my sharp nails into the pink, fleshless wound on the side of Peter's head where his ear used to be. Then I raked them down.

Peter flung himself off me, shrieking. I turned over and lifted myself to my knees, flailing through the pile of fallen books, looking for the gun. I spotted black metal under the couch and dove for it. I pulled the heavy gun up off the floor, in toward my stomach, and slipped my finger over the trigger.

Swinging it around at Peter, I squeezed. Nothing happened. The trigger wouldn't move. I pushed the safety in with my thumb and then raised the gun again. It still wouldn't fire.

I screamed as Peter booted me in the side of the head. The gun went flying out of my hands. It spun as it sailed over the hardwood, down the hallway, and toward the bedroom.

"It's called a double-action pistol, you dumb bitch. You need to squeeze the trigger really hard in the beginning to get off the first round," Peter said, stepping toward it. "Allow me to demonstrate."

I jumped up and ran in the opposite direction. I was going to run out the front door screaming for help, but I knew what Peter would do to Emma.

I turned at the last second and ran into the kitchen. I grabbed at the knife block beside the stove. The big eight-inch Henckels slid easily into my grip. I raised it over my head and ran back into the living room.

Peter, standing by the bedroom doorway, now had the gun trained at my face. He actually laughed as he watched me coming.

Still chuckling, he tried to pull the trigger.

Nothing happened. Instead of disengaging the safety, I must have put it on!

I kept coming and swinging as I dove forward. The barrel of the gun hit me in my mouth, knocking two of my teeth loose. I still kept coming.

My knuckles brushed the smooth underside of Peter's freshly shaven chin as I came down with all my might.

I opened his throat and buried the knife to the hilt in his collarbone.

He fell back into my bedroom, making a wet, gagging sound. I remember warm blood in my eyes and on my cheeks as I turned and ran for Emma. Kicking books away, I found Emma's hand and dragged her to the door before she groggily got to her feet. We hobbled out of the apartment and down the stairwell, clutching each other.

A woman with a bad face-lift, walking her Labradoodle, screamed and took off sprinting when she saw me come out of the building's service entrance onto the sidewalk in my bloody bathrobe. When we got to the Korean grocery store on the corner of Third Avenue, I stopped by the florist sink beside the racks of cheap roses. I was still hosing the glass out of Emma's eyes when the first cop car jumped the curb.

Epilogue

ONE YEAR LATER

Chapter 117

"Jeanina! Get in here!" Charlie screamed from the office at ten to seven on Saturday morning.

I lifted my head off the pillow and sighed at the pet name Charlie had invented on the way back from our honeymoon the month before.

Charlie's was the first face I saw when I woke up in the hospital a day after Peter's attack and the last one I'd seen every night since. Not only had he forgiven me, but he'd done the impossible: helped me to forgive myself.

I'd also underestimated the response

from my boss and firm. Tom couldn't have been more supportive or under-standing once everything came out. I even got a postcard from Justin Harris. It was from Antigua, where he'd relo-cated after he was finally cleared. He'd given me a standing offer to visit any-time.

He was going to be waiting awhile. I didn't think I'd be heading back down to the Caribbean any time soon.

"Jeanina!" Charlie called again.

I crawled out of bed and stepped into the hall.

"What's he hollering about?" Emma said with a groggy smile as she poked her head out of our new Upper West Side apartment's second bedroom.

"No idea," I said, happily noting the lack of bags under Emma's eyes. She'd been having fewer and fewer night-mares. She was definitely moving on and so was I. We'd just about wiped the last of Peter off our shoes.

"Jeanina!" Charlie screamed again as I walked into his office. "Oh, there you are."

"What is it?" I said.

"We need to celebrate," Charlie said, springing up from his office chair.

He clicked a button on his laptop. The printer turned on with a long beep before pages start spitting out.

"I'm done!" he said triumphantly. "My book is finally done."

"You're done? Congratulations! Oh, Papa Charlie," I said, giving him a kiss. "But wait a second. What's your story about, anyway?" I said coyly, as if I hadn't been editing the damn thing for the last year.

It was actually a really good lyrical detective story set in Dallas, where Charlie had grown up. Charlie had talent. Tons of it, in fact. Grisham had to watch his back.

"OK, here's the pitch for Spielberg," he said, his bathrobe billowing as he raised his hands. "It starts out with this young, very attractive girl on spring break in South Florida."

He was joking, of course. I decided to go along. I'd go along with Charlie anywhere from here on out.

"A young Gisele Bündchen type?" I said, leaning in and kissing him.

"Exactly," Charlie said with an intense nod. "She falls in love with this unbelievably handsome, muscular lawyer."

I grabbed his biceps. "So it's a romance with a sexy lawyer? I'm liking this already. Is there a trial?"

"Better," Charlie said. "They get a guy off death row."

I smiled at him, started laughing. "Does everyone live happily ever after?"

Charlie stopped. He grabbed his stubbled chin, thinking it over, as he looked up at the ceiling.

"You'll just have to wait for the sequel," he finally said with a grin.

About the Authors

JAMES PATTERSON has had more *New York Times* bestsellers than any other writer, ever, according to *Guinness World Records*. Since his first novel won the Edgar Award in 1977, James Patterson's books have sold more than 205 million copies. He is the author of the Alex Cross novels, the most popular detective series of the past twenty-five years, including *Kiss the Girls* and *Along Came a Spider*. Mr. Patterson also writes the bestselling Women's Murder Club novels, set in San Francisco, and the top-selling New

York detective series of all time, featuring Detective Michael Bennett.

James Patterson also writes books for young readers, including the award-winning Maximum Ride, Daniel X, and Witch & Wizard series. In total, these books have spent more than 200 weeks on national bestseller lists, and all three series are in Hollywood development.

His lifelong passion for books and reading led James Patterson to launch the website ReadKiddoRead.com to give adults an easy way to locate the very best books for kids. He writes full-time and lives in Florida with his family.

MICHAEL LEDWIDGE is the author of *The Narrowback, Bad Connection,* and, most recently, the coauthor, with James Patterson, of *Tick Tock.* He lives in New York City.

Books by James Patterson

FEATURING ALEX CROSS

Cross Fire • *I, Alex Cross* • *Alex Cross's* Trial (with Richard DiLallo) • *Cross Country* • *Double Cross* • *Cross* • *Mary, Mary* • *London Bridges* • *The Big Bad Wolf* • *Four Blind Mice* • *Violets Are Blue* • *Roses Are Red* • *Pop Goes the Weasel* • *Cat & Mouse* • *Jack & Jill* • *Kiss the Girls* • *Along Came a Spider*

THE WOMEN'S MURDER CLUB

10th Anniversary (with Maxine Paetro) • *The 9th Judgment* (with Maxine Paetro) • *The 8th Confession* (with Maxine Paetro) • *7th Heaven* (with Maxine Paetro) • *The 6th Target* (with Maxine Paetro) • *The 5th Horseman* (with Maxine Paetro) • *4th of July* (with Maxine Paetro) • *3rd Degree* (with Andrew Gross) • *2nd Chance* (with Andrew Gross) • *1st to Die*

FEATURING MICHAEL BENNETT

Tick Tock (with Michael Ledwidge) • *Worst Case* (with Michael Ledwidge) • *Run for Your Life* (with Michael Ledwidge) • *Step on a Crack* (with Michael Ledwidge)

OTHER BOOKS

Now You See Her (with Michael Ledwidge) • *Toys* (with Neil McMahon) • *Don't Blink* (with Howard Roughan) • *The Postcard Killers* (with Liza Marklund) • *Private* (with Maxine Paetro) • *The Murder of King Tut* (with Martin Dugard) • *Swimsuit* (with Maxine Paetro) • *Against Medical Advice* (with Hal Friedman) • *Sail* (with Howard Roughan) • *Sundays at Tiffany's* (with Gabrielle Charbonnet) • *You've Been Warned* (with Howard Roughan) • *The Quickie* (with Michael Ledwidge) • *Judge & Jury* (with Andrew Gross) • *Beach Road* (with Peter de Jonge) • *Lifeguard* (with Andrew Gross) • *Honeymoon* (with Howard Roughan) • *Sam's Letters to*

Jennifer • *The Lake House* • *The Jester* (with Andrew Gross) • *The Beach House* (with Peter de Jonge) • *Suzanne's Diary for Nicholas* • *Cradle and All* • *When the Wind Blows* • *Miracle on the 17th Green* (with Peter de Jonge) • *Hide & Seek* • *The Midnight Club* • *Black Friday* (originally published as *Black Market*) • *See How They Run* (originally published as *The Jericho Commandment*) • *Season of the Machete* • *The Thomas Berryman Number*

FOR READERS OF ALL AGES

Daniel X: The Manga, Vol. 2 (with SeungHui Kye) • *Middle School: The Worst Years of My Life* (with Chris Tebbets, illustrated by Laura Park) • *Maximum Ride: The Manga, Vol. 4* (with NaRae Lee) • *ANGEL: A Maximum Ride Novel* • *Witch & Wizard: The Gift* (with Ned Rust) • *Daniel X: The Manga, Vol. 1* (with SeungHui Kye) • *Maximum Ride: The Manga, Vol. 3* (with NaRae Lee) • *Daniel X: Demons and Druids* (with Adam Sadler) • *Med Head* (*Against Medical Advice* teen edition; with Hal Friedman) • *FANG: A Maximum Ride Novel* • *Witch & Wizard* (with Gabrielle Charbonnet) • *Maximum Ride: The Manga, Vol. 2* (with NaRae Lee) • *Daniel X: Watch the Skies* (with Ned Rust) • *MAX: A Maximum Ride Novel* • *Maximum Ride: The Manga, Vol. 1* (with NaRae Lee) • *Daniel X: Alien Hunter* (graphic novel; with Leopoldo Gout) • *The Dangerous Days of Daniel X* (with Michael Ledwidge) • *Maximum Ride: The Final Warning* • *Maximum Ride: Saving the World and Other Extreme Sports* • *Maximum Ride: School's Out—Forever* • *Maximum Ride: The Angel Experiment* • *santaKid*

For previews of upcoming books and more information about James Patterson, please visit his website or find him on Facebook or at your app store. www. JamesPatterson.com

donation